AF580745

How to Survive a SLASHER

Also by Justine Pucella Winans

The Otherwoods

Wishbone

How to Survive a SLASHER

JUSTINE PUCELLA WINANS

BLOOMSBURY

NEW YORK LONDON OXFORD NEW DELHI SYDNEY

BLOOMSBURY YA
Bloomsbury Publishing Inc., part of Bloomsbury Publishing Plc
1385 Broadway, New York, NY 10018

BLOOMSBURY and the Diana logo are trademarks of Bloomsbury Publishing Plc

First published in the United States of America in March 2025 by Bloomsbury YA

Library of Congress Cataloging-in-Publication Data
Names: Winans, Justine Pucella, author.
Title: How to survive a slasher / by Justine Pucella Winans.
Description: New York: Bloomsbury Children's Books, 2025.
Summary: Queer teen CJ must rely on their knowledge of horror-movie rules to survive when a prophetic manuscript thrusts them into the center of a new murder spree in a town notorious for its past massacres.
Identifiers: LCCN 2024036387 (print) | LCCN 2024036388 (e-book)
ISBN 978-1-5476-1631-2 (hardcover) • ISBN 978-1-5476-1632-9 (e-pub)
Subjects: CYAC: Murder—Fiction. | Psychic trauma—Fiction. | Survival—Fiction. | LGBTQ+ people—Fiction. | Horror. | LCGFT: Horror fiction. | Novels.
Classification: LCC PZ7.1.W5833 Ho 2025 (print) | LCC PZ7.1.W5833 (e-book) | DDC [Fic]—dc23
LC record available at https://lccn.loc.gov/2024036387
LC e-book record available at https://lccn.loc.gov/2024036388

Book design by Jeanette Levy
Typeset by Westchester Publishing Services
Printed and bound in the U.S.A.
2 4 6 8 10 9 7 5 3 1

To all the storytellers who inspire me
Your incredible worlds allowed me to survive this one.
Thank you.

How to Survive a SLASHER

WELCOME TO SLASHERVILLE, OHIO!

Guest post by Moon Satter on VisitSatterville.com

From a distance, Satterville, Ohio, seems like the ultimate suburban dream. Outside the city of Cleveland and nestled right on Lake Erie, the town is a sparkling community with a handful of restaurants, one movie theater, and even an independent bookstore. While it isn't necessarily a rich area, it is clean and surrounded by nature. Idyllic. Quaint.

Except for all the murders.

It started in the summer of 1996, at Camp Satterville. On June 6, around 9:15 p.m., a murderer clad in a cheap wolf mask (later to be dubbed the Satterville Wolf Man) took the lives of four of the seven camp counselors and eight campers, resulting in the end of the camp and the start of a legend. The killer was revealed to be Brett Miller, a Satterville High School student who had tumultuous relationships with many of his classmates working at the camp. He was killed by two of the three surviving counselors, Maria La Rocca and Anthony Volkov. (The third survivor, Christian Smith, was left unconscious and bleeding out after a valiant effort to stop the Wolf Man, but miraculously recovered from his injuries.) Now the campgrounds sit abandoned, aside from the ghost-loving, true-crime-junkie tourists who like to spend the night hoping to see some not-so-restful spirits.

Such an event would be bad enough, if not for what followed in 2019.

Evan Miller, younger brother of Brett Miller, tracked down and killed the three remaining survivors, donning a copy of the unsettling (and perhaps a bit poorly constructed) wolf mask that his brother had worn during the initial murders. While the look of this Party City Costumed Killer might not strike fear into the hearts of my dear readers on images alone, I can assure you, the crimes themselves will.

On the twenty-third anniversary of the Camp Satterville Slaughter, Miller murdered the forty-two-year-old La Rocca, forty-year-old Volkov, and the last surviving camp counselor, forty-one-year-old Christian Smith. The families of La Rocca and Volkov were also killed in the attacks, but Smith's family was lucky: His wife had given birth to twins the month prior and, as is common with twins, the children remained in the NICU for additional care. Mrs. Smith was with them that night while her husband stayed with their two older children. Cassiopeia Jane, better known as CJ (eleven years old at the time), and Orion (then seven years old) were found hiding in a closet unharmed.

Miller was found dead in the Smith residence, believed to have been killed by fatal wounds inflicted by Smith before his passing.

And thus a town that one would expect to be nothing more than a pit stop on the way to Cedar Point gained its own reputation and the delightful nickname of Slasherville. It was even painted over the town's welcome sign and has gotten to the point where those who aren't residents probably haven't even heard of *Satterville* but can tell you fifty different stories about the events that occurred in the *real* mistake on the lake, Northern Ohio's very own serial killer's wet dream.

These horrific crimes served as the inspiration for my two critically acclaimed novels, *New York Times* bestselling *Camp Slasherville* and the sequel, *Welcome to Slasherville*. Both heavily researched, my books aim to provide a fictionalized account of the heroic efforts of Maria La Rocca, Anthony Volkov, and Christian Smith, all while entertaining readers with the gory history of Satterville, Ohio. Both have e-book editions that are currently on sale for only $2.99 (linked below).

Subscribe to my newsletter to be the first to get updates, and support Satterville by visiting for their annual Slasherfest, an event created to honor the victims and bring the community together.

Moon Satter is the authority on all things Satterville, Ohio. An accomplished true-crime fiction writer rumored to live in the town themself, they are an extremely private person and not open to public appearances. Their debut novel, *Camp Slasherville*, was an instant hit that sold more than five hundred thousand copies worldwide. The sequel, *Welcome to Slasherville*, received critical acclaim. They are currently working on their next novel.

---

1 Comment

CJ Smith: fuck you and your trash books you inconsiderate dickface

> **Moon Satter:** Would you be interested in an email interview?
>
> **CJ Smith:** eat shit and die

1

The Story Unfortunately Begins

Everyone wants to be the hero of their own story, but they should take time to consider the genre first. If your life is a romantic comedy or a fun fantasy or some kind of heartwarming, family-friendly animal tale, sure. Hero away.

Some of us aren't so lucky.

Some of us live in the kind of B-list, vintage '90s horror movie where one bad decision can lead to your gruesome death. Being a hero in *that* story usually just means you'll die even faster, and the people watching will criticize your unrealistically selfless behavior as a fountain of blood spurts from your severed neck. In the horror story that is my life, it's better to get by as a nameless extra.

Honestly, it's the only way to avoid a horrific demise in my hometown of Slasherville. Well, that and family survival drills in Satterville Towne Park, according to my mom.

Mom cups her hand over her mouth to help her voice carry in the breeze. "All right, CJ. You're the chaser this time. Ten minutes on the clock. Ready . . ."

Mom really missed her calling as a drill sergeant. Most of the time, she dresses like a bubbly kindergarten librarian who finds dark clothing a personal affront to her energy. But that changes during what she calls our life-or-death drills. In a white tank top that shows off muscled arms and shorts, she is in full gym teacher mode.

This isn't our first rodeo doing drills at the park, so I wait for my younger siblings to get their head start, right at the edge of the playground. Leo and Lyra, the twins, are still too young to get Mom's reason for this training, instead thinking of it as regular playtime. Orion, the thirteen-year-old little shit he is, wears the ever-annoyed smirk he always does, but still has his muscles tensed, ready to run.

"Go!" Mom shouts.

I take off.

The twins erupt in delighted squeals, racing around the playground. I dart around the swings, keeping my pace slow so their little legs have a chance. Leo scrambles up the rock wall of the play structure, so I target him first. I jump up, grabbing the last monkey bar, and pull myself up so I land next to the top of the rock wall, snatching my little brother by the back of his shirt just as he tries to dart away.

He screams, laughing, as I make monster sounds.

"Leo's out," Mom says. "Come here, kid, you're dead."

Leo makes a show of his dramatic death scene, coughing and pretending to choke until he falls down onto the slide, body slowly getting pulled to the bottom. He smacks against the soft mat beneath us before giving me a huge smile.

Lyra's next. She's not as silly and chaotic as Leo. She might be only six, but she's a budding genius, always reading and far too clever for her own good. I scan the playground from my vantage point. I don't see her running around, like Leo was. She's doing what she does best: hiding.

Unfortunately for her, there are not a whole lot of places to hide here. I slide down the fireman's pole, turning to the underside of the jungle gym. It's a big one, enough that there's plenty of space to walk under.

I walk toward the middle of the jungle gym, where the ceiling is higher due to an opening that leads to the tallest point of the structure. Lyra is there, perched on two bars.

I spring into action, reaching for her, and she tries to kick me off. Good. Still, I'm able to climb up with ease and grab her, making the same monster growls that always get her and Leo to giggle.

"If I had a weapon, I would've got you," Lyra says proudly.

"You're, like, ten years too young for a weapon."

She frowns. "But you've had Dad's knife since *forever*."

She's almost right. Dad always carried his knife around, and he bought me an exact copy to give to me when I started high school. I ended up getting it earlier than planned, at eleven, on the night we lost him. The same way Dad kept his, I'm never without mine. It's even tucked in my pocket now. But he only gave it to me when he did because he had no other choice. Because he knew he might not be able to protect me that night. That's not something you can easily explain to a six-year-old.

Fortunately, Mom saves me.

"Lyra, you're dead!" she calls.

Lyra doesn't make a performance out of her pretend demise. She just jumps to the ground and skips over to join Mom and Leo on the sidelines.

"Five minutes left!" Mom calls.

I glance to the opposite end of the jungle gym and spot Orion standing there. He looks the most like me out of all my siblings, with his straight, dirty-blond hair and eyes that look amber in the sunlight. He's also already taller than me, and my only actual real drill opponent. Leo and Lyra are basically babies—Orion has been doing Mom's death drills with me since day one.

As if to prove that, with his back to Mom so she can't see, he lifts his middle finger right at me, poking out his tongue.

That little shit.

I charge after him, and he darts around the corner, scrambling up to the second level of the jungle gym. I'm a little tired, to be honest. This is, like, the fourth drill of the day, plus we did sprints earlier, which I hate more than anything. Normally, Mom isn't so vicious with training, but with Dad's death anniversary approaching, she's in full prep-and-protect mode, and my sore muscles feel it. Orion at least had a moment to rest while I was focused on the twins. Part of me wants him to be able to get away, since that's the whole reason for the drill, but I also don't want to give him the satisfaction of winning against *me*.

Orion dodges obstacles, tearing through the playground with me close at his heels. He's faster than me, unfortunately, which means I have to be strategic.

I feign reaching out to his left, so Orion twists to the right—exactly where the one step that everyone always trips on is. He's just grazing by me, so close to his victory, before his feet stumble beneath him and he falls with an "Oof!"

I'm not a total jerk of a big sibling, so I reach out a hand to help him up.

"Orion, you're dead," I say at the same time as Mom calls it.

Orion ignores my hand, instead choosing to hoist himself back up to his feet.

"I let you win that one," he says. "Just wait until I'm chaser."

"You were, earlier, and you didn't get me in time."

"Yeah, well, I did stealth way better than you."

He's right. Orion is completely silent when he walks. Scares the shit out of me all the time at home.

"Hey, it's not a competition," Mom says, marching up to us with one of the twins' hands in each of her own. "What's important is that everyone survives." She smiles. "Speaking of working together more, I heard about this serial killer–themed escape room that opened up in downtown Cleveland. I think we should have you two do that one. It might be too scary for the twins, but supposedly it's realistic."

I frown. "I don't think the Wolf Man is going to lock us in a room with puzzles, Mom."

"You don't know what sick murderers get off on, CJ."

I don't argue, even though out of everyone left in our family, Orion and I are the only ones who actually had a run-in with a real serial killer. The Satterville Wolf Man took a lot from Mom, but she never actually crossed paths with him. Still, I know everything she does is out of love.

"Sure, Mom. Let's do it."

She clasps her hands together. "All right, kiddos. Let's get home before that old lady calls the cops on me again."

To be fair, maybe it wasn't the best idea to show us how to escape from rope arm restraints in a public park during the day.

"Mom, I don't want to go yet," Leo whines.

"What if we get ice cream?" she bribes.

There's not even a real response, just a screech of *icescream!* as both he and Lyra sprint ahead to the car. As much as Mom wants us Smith siblings to work together and take care of one another, I'm ninety-six percent positive both of the twins would sell me out for Dairy Queen.

A few other families give us looks as we pile into Mom's SUV. While I feel instantly defensive with so many eyes on us, I can't *really* blame them. Like, I know this shit is weird. While everyone else is at the park doing things like dog walking, picnics, or frisbee, we're doing cardio focused on evading potential kidnappers and killers. Normal families don't do that.

But normal families don't have our history either.

Mom can be a little . . . much, to say the least. But it's not easy to raise four kids basically alone. Especially not after losing your husband in a sudden, horrific way. Since the night of Dad's murder, Mom vowed to not let anything like that happen to us again. To dedicate a major part of herself to protecting us from any future Wolf Men. That meant trying her best to teach us how to keep ourselves and each other safe.

I can't blame her for that, even if it made it a lot harder for me to make friends. I was never the most popular kid to begin with, and if being the queer kid whose dad was killed by the last Wolf Man wasn't bad enough, our small apartment practically looks like a doomsday bunker. Imagine having a friend over, only for the twins to come in screaming that they're being attacked by a serial killer and lock themselves in the bathroom with the burner phone while Orion runs out with a mask and fake weapon.

Whatever. It's not like it matters. I have my family, that's what is most important. I don't need anyone else, especially when there are people out in the world like the Miller brothers. Or like Moon Satter, for that matter. They'll eagerly profit off "fictionalized" books based on their town's collective trauma but are too chickenshit to show their face.

And, okay, I guess no one knows for sure that Moon Satter actually lives in Satterville, but that's what all the rumors say. While I would rather choke on my Reese's Peanut Butter Cup Blizzard than read a Slasherville book, from what I've heard, Moon knows too much to be an out-of-towner—even the biggest gossips wouldn't have spilled all the details Moon wrote about. Which is probably why Moon insists on remaining anonymous.

Yet another reason why I only need my family.

Leo eyes my Blizzard hungrily, trying to stick his spoon into my ice cream from behind me in the back seat. I swat him away. "Hands to yourself, kid."

He frowns. "But I want peanut butter."

"Why did you get Oreo, then?"

"I want *both*, but Mom never lets me get two!"

"Orion got peanut butter, too."

Leo moves his spoon over toward Orion before getting a sharp look.

"Come one inch closer and this spoon becomes a murder weapon," he snaps.

Leo starts to pout so I relent, letting him steal one spoonful of my ice cream. Of course, that means Lyra also takes a scoop. And prompts Mom to ask me to feed her a bite while driving. Maybe Orion has the right idea.

I continue to fend off Leo's and Lyra's spoons the rest of the way home. On the walk up to our apartment, I hold my Blizzard high above my head, yelling to Mom to open the front door quickly so I can eat in my room in peace. Mom only laughs, bending down to pick up a package on our doormat (which features a grumpy-faced cat with the words "GO AWAY" over it).

She looks at me. "Did you order something?"

I shake my head. "Is it for me?"

She tilts the package toward me, where "CJ SMITH," along with our address, is written in Sharpie. There doesn't seem to be a return address, though. Weird.

Orion bites his ice cream. "Maybe it's from a pervert."

Mom glares at him. "I'll open it first to be safe." She takes a few steps down the hall before tearing open the package and peeking inside. "Looks like a book. Seems safe. Maybe Ms. Maeda sent it."

She tosses it over to me, still in its envelope, and I only just manage to catch it with my free hand.

Ms. Maeda is the owner of the local independent bookstore, my favorite spot in town and pretty much the only place I go outside of school and home. I don't know why she'd mail me a book, when I'm at the shop so often, but I'm also not going to complain about a free book.

Mom finally opens the apartment door, and Leo and Lyra run in. "Hey, hey, watch it with that ice cream!" Mom calls after them. Orion takes his spot on the couch, wordlessly scrolling his phone and ignoring us as usual, while Mom does up the locks. First the dead bolt, then the chain, then the one on the doorknob. She even taped a picture on the door of an otter with the speech bubble "You otter remember to always keep the door locked!" which she finds hilarious. I don't know how she even got permission to add all that, but then again, this is Slasherville.

I let out a huge yawn. I didn't sleep well last night—I never do when the anniversary's approaching—so I feel even more tired than normal after running around at the park all afternoon. "I'm sweaty. Anyone need the bathroom before I shower?"

None of my siblings respond.

"Aren't you going to help me with dinner?" Mom asks. I give her a look with pleading eyes.

"I'm kidding. I'll call you when it's ready, just set the table."

I drop off the package and ice cream cup in my bedroom and pick up my towel and fresh clothes. I barely turn toward the bathroom when Leo shoots up.

"Wait! I have to poop!"

He rushes past me, slamming the door in my face.

"Not like I just asked if anyone had to go," I mutter.

I lean against the wall, right across from the hallway shelf that holds Dad's ashes. It's something like a small shrine—the nice urn that acts as his final resting place and a photo of him, just as I remember. His bright eyes, the same as me and Orion, and the huge smile he always wore.

In a few years, he'll have been out of my life for longer than he was in it. The pain of losing him has a way of nestling into my gut and overwhelming me at the strangest moments, like now.

"You'd think the drills are weird as hell," I whisper to him. I wipe my face. "Miss you."

Thankfully, Leo doesn't notice my watery eyes as he walks out. I have to open the bathroom window (like, *ugh,* is he lactose intolerant or something?), but at least the hot water of the shower is the perfect mask for crying. This time of year is always tough, but Slasherfest makes it even worse. I would assume most people remember their grief anniversaries based on the related emotions alone, but it is truly impossible to forget when your town has a freaking festival every year on that date. It was originally supposed to be more of a memorial, or celebration of the victims' lives, but then all the true-crime and horror-movie-obsessed freaks caught wind, with their big pockets, and it became something else entirely. Not exactly helpful when trying to get over this kind of trauma.

But even without Slasherfest, there's nothing that can make grief go away completely. Chocolate and peanut butter ice cream and hot showers certainly help, though.

My eyes and nose are still red when I'm dry and clothed, so I sneak into my room to be alone. I flop down on my bed, making the package from Ms. Maeda bounce. A new read could be just the distraction I need, so I grab the envelope and pull out the book. Except it's not quite a book—more like a printed-out Word document that was bound together to *look* like a book.

Then my eyes land on the cover page and my blood runs cold.

Return to Slasherville by Moon Satter.

What the fuck? Moon actually wrote another book? I don't know what they could have written about—the dickface seems incapable of coming up with any ideas of their own, and the most horrific thing to happen in Satterville recently was Max Dolan flashing the crowd at the homecoming game last semester (which, ironically, was an away game, as most of our rival schools refuse to play in Slasherville).

The point is, there hasn't been another crime since Dad died. And even if there had been, or if Moon Satter was making up their own murders now, why the hell would they send this to *me* of all people? My family has refused interviews for years, and our distaste for what Moon did isn't exactly a secret (I personally rated both books one star across various websites). Do they think sending me this means I'll give it a chance and promote the book or something? If that is the case, then they're freaking delusional.

I jump out of bed and throw the book into my trash can, where it belongs.

I grab my remaining ice cream and shovel three melty spoonfuls into my mouth. How *dare* they send this crap to me? And so close to the anniversary of the Wolf Man attacks, too. It's not like Moon doesn't know it's coming up—they wrote two freaking books about it. What is there even left for them to say? Why even write a third book? I stare daggers at the pages peeking over the rim of the trash can.

Rage-driven curiosity takes over me. Against my better judgment and armed with another bite of delicious chocolate and peanut butter, I fish the book out of the trash and open to the first page.

While Taylor Topper didn't interact with the Wolf Man, or anyone who had, it seemed inevitable that she would be the next Final Girl.

Taylor Topper? As in, the same Taylor Topper that's been in my class since fourth grade? Is Moon really such a bad writer they can't even come up with fake names anymore? I know they at least did that much with the first two books (not that anyone actually believed it was "fiction"). Seems like it would be a legal nightmare to use the names of real, living Satterville teens in a spin-off.

So . . . what is this?

I should stop reading.

But, out of some combination of curiosity and spite, I keep going. The first chapter literally takes place on tomorrow's date, May 26, which seems too suspicious to be coincidental. But that's hardly the weirdest part—*everyone* in the book is someone I know.

My eyes practically bug out at the sight of my own name.

Taylor was already running late when someone nearly smacked into her. A curse word died on her tongue as she brushed off her dress and took in the person in front of her. It was a rather spooked (and a little suspicious-looking) CJ Smith. Clearly, they were having a morning, wearing an ill-fitting shirt that looked like they got it for free in middle school, their unplucked brows knit together in what seemed to be stress.

My hand brushed my eyebrows. Are they that bad?

No. It's just a stupid book.

Before Taylor could say anything, the announcement bell went off. "Good morning, Satterville Salamanders. Just an update that the women's restroom on the first floor near the office is temporarily closed due to flooding. A reminder to not flush anything down the toilet that isn't toilet paper. They are not magic, they will clog. Thank you."

Gross. CJ opened their mouth to mumble a "Sorry" before scurrying down the hall like they had somewhere to be. Taylor almost felt bad. They could be cute if they didn't have to share clothes with their little siblings or whatever led to that unfortunate outfit choice.

I'm going to punch Moon Satter right in their smug face. There's nothing wrong with how I dress, even if Taylor Topper would probably disagree. I guess I at least have to give Moon credit for using "they" pronouns. While I'm not exclusive to any, the inclusion is nice.

But this is weird. And not like life-or-death-drills weird, but like, *actual freaking creepy, hell no* kind of weird.

An eerie feeling settles over me as I continue on to the second chapter. Taylor learns in her fourth period class that someone made a report of seeing a Wolf Man outside the school that morning. All her friends are making fun, cracking jokes about the town legend coming back right in time for the questionable yearly event that commemorates the slayings: Slasherfest.

My chest tightens, and it only gets worse as I read more.

After lunch, Taylor thinks she sees someone suspicious and goes down the ultra-sketchy hall behind the cafeteria that leads to the shop room. The lights flicker, almost go out. She gets inside the shop room to come across the murdered body of Nadia Martínez and a message written in blood: *Cheer up, little queen, I'm not done yet.*

I throw the book across the room. It smacks against the wall before hitting the floor.

My breathing is heavy and my hands are shaking. What the hell is that?

The book is saying there's going to be another Wolf Man? While it's something my family constantly prepares for, the idea of it actually happening, and *tomorrow,* makes my head spin. No. He can't be back. He can't be here.

This is just some sick fucking money grab. It *has* to be.

"CJ, this table isn't gonna set itself!"

I jump at Mom's voice, half expecting her to come in the room to get me. There's no way I can have this book lying around where anyone can find it, especially not now, when Mom is already on edge. I scramble to pick up the book and look around my room for a good hiding spot. Lyra sneaks in here too often to steal books (despite Mom saying she's not old enough to read them), so I can't slip it on my bookshelf. In a space this small, options are limited.

"CJ! Did you hear me?"

"Coming!" I yell back. Panicking, I grab my backpack and shove the book in there, zipping it closed. That will have to do for now. It's not like anyone is interested in my finals prep work.

I throw my bag back on the floor and take a breath before facing my family.

I can't act freaked out. It's only a prank. Honestly, I don't even know that it's actually from Moon Satter. There wasn't a return address on the envelope, after all. Maybe some asshole fed Moon Satter's books into an AI generator and made sure it used the names of real people. With the anniversary of the Wolf Man incidents coming up, it's possible someone is trying to fuck with me. It wouldn't be the first time. Mom has shielded us from a lot, but she can't protect us from everything. Making an entire fake book is . . . a lot, but there are some ridiculous, shitty people out there.

It doesn't exactly make me feel better, but it's not like someone is actually going to die. I try to count my breathing, slow the pace of my heart, and calm down.

It's just some screwed-up joke.

I mean, it has to be.

My life is already enough like a horror movie. The absolute last thing I need is another unwanted reboot.

2

More Than Fiction

There's nothing I want more than to crawl back into bed, especially with the shrieking outside my door. Apparently, Leo doesn't want to wear clothes today. My room feels like a temporary sanctuary from the rest of the apartment, which has Mom scrambling to get ready for work at the same time she has to wrangle the twins into getting ready for school. Orion and I are lucky to get any bathroom time. All the bathroom time in the world couldn't fix my bloodshot eyes at this point, though.

I barely got any sleep last night thinking about the book. I don't understand why someone would go so far just to freak me out.

I check the clock. Shit. We're already running late.

I quickly clean my glasses, even though I know they'll get dirty again in approximately four seconds. I do a once-over in the mirror, but there's no time to improve my appearance. I'm wearing an old *Satterville Reads!* T-shirt from a library reading challenge, and my hair is frizzy. I try to tie it back, but that just makes me look like a twelve-year-old boy. I twist it in an attempt to smooth it down. It's a temporary fix, I guess.

Whatever. This is just how I'll have to look today. Peak *it's a good thing I haven't grown in four years, since clearly we haven't bought new clothes in some time.* At least I support libraries.

Clearly, they were having a morning, wearing an ill-fitting shirt that looked like they got it for free in middle school.

I frown, Taylor Topper's fictional voice in my head. I snatch up tweezers and clean up my eyebrows. At least those are on point behind my glasses. That's already something different from the stupid book.

Gathering my backpack with the review materials for finals I'm super not prepared for and the book no one could ever be prepared for, I head out of my room and into the kitchen. Mom's pouring coffee into her mug with one hand and steaming Leo's shirt with the other as he sits on the floor in only his pants. There's no way I'm making it on time today.

"Mom," I complain, "I'm going to get detention if I have another tardy, the twins should be dressed by now." I twist toward the hallway and raise my voice, my glasses slipping down my face. "ORION. Hurry the hell up, you've been in the bathroom for like twenty minutes!"

"I'm *coming.* Jesus," his voice snaps back.

"Did I have that much attitude when I was thirteen?" I ask Mom.

She gives me a look. "You were, and still are, even worse."

"Lies."

I storm to the fridge, snatching up the twins' lunches before they forget them. I drop Leo's lunch box onto his lap and then hand Lyra hers. She's at least fully clothed, but stretched out on the couch with her nose buried deep in a book. I'm the only one in this family with any sense of urgency, I swear.

"Lyra, can you dog-ear that? I get you're a genius, but we've got to go."

"I can't bend the pages, CJ," she scoffs. "Mrs. Antonella says that's against the rules."

"There are no rules if you paid for it," I tell her. "Now, let's go."

"Okay, I'll finish the chapter first."

I let out a long sigh. At least it's a chapter book. How long can it be? Mom is shoving Leo into his shirt as he tries to twist out of it like a spooked kitten. "Leo!" I snap. "Put on your clothes *now*."

He goes slack before pushing his arms through. Leo always listens to me. Mom will baby the twins, but since I didn't give birth to them, yet still had to clean up after them one too many times, I fell into the role of scary big sibling. For some reason, I think that made me the favorite.

Once clothed and with his lunch box in hand, Leo rushes over to me and clings to my leg.

"Can't I go to school with you?" he asks.

"I would just like to go to school at all at this point," I mutter, ruffling his hair before twisting to the hall again. "Orion, the damn Coast Guard called about the water you're wasting!"

The sink shuts off and he stomps out of the bathroom, both his hair and scowl in place. "You sound like a dad."

"Well, I'm the closest thing we have to one in this house, so get your shit together."

Mom rolls her eyes. "Do you have to swear so much?"

"Yeah, I actually have a sponsorship deal with Urban Dictionary." I pull on my backpack before picking up Lyra's and handing it to her. "Can we go now?" I check the time on my phone. Shit, it's already 7:10. The drop-off traffic line will be terrible, and we have three different schools to go to. Detention is the last thing I need so close to summer.

"I'll drop you off first," Mom says, ignoring my sarcasm. "It'll be fine."

Of course, it's another thing to actually get everyone out of the apartment and into the car. By the time we're all strapped in and ready to go, it's already 7:23. School starts in seven minutes.

My stomach growls. In the general chaos of the morning, I forgot to grab even a shitty Pop-Tart for breakfast. I'll have to try a vending machine. Maybe I can convince someone in the cafeteria to slip me something. I'm already on the free lunch program, so what's the difference?

"All right," Mom says. "Time for family rules. What does the Smith family always do?"

Normally I don't mind the daily routine, but we don't have time for this. I mutter a "Seriously?" but Mom gives a hard glare.

"Stay safe, stay alert, and stay the heck away from reporters," the kids and I all say in unison, with varied degrees of sass.

Mom smiles, bubbly as ever. "That's right, kiddos."

We've barely pulled into the street before the twins start shoving up against each other, Leo trying to read Lyra's book and her responding by elbowing him in the face.

"Can you two stop being so annoying?" Orion snapped.

"Moooom," Lyra whines from the middle seat. "Orion's being mean."

Lyra's wildly mature for her age, but something about our brothers gets on her nerves and makes her act like the little kid she is. I really am the best sibling.

Well, maybe not according to Orion. We're likely all in a three-way tie for his least favorite.

"Orion's always mean," Mom says, causing him to eye-roll directly behind me. She glances up at the rearview mirror before turning her eyes to the road. "But if you don't behave, I'm going to tell Uncle Ian he can't take you out for ice cream this week."

The twins break out in gasps and NOOOs like Mom just said she snapped Bluey's neck with her bare hands. Like we didn't already get ice cream yesterday. Still, part of those complaints might have more to do with not seeing Uncle Ian.

While he isn't related to us by blood, Uncle Ian is the only family we have left. He was best friends with Dad from when they were little kids, and was even the one to introduce Mom and Dad in high school. After losing Dad, he really stepped up, helping Mom and taking care of us. He lives close by, his house an inconvenient but possible walk away, so he makes an effort to be present and see us often. I honestly don't think we would've made it these last few years without him.

"Behaving means shutting up," Orion mutters before putting on his headphones.

Lyra and Leo stop the protests immediately, making a show of puffing out their cheeks but keeping their lips closed tight.

At that point, we've basically reached the high school, but the drop-off line is a nightmare. We can't even turn in to the school with all the traffic, instead waiting in line on the street bordering the wooded area near the football field. I check the clock. Oof. Homeroom is already a bust, but with hustle and a dream, I can maybe make it to first period on time and pretend that I was marked absent by accident. Although, I can't necessarily guarantee it.

"Just let me out here," I say, gripping my backpack. "I'll walk up."

Mom's forehead creases in worry. "Are you sure?"

"Tons of kids walk this way, it's fine." I pop the door. "We're already running late and you've got two more stops." Both the elementary and middle school start at eight, so they at least have a chance of making it on time. I'm already past that point and have detention on the line, but I don't want to make Mom feel bad. I pat the small side pocket of my backpack. "Besides, I've got my pocketknife and pepper gel."

Am I allowed to bring them onto school grounds? Likely not. Will Mom allow me to leave the house without them? Also no. But I fly low enough under the radar that no one has bothered checking thus far, and my family history is well-known enough for the principal to understand. Maybe.

"Okay," Mom said. "Love you, and text me once you're in class."

"You got it." I keep my phone in one hand. "Love you. And all you, too," I add for the back. "Even Orion."

He flips me off as a goodbye, earning a glare from Mom. Leo and Lyra give me big waves.

With that, I head out, close the car door, and adjust my backpack so I can start up the dirt path to the school. It's kind of calming, despite all the traffic right behind me. There are enough trees on the path to make it feel separated from the rest of the world, even if it isn't that far. It's a little wooded corner, which seems like a terrible place to walk alone, but desperate times call for desperate measures.

With nothing else to distract me, my mind wanders to *Return to Slasherville*, or at least, the part of it that I read. Not only did someone send me this messed up book, they made sure the dates lined up so I would get it the day before the murder supposedly takes place. While I know it isn't real, I hate that it still has me feeling unsettled. That in this weird world of the book, someone I know will die today.

That's fucked.

I take a deep breath. Focus on the way the individual leaves look sharp and clear with my recently updated glasses prescription. Listen to the birds chirping. Spot the squirrels running around in the trees and hope they don't end up as roadkill on the street I sometimes have to take home.

Peaceful thoughts. To forget fictional murders of real people.

Except now I'm thinking about it again. *Squirrels, CJ. Look at the squirrels, dammit.*

Maybe it's because I'm already so late, but usually there are a few other students on the path and it doesn't feel quite so isolated. But there's no one else around now. I reach back and grab my pocketknife. While the pepper gel is supposed to be more effective than the spray variety, even in the wind, the breeze is picking up and I'm not sure I want to risk it.

It feels darker with the cover from the trees, and my arms prick from a sudden chill. I'm just overreacting. I can't let the book spook me.

My chest still tight, I pick up the pace. I'm almost to the end of the dense trees and to the football field, which at least has better visibility. Once I make it there, I'll be okay. That's how I manage, focusing on the next step, the thing that is within reach.

Only a few feet away.

A large *snap!* expands my vision from the focal point of my goal. I should just break into a run. I'm already late, who cares if I draw more attention to myself? But I'm also determined not to let this stupid prank get to me.

Then I make the mistake of turning around.

And I see him. The Wolf Man.

Panic surges in me. My hands start to shake and my eyes sting. My throat goes dry. There's no breathable air.

It's not him, not really. Not the one from six years ago. He's dead. They found him dead. I saw the blood, all the blood, a few feet away from Dad. I saw his body.

It's not the same man. But it's the same mask. That's all it takes. He's hidden between branches, but I can't miss him. Except this can't be real. That book is just a fucking story. I must be imagining it. The Wolf Man isn't back. He can't be.

He ducks behind a tree.

That sure looks pretty fucking real.

Logically, I know it's the person pranking me. Emotionally, I'm losing my shit.

I grip the pocketknife. I have to get as far away from here as possible.

A panic attack is inevitable at this point, but life-or-death drills aren't for nothing, and I am prepared with my comfortable shoes that were made for this moment.

So I run.

3

When Therapy Works a Little Too Well

Instead of first period, my panic attack took me directly to my guidance counselor, Mr. White. Given that he's been dealing with me since freshman year, he knew exactly how to help me ground myself, calm down, and explain what happened. At least enough to get the point across and have the woods immediately searched. He also promised that I wouldn't get detention, which does admittedly help slightly. I sip the juice box Mr. White gave me before a police officer asked to speak to him in the hallway, a weighted plushie from his bookshelf on my lap. It's a stegosaurus named Happy, which is perhaps a little silly, but also, if I didn't have this ridiculous dinosaur to hold, I'd literally die.

When Mr. White steps back into the office and gently closes the door behind him, I can already tell from his expression that they didn't find anyone. I know where the conversation is going to go. Kind and educated words about trauma and PTSD and how I should probably see a psychiatrist that we'd never be able to afford because the insurance deductible alone is more than my savings.

"They didn't find anyone," Mr. White confirms, sitting at his desk across from me. "That doesn't necessarily mean someone wasn't there, though, and they'll keep an eye out." He sighs. "I know we've had some incidents in previous years with students getting a little excited around Slasherfest, and since that's coming up soon . . ."

As if I could forget when Slasherfest is. It's like the whole town can't shut up about the masked murderers who first failed and then succeeded at killing my dad. But to everyone else, they're just stories at this point. It's almost like if the tragedies can feel like fiction, the town doesn't have to admit how much it was actually hurt by them. The families that left. The ones that never had a chance to, like mine. If you shove the grief and horror behind food and drink and merch, you almost forget they're there. Not that it works for us.

My family knows that there's no escaping the ghosts that haunt you. Which is why Uncle Ian normally takes us on short trips to Cleveland or Sandusky to avoid the worst of the festival. He couldn't get off work this year, though, and money's especially tight at home, so a little escape is probably out of the question.

"It's okay," I say, trying to reassure myself just as much as Mr. White. "He didn't hurt me or anything. It is probably just a prank." Like the book that said the Wolf Man would return today. That he would kill one of my classmates. Just a prank.

Mr. White's mouth is a hard line. "When we find out who was involved, there will be absolutely zero tolerance for that kind of behavior on campus."

"Right."

I know he means well, but I'm not exactly convinced. While no one has gone to extreme lengths like this in the past, I'm sort of an easy target for people who get into the Slasherfest hype. Orion and I are the only people left in Satterville who had a run-in with the Wolf Man, after all. There've been pranks before: students trying to wear Wolf Man masks to school or writing messages on my locker. Two years ago, Mom had to pick up Orion from school because a couple little shits dressed up as the Wolf Man and scared him in the bathroom. He peed his pants, but fortunately, it was during class, so only the two instigators saw.

I'm pretty sure they just got suspended for a few days. Big whoop.

Still, Mr. White wears his concern well. "Have you noticed anything strange? Has anyone said or done anything to you recently?" he asks.

I squirm in my chair. Sending a book predicting the return of the Wolf Man is pretty freaking strange. "Someone left a message at my house yesterday," I say finally. "I think it was trying to spook me. So it's probably the same person."

I don't really think he'll be able to do anything about it. I guess I just want someone else to confirm it's a prank and that I don't have to be worried.

Mr. White's eyes widen. "Did you go to the police with it?"

I shake my head. "It's not worth it."

The police haven't helped with harassment from reporters and Moon Satter fans in the past. At least, not enough. I'm sure this would just be another report that would die on someone's desk. Especially since they are likely preparing for all the out-of-towners getting drunk at Slasherfest.

"It is definitely worth mentioning. What was the message?" Mr. White asks.

"I don't really remember," I lie. I don't want any rumors about the book getting out. Besides not wanting my mom to find out, I can't imagine how Nadia and Taylor would feel. Unless one of them is behind the prank? That would be a little obvious, though.

I swallow. But . . . maybe Taylor? After all, she is the protagonist.

I realize I've been in my head, Mr. White watching me carefully. "If anything else happens, I'll definitely report it. And you all can still investigate, but . . . this just stressed me out and I'd rather move on from it, you know?"

Mr. White gives a smile that's weaker than my will to move. "Okay. Whatever feels right to you. Take all the time you need," he says. "I'll write you a pass and email your teachers."

"Thanks," I say.

A moment passes. I squeeze Happy a little bit tighter.

"Do you want to talk about anything else?" Mr. White asks. "Anything that might be on your mind with Slasherfest coming up?"

"Like what?" I ask. Now it's Mr. White's turn to squirm. "You mean like that night?"

Mr. White knows everything from my first crush on Hana Maeda to my anxiety about being in small spaces, but I haven't told him much about the night Dad died. He's never pressured me to talk about it.

Sometimes, it feels like that's all anyone wants to know about me.

How did those kids survive?

"Whatever you're comfortable with," he answers, like he hasn't wondered himself.

My heart ticks along with the red second hand on Mr. White's old clock.

What exactly happened the night Christian Smith died?

"Go," Dad said. He put a pocketknife in my hand, closing my fingers around it. It was exactly like the one his fingers gripped. His hand was warm, but his eyes were panicked. "You have to protect your brother, okay, Cassie?"

"Dad, what's happening?" I asked. My eyes burned from tears.

"Hey, hey, hey," he said quickly, voice a controlled whisper. His free hand cupped my face. "You're my strong girl. It'll all be okay. You know this. We planned for this, didn't we?"

I nodded.

"What do we do when Daddy says to go?"

A crash from downstairs. Glass breaking. Orion started to cry.

"I take Orion and I hide."

"And when do you come out?"

"Only when you or Mom comes to get us."

"No matter what you hear?"

"No matter what."

He kissed me and Orion big and wet on our foreheads and pulled us in tight. I thought it was to make us brave. I think it was to say goodbye. Footsteps thundered, someone howled like a wolf.

"*Go,*" Dad said.

That time, I knew there was no question, no argument. I took Orion's hand and I ran into the closet. Through the slotted doors, bits of the room were still in view. I pulled Orion back into the shadows, clothing draping over us. I covered his mouth with my free hand, not moving even when snot and spit dripped onto it.

I held out the pocketknife with my other hand. Between that and my brother against me, I told myself that everything would be okay. That Dad would protect us, no matter what. That Dad knew what to do. Because we had prepared for it. And I had to focus on the next step. The one task.

Don't move and don't leave. No matter what.

So we stayed quiet and still.

Even as the man in the wolf mask walked into the room.

Even as we heard them fight, shadows moving across the closet floor in front of our trembling feet. Even as a sourness filled the air and I felt Orion's pee warm against me. Even as the blood poured under the closet door, staining my pink pterodactyl socks a sickening red.

Dad killed that man before he could find us, but his wounds were too much. He didn't have his healthy teenage body like he did when he survived the first slaying. There was too much blood. So much blood. Too much blood.

But we didn't leave the closet, Dad, we didn't leave, we didn't—

A choking sound escapes me, bringing me back into Mr. White's office. I'm panicking all over again, tears filling my eyes, gasping like a fish out of water. I'm at school. I'm in Mr. White's office. He's at my side now.

"You're here, you're in this chair," he says in a calm voice. "You're safe."

I'm safe.

"Would you like me to call your mother?" Mr. White asks.

Hell no. She has work today. The last thing she needs is to have to pick me up because a fake book scared me. I need to calm down. The Wolf Man isn't back.

He's dead.

"No, I'm fine," I quickly say. "I actually should get to class. Finals review and all that." I'm in such a rush to grab the pass, I almost take Happy with me, too, but throw him back on the chair at the last moment as I tear out of the office. I'm so distracted, trying to convince myself I'm fine, that I almost run directly into another girl.

"Sorry," I mumble.

I glance up. It's Taylor Topper. She looks unfairly put-together, with her smooth, bright blond hair and clearly new dress.

"Nice shirt," she says in a way that makes it clear she means the exact opposite.

"Thanks, I won it myself."

Before she can try to come up with a response to that, the PA system rings with an announcement. "Good morning, Satterville Salamanders. Just an update that the women's restroom on the first floor near the office is temporarily closed due to flooding. A reminder to not flush anything down the toilet that isn't toilet paper. They are not magic, they will clog. Thank you."

My heart pounds.

That's the same announcement that was in the book. Which means whoever is trying to freak me out went as far as clogging the toilet, or at least faking the announcement. And it happened right after I ran into Taylor, too. She *has* to be involved—it's too big of a coincidence for her not to be. Right?

It wouldn't be super surprising if she was, to be honest. Taylor is known for being a bit of a bully. I just didn't think she had anything against *me.* I twist toward her, studying her face for some kind of giveaway. I can't let her know how this has been affecting me, but I want to test her somehow.

"Are you going to the shop room?"

She gives me a look. "What? No, I'm not going to the *shop* room."

With her tone, I didn't have to hear the "creep" to know it was there. Of course, that probably wasn't the best way to ask. That doesn't mean she isn't involved, though. She could just be good at bluffing.

"Yeah, never mind," I say quickly. Before I can embarrass myself any further or reveal how freaked I am, I turn on my heel and head toward class.

It's fine. Everything's fine. The Wolf Man isn't back and some kids (probably Taylor) are pranking me and I'm totally fine and can get through the day, no problem.

It's a mantra I repeat to myself, even during class, when I am totally not fine and totally not getting through it. My mind won't stop racing. What did the book say was going to happen after I ran into Taylor, again? What period was she supposed to find Nadia's body?

I casually pull the book from my backpack, trying not to be too obvious. I lay it flat over my open Chromebook like it's some supplemental history material. I don't fully reread the opening, but skim for the basic details. While the book doesn't have any dialogue between me and Taylor, the announcement is practically word for word.

What. The. Hell.

Okay. So she clogged the toilet and wrote the announcement. Multiple people can be involved, too. Plenty of kids have a work-study in the front office. It's not like the book is predicting the future. That's absurd. Impossible.

Right?

I rub my eyes. I think I'm losing my mind.

As Mr. Liu continues the final exam prep I'm fully paying attention to, I flip through the pages of the book. I can't bring myself to reread the murder in the shop room, so I focus on the details before. Taylor goes to her morning classes, goofing off with friends. During lunch, it rains, so even the seniors have to eat inside and the lunchroom is crowded as people make their plans to get drunk as shit at Slasherfest. Afterward, when everyone is back in class, Nadia goes to the shop to pick up a birdhouse she made, and Taylor is heading to the office when she notices a figure that sends her toward the crime scene.

I check the weather on my phone. There's barely even a chance of rain today. A sigh of relief escapes me. I feel silly needing reassurance that the story isn't real, but it's still nice to have this proof that it's wrong. Hopefully this weird prank will end soon so I can get on with my life and forget this day ever happened.

At lunch, it rains.

And I'm panicking a little.

Like, okay, no, I don't believe I have some kind of prophetic book, because that is impossible and, like, weather apps exist and it wasn't a zero percent chance, but I'm just *concerned* because I don't know how far this prank is going to go or what else they are planning.

I sit at my usual table of stoners who think I'm funny enough to sit with but don't care enough to hang out with me outside of lunch, and while Peyton is clearly high and usually clueless, even he asks if something's wrong.

"I'm good," I say. "Great."

"Okay, just know, you can always talk about shit with me, man," he responds. "I get it. My mom's a therapist. Well, a pet therapist, but I think some principles can apply." He places a hand on my shoulder. "If you meowed right now, I would sense the anxiety."

"Um . . . okay. I'm cool, though. Really."

"Sweet," Bethany says from across the table. "Because if you don't have plans, we're figuring out what we're going to do for Slasherfest, and my older brother is down to buy beer."

Great. I can't even escape the scripted lunchtime conversation. I go along with the Slasherfest excitement without actually committing to anything. But my mind is elsewhere. I can't focus. I practically feel out of my own body. I keep looking over my shoulder like the Wolf Man is right behind me. I even try to see if I can spot Nadia to, I don't know, confirm she's here? That she's still alive? But the cafeteria is too crowded. When the bell rings, I say goodbye to my table, but I don't start toward my next class.

I stand outside the lunchroom, in view of the route that leads to the shop room. Nadia will have to come this way if she does head over there. If she doesn't, that's fine. Great, actually. Either way, at least I'll know for sure.

If Taylor is behind the book, I can easily see her involving Nadia. There's no way she'd actually kill her, but that doesn't mean there isn't something awful planned. A *Carrie*-style prank, maybe? Things have been so weird today that I don't want to risk it.

Even as everyone files into their classes and the hallway empties, no one gives me a second glance.

Maybe the fake book is right and I really do give off unnoticeable-extra vibes.

Then I see her, walking down the hall, eyes down on her phone.

"Nadia!" I rush toward her.

She jumps, her phone clattering to the floor. It's open to a web-comic with a clearly steamy Boys' Love scene. It's hard not to look and she notices.

"Um, would you believe me if I said I read it for the plot?" she starts, bending to pick up her phone.

"No, I mean, yes, I get it, I read a lot of manhwa and webcomics."

Her eyes widen in excitement. "Seriously? I don't have any local friends who do and I am in desperate need of someone to fangirl with, so I think I might have to make you my best friend now." She laughs, all energy that shouldn't be possible during the school day. "Not to be too pushy, but I've always wondered why we weren't close, because I feel like we'd vibe well, and this seals it."

I blink. She thinks we'd vibe well? I can't imagine why she'd think about me at all, since no one seems to unless it is in connection to Slasherfest and the Wolf Man. Is that just something nice, pretty girls say to everyone?

I don't have to ask, because Nadia keeps talking, rapid-fire. "What do you read? I read way too many, it's a little embarrassing. I'm on Webtoon, some on Tapas, but just the Wait Until Free ones, oh, definitely Manta . . ."

"Romance, mostly?" I say, thrown by the direction this conversation is taking.

"Same! I read contemporary romance, and BL and GL of course, but I honestly love romance fantasies, especially the reincarnation and isekai kind of stories."

On a normal day, I would say *No way, me too* or ask which titles she's into. But today isn't a normal day, since I almost had a PTSD breakdown in the guidance office and have a horrifying, ongoing prank involving a fake future-telling book being played on me.

"Are you heading to class?" I ask, trying to sound casual.

Nadia adjusts her backpack. "Nah. This is my free period, but I was making up a presentation during lunch and I asked Sebas to pick up my birdhouse in shop. My presentation didn't run over that long, though, so I thought I'd meet him."

Shit, so the birdhouse thing is real. That's not good. That's really not good. But even if they are planning something in the shop room, at least Nadia is *here.* Wait. My brain finishes processing everything she said.

"Who's Sebas?"

There's no Sebas in the school that I know of, and certainly not one in the beginning of *Return to Slasherville.*

"Oh, my cousin Sebastián. You don't know him, he just moved here from Costa Rica. He already finished up the school year down there, so he's just in this week to get ready to officially transfer next year. And run errands for me, of course."

"So he's in the shop room? Now?" I can't contain the panic in my voice, and Nadia is clearly weirded out.

"Uh . . . yeah?" Nadia says.

Shit. Shit shit shit.

I have to get him out of there. I hope I'm overreacting, I really do, but what if I'm not? Whoever is behind all this has *something* planned in the shop room. Even if Nadia is the original target, her cousin could end up hurt.

"Is everything okay?" Nadia asks. "Honestly, maybe you should just ditch with me and read comics. This new one just dropped where a girl is reincarnated into the *male lead* and I am living for how gay that sounds."

That does sound incredible and like it will give me all the gender feels, but I'm kind of in the middle of spiraling.

"Sorry, I have to go. Wait here," I say to Nadia, voice hard. "Don't follow me. I'll explain later."

Cursing myself over and over, I do the one thing that people potentially living inside a horror story should never do, and sprint in the direction of the shop room to be the hero.

4

A Messed Up Murder Meet-Cute

It's probably nothing.

That's what I have to remind myself as I step into the hallway that leads to the shop room. It's not like Taylor would murder someone for a prank. There's just a lot of potentially dangerous stuff in the shop room. Accidents could happen.

They won't, though. It will all be fine.

It might be easier to convince myself of all that if this particular hallway didn't look like a literal set from *Evil Dead*.

It's an area of the school that feels a world away from everywhere else, a practically hidden hallway. Aside from the shop room, which I think only has classes first and last period because it's not the most popular elective, the hall holds a bathroom that's widely considered *Emergencies Only* because it's by far the worst one and hardest to get to. Even with a women's restroom out of order, this one is still empty. If you're not about to shit your pants from cafeteria food, there's no reason to head over here in the middle of the day.

The normally gross fluorescent lights even seem to be flickering a little bit more than usual. It feels like I stepped out of the school day and wandered into some other dimension. I keep my steps light, pace slowed to not draw attention to myself. My heart pounds in my chest, so loud I almost feel like it would alert someone to my presence.

The lights of the hallway turn off, covering me in a thick blackness. A scream catches in my throat. I reach into my pocket and pull out my pocketknife. I don't care if I'm just getting messed with. This is too much. The hairs on my neck all rise on end, almost like there is someone here with me. Someone who can see me through the dark.

A breath on my shoulder.

The lights flicker back on as I spin around, but nothing is there. Shit. Maybe I am actually losing my mind. I quicken my pace down the hall.

The light is bright in the shop room, the door ajar. Small blade at the ready, I peek into the room, half expecting to see some horrific scene. But no, instead there is a very much alive and very much attractive guy who turns to me. He shares some features with Nadia, but his skin is a darker shade of brown and his face narrower.

His expression looks confused as he takes in the pocketknife and what I'm sure is a crazed look in my eyes. The room, however, is masked-killer free. I quickly rush inside.

"I know this is weird," I whisper, "but I think you should get out of here. Now." Oh no, that's coming on way too strong. "I mean, Nadia is looking for you. You're her cousin, right? Sebas?"

I figure name-dropping his cousin will be more effective, even if I'm sort of reminding myself of those creepy child abductors in movies telling a kid their mom sent them.

"Yeah . . ." he starts, eyes darting down to my hand.

I follow his gaze to the knife there before looking back to his face. Yeah. This was definitely a bad idea. As if it wasn't bad enough that I look *far* from my best, I'm coming across as a complete weirdo.

"Sorry," I say. "Lights went out in the hallway and I freaked out a little."

I'm not sure I'm making this any better, and the fact that he is hot only makes matters worse. I can feel my face heating. I'm horribly inexperienced with people I'm attracted to. Being the kid whose dad was killed by one of the town's bogeymen hasn't exactly been a sexy selling point for me. I try to avoid his dark brown eyes and unfairly long lashes, instead focusing on his black hair that looks just long enough to run fingers through.

No. That's a weird thing to think about. I need to focus. I'm trying to avoid a potential bad situation, not ask him to dinner.

"What happened? Is Nadia okay?" Sebas has a nice voice, light and soothing, with an accent from I've already forgotten where because every other detail Nadia gave me was lost in the panic.

"She's fine, but we should get going," I say.

"Is there an emergency?" A line forms in the middle of his forehead. "Is Samuel okay?"

Samuel? Great. Another person I don't know. I hope they're not also coming here. "I think so. We're the ones in a dangerous spot."

"Well, yeah, but I'm not using the tools. I'm just picking this up." Sebas lifts the birdhouse. "Plus, you're the one with the knife."

I glance around the room, face hot. There's at least one big table saw, although thankfully, it's covered, plus an assortment of other tools. I'm surprised the room was even open. There are, like, at least fifteen different ways someone could have a gruesome slasher death here, and that's *not* including the obvious table saw brutally slicing someone in half. I glance at the clock on the wall. We have a few minutes before whatever is planned goes down. Maybe.

"Yes, but I told you, it's just because I got scared." I sigh. "It's a long story, but essentially, I think someone is pranking me because

Slasherfest is coming up, and I don't want you to accidentally get involved."

Sebas looks confused. "The festival that's happening soon? Why would they prank you because of that?"

Oh right. He just moved here, so there's no way he knows who I am. For some reason, a bit of excitement rushes through me. I've rarely left Satterville, so I'm not used to anyone not knowing me as the oldest surviving Smith kid. I've been trapped in the shadow of the Wolf Man so long, it's like I forgot that outside of this town, people don't care.

It's kind of nice.

"You really don't know anything about this town, huh?" I ask, almost able to hide my excitement.

"Um . . . I guess not?"

"That's amazing," I mutter.

"What?"

"Um, I just . . . people tend to get a little obsessed with the whole Slasherfest thing. It's not like *I'm* a target. It could be anyone. I'm just, like, a random extra." Shit. Who talks like that? The book is a little too in my head. "I mean, person. Like . . . I think this is the *location* of the prank, so I just want to avoid it while we still can. If there isn't anything planned and you follow me, I'm just a weirdo and you're fine. If something does happen and you don't follow me, you could get hurt or embarrassed or something. Worse than I'm embarrassing myself right now." I give a weak smile. "So can you take the better option and just get out of this creepy-ass hall with me?"

Despite my winning logic, I expect him to question me more. I *know* I'm being ridiculous. If a random stranger came up to me with a knife and said we needed to get out, I'd probably . . . well, actually, I'd probably listen. At least in the sense of getting away from a dangerous area. But most people didn't spend their childhood playing strategic games on horror-situation survival with their moms.

Sebas, however, goes along with it. "If you're Nadia's friend, I'll trust you. Besides, it is creepy in here, you don't have to ask me to leave twice."

Keeping the birdhouse in his arm, he follows me back toward the door with slow steps. He does keep some space between us, probably because of the knife. Can't blame him for that. I put it back in my pocket.

The classroom has glass windows that look out into the hallway, although most of them are covered with a pale beige paper. We're almost back at the door, still slightly open, when my eyes lock on one of the uncovered spots in the window.

Where a Wolf Man walks out of the bad bathroom, a large blade protruding from the baggy sleeves of his dark gray cloak.

I freeze.

"Do you see him too?" I whisper, voice barely above a breath.

"Yeah," Sebas says. "This is the prank?"

My stomach drops so low I nearly give birth to it. It's like a black hole opened inside me, sucking up all my insides and the air around me.

The Wolf Man turns toward the shop room.

Is this a prank? Because that knife looks pretty freaking real.

Whether or not he actually wants to hurt us, I can't take my chances. Mom prepared me for this, and I'd rather overreact to a fake Wolf Man than underreact to someone actually out for blood.

"I don't know," I admit.

If we run, we might not make it. At least, I won't. Despite all Mom's training, I have short legs and the Wolf Man is right outside the exit. Without a head start, I'm screwed. We can't get out of the room safely.

I'm already looking around the room to calculate our best option. My chest feels like it's caving in, but my brain seems to detach itself from the chaos of emotions. It's just like the drills I've done for years now. If escaping isn't going to work, there's hiding and stealth. I grab on to Sebas's sleeve and yank him into the storage closet with me, quickly shutting us in.

My panic surges, my chest tight. It's like all the air is being sucked out of the closet. I close my eyes and try to imagine I'm anywhere else.

Sebas speaks and I try to focus on his voice. "I'm not saying I'm against this," he starts, "but usually, I'd like to get to know you first. There's a great taqueria near my house. Less creepy, and amazing birria."

As embarrassed as I am, the normal conversation actually helps. At least in the dark closet, he can't see me blush. There isn't much space for standing in the closet. With the tall shelves and random items packed along the edges, we're practically pressed together, Nadia's birdhouse the only thing keeping space between us. If I focus on him, I don't have to focus on the tight walls closing in. The way this situation is far too similar to that night all those years ago. I shove the thoughts away, my breathing still far too quick.

"No, it's not like . . . I'm not trying to . . . Not that you aren't . . ." I internally groan, keeping my voice in a whisper. "I don't know if this is a prank anymore. That knife looked real, and I don't think we should let him know we're here."

"The guy in the weird mask?"

Wait. Does he not even know what that mask means?

"That's not just a mask," I whisper back. "That's the reason they call this place Slasherville. That's the Satterville Wolf Man."

"You're saying we're being chased by . . . the Satterville Wolf Man?"

He still seems confused.

"Do you not know about the Wolf Man? Seriously?"

He's quiet for a moment. "Do you want me to?"

Is he trying to act cute with me? It's either slightly weird flirting or he really doesn't know the Wolf Man. That might be more likely. It's not like cute people are known to hit on me. Oh my God, he seriously moved to Satterville without knowing anything. I can't believe Nadia didn't even prep him. Still, as rough of an awakening as this will be for him, it's better than I ever could've imagined. Not only does he not know who I am, he doesn't know the Wolf Man or my connection to him. He won't want some scoop about how my dad managed to kill the last Wolf Man before dying, because he doesn't even know to ask. To him, I'm fully just another extra. A nobody.

I like the idea of that.

"No," I say, finally answering. "I mean. Yes? It's a masked murderer who might kill us if he finds us. That's the most important part." I try to think of a way to explain when my vision almost tunnels and I stifle a scream. "What is that?"

He glances behind him. "Don't worry, it's just a model. For clothes."

Because of course the scary woodshop needs mannequins in the closet. What the fuck are those even used for? Practice in dismembering a body? Do I have to look into whoever the shop teacher is?

"Sorry, I'm just a little freaked out. Even if this is just another student, they have a knife and we could accidentally get—"

However I was going to finish that sentence doesn't matter, because I hear the door to the room creak open. Footsteps sound from right outside. My vocal cords freeze, along with the rest of me, because it's like I'm right back in that closet with Orion six years ago.

The steps sound louder. My heart pounds. The pocketknife is slick with my palm's sweat.

"Can you see him?" The softest whisper.

I'm not with Orion. I'm with Nadia's cousin. The guy who isn't even supposed to be here, according to the book. I can't answer. I don't know where the Wolf Man is outside, and I'm waiting for the door to be thrown open to reveal him right there. I see something red drip under the door, but no, that has to just be my mind, right?

All that blood. So much blood.

I see it on my hands. No, my socks. Everywhere, I . . .

Dad, did I fuck up?

Next to me, the boy continues, voice soft, barely audible, "If he finds us, I'll distract him. You run and call for help, okay?"

I'm so shocked I find my voice. I'm slightly more grounded back in my body. "I can't leave you."

Even if it is all scare tactics, the person is armed. Sure, I technically am too, but the blade he has makes my pocketknife feel like the danger level of plastic cutlery. This person is long past going too far.

Sebas smiles. It's a nice one, even in the dim light of the closet. His teeth are crooked and short and he has a few braces in the front I didn't notice before. Somehow that makes him even cuter. It's easy, a light summer breeze behind his lips.

"Don't worry about me," he says. "I've always been very lucky."

"I've always been very unlucky, unfortunately."

He leans in, ever so slightly, and I feel his breath tickle my skin. "Well, then we balance each other out."

Something about the way he says it makes my panicked heart skip a beat. Maybe he isn't joking and he really *is* flirting with me. I can almost forget the Wolf Man outside. I can almost forget that I'm one of the Smith kids. That, maybe, in some other universe, I could just be someone this cute boy is possibly interested in. And we could be good together. And we could balance each other out.

Instead of probably getting stabbed to death in a fucking storage closet.

"Once we get out of this . . ." he says slowly, only for my left ear to hear, "do I get to know your name?"

"Maybe," I whisper back. "Do I get birria?"

"Bir*ria*," he teasingly corrects. "If the werewolf doesn't kill us, first thing we'll do is learn to roll your *r*'s."

"It's not a werewolf—"

One of the shelves behind him gives, and things slide and tumble off. All too much noise thunders as things smack and clatter against the wall and closet door. We both jump slightly, staring at each other with wide, panicked eyes.

Footsteps. Closer. My heart is in my throat.

His fingers brush my wrist and I can't help myself. I grab on to them. He doesn't say anything as I squeeze his hand, the callused warmth providing the smallest amount of comfort. We wait for the door to open. For . . .

I don't know. I don't want to.

The footsteps stop right outside the door. The shadow of a person, of the Wolf Man, blocks the light. Next to me, Sebas squeezes my hand back.

My phone lights up in my pocket. I chance a look at the time. 2:13. In the manuscript, it was right around this time that the body was discovered. What are they planning? Is it Taylor in the costume, or is she supposed to show up to make fun of me?

I try to tell myself it's just a prank. It sounds like a lie. This is just like the last time. With the Wolf Man.

But he didn't find us he didn't he didn't.

It's too similar. Like this isn't just a prank. Like this is actually life-or-death.

With the Wolf Man right on the other side of the door, death is currently the more likely option.

And because I didn't take this threat seriously enough, it feels like it's all my fault.

5

The First to Die

Time speeds and slows at once. It's like we were in the storage closet for hours, but also, it goes by so quickly. I'm preparing to maybe use my pocketknife, or maybe just run for my life, like I probably should have done from the beginning. Still, with Sebas's hand squeezing mine, I don't regret coming.

Not even if the door opens.

But it doesn't. The footsteps move away from the other side of the door, seeming to pick up speed as they get quieter, farther away.

Did the Wolf Man really just . . . leave?

"Is he gone?" Next to me, Sebas's eyes catch mine through the darkness.

"I think so?"

My heart still pounds, all the pent-up fear and panic not sure what to do after the supposed killer's anticlimactic exit. If he leaves without killing anyone, what does that mean? Does Taylor find me and Sebas in the closet instead? Does the story change genres from horror to coming-of-age romance?

Or the whole point was just to scare me. Mission fucking accomplished, in that case.

"Um . . . I know we potentially got through something together here, but it's kind of strange that you're touching my butt."

I drop Sebas's hand. "What?" I lift my other hand with the knife. "Literally how would I be touching your butt?"

We share a look, and with little regard for the fact that a killer was just outside, I push the door open and we spill out into the empty woodshop room. I look back toward the closet, to whatever was touching him.

My heart nearly stops.

"Is that . . . ?"

A hand reaches out from under a tarp, suspiciously stained in red. Fuck. No.

"It's probably one of the mannequins," Sebas says next to me.

I give him a look through my blurring vision. The hand is white, but it's not mannequin white. That is *skin*. That is a *human fucking hand*. I rub my own hands over my face. This can't be happening. This can't be real.

One thing's for sure: this is no prank.

The Wolf Man is back.

My whole body turns to ice and I want to throw up. The Wolf Man didn't leave because he just wanted to scare me or decided not to kill today. He left because he *already had*.

That's probably why he was coming from the bathroom. He was washing off the blood.

I eye the hand sticking out from under the tarp, the only visible part of the body. Did Nadia follow me? Take a shortcut I don't know about? Or . . . is it someone else?

I don't want to think about it. I don't want to think about any of this.

"Can you call for help?" I ask Sebas. He's staring at the hand, clearly freaked. It takes a moment for him to react to my voice, but he nods, taking out his phone.

I take a step toward the body, Sebas's voice on a call with 911 fading into white noise. My stomach gurgles. You'd think I'd be better equipped to deal with this kind of situation, but it's not exactly something you get used to. If anything, I'm pretty sure my trauma makes me *less* equipped for this shit, but I'm trying to compartmentalize and not really think about it.

Should I move the tarp?

No. You're not supposed to mess with a crime scene. Then I'll just get my fingerprints on it and that will make everything worse. Shit. Who the hell is it?

This is so wrong.

The fake manuscript wasn't sent to me as part of some harmless prank. It was a warning. The Wolf Man is back—and this copycat already claimed his first victim.

I turn away from the pale hand and look back to Sebas.

"We're supposed to wait here," he says, tucking his phone back in his pocket. "They're on the way."

Great. Exactly what I want to do. Wait in a room with a dead body.

He's looking back at me with a strange expression. Or, past me. He points over my shoulder. "What's that?"

I follow his finger. There's a streak of red on the left of the open storage closet door. Our fingerprints are already all over it, so it probably can't hurt to see what's there. I move the door to reveal the other side.

There, painted in a bright red:

HIDING IN CLOSETS WON'T WORK ANYMORE, LITTLE SHEEP

My chest seizes. The killer left a message in blood in the book, too, but it was different. *Cheer up, little queen, I'm not done yet.* I remember thinking it was kind of silly when I read it, but it was clearly meant for Taylor, this year's prom queen and the book's Final Girl. This message is different. It's not meant for Taylor.

It's meant for me.

The Wolf Man knew it was me hiding. He left the message for me, just like he had in the book for Taylor.

But I'm just an extra. A blip in the story. Or at least, what I read of it.

Shit. Maybe I should have kept reading.

My breathing starts to come out quicker as my hands shake. Panic rises in me. It's like the floor shifts under me as my balance is tested by my own lightheadedness.

I don't think Sebas understands the threat on the door—how could he when he doesn't know who I am? But he's at least able to catch on to the fact that the killer knew we were hiding in there, so he steps closer to me.

"Is it okay if I touch you?" he asks softly.

I nod.

He turns me around, away from the threat and the still arm peeking out from the tarp. His hand grasps mine. He tosses on a smile, not enough to show in his eyes, but enough to reveal his braces in the light.

"It's going to be okay. They'll catch the guy. We're safe."

"Yeah," I choke out. "Yeah. He's gone. We're safe."

Somehow, saying the words aloud helps, even if I don't believe them. His hand is warm in mine, and I'm not shaking quite as badly now.

"Just keep breathing . . ." He says it like he has to convince both of us, but at least he seems to be holding it together. "You promised me your name."

"Cassiopeia," I say. "But everyone calls me CJ."

"Cassiopeia," he repeats. "Like the constellation."

I nod. I've had a bit of a love-hate relationship with my full name, but something about the way he says it doesn't have me minding so much. Maybe it just sounds a lot better without everyone emphasizing *pee*. "My mom has a thing for stars, I guess."

"Mucho gusto, Cassiopeia," Sebas says. "Or CJ. Although I kind of wish we were meeting under different circumstances."

I almost snort, despite everything. I don't want to admit that the circumstances aren't all that unheard-of for me. "Yeah," I mumble. "Next time, let's meet in math class or something. Maybe a bookstore."

He bites his lip. "I'm not really a math person. Or a big reader."

"Well, then something else a little less memorable. Take your pick."

He laughs. I have to admit, the distraction is helping.

"Nadia said you just moved here?"

Sebas nods. "A few weeks ago. I'll officially start school here this fall. Just for my last year."

I give an apologetic smile. "What a fucking welcome to Slasherville, huh?"

He tries to play it off, but his eyes seem freaked out. "I thought my last school had problems, but they don't compare to this."

"To the school's credit, this is the first dead body I know of here."

Only because the other incidents weren't at Satterville High, but I don't mention that. It's already bad enough without me freaking him out more.

I push my lips together. I feel like crying, but I force myself to hold it in as I meet his eyes. "I'm sorry you got dragged into this, but thank you for listening to me. For staying with me. I'm . . . I'm not sure I would've gotten through that alone."

"I definitely wouldn't have, because I didn't even know anything was wrong, so thank you." His expression shifts slightly as he takes me in. "But, I still don't understand how you knew to—"

His question is somewhat fortunately cut off as police and paramedics arrive. It's like time had frozen, with the two of us distracting each other from the horror we went through, but the seconds rush forward once more with the arrival of others. The room fills with sound and footsteps and faces a strange mix of panic and focus. Not only are they professional, they work in Satterville.

Just because it's been six years doesn't mean they weren't prepared for this to potentially happen again.

My senses are in overdrive and the adrenaline starts to wear off. I feel so drained, I barely remember to slip the pocketknife back into my pants. I don't know if anyone saw it, but I'm not sure anyone would care. Or, at least, they might understand why I have it once Sebas and I explain what happened.

If I can even explain. I don't know what to think. Do I turn over the book? I feel like I'd at least need to make a copy first. If the police take it, I won't ever know what the rest of the book says, which means I can't use that knowledge to my advantage. To stay safe.

Because, clearly, someone is trying to make this fucked up fan fiction come true.

What if someone in my family is targeted next?

I swallow. Maybe I should keep the book quiet for now.

Sebas and I start to get ushered out of the room, but not before I see them pull up the bloodied tarp. The image immediately sears into my mind. Blond hair matted down with blood, blue eyes wide and lifeless. I'd recognize her anywhere. In fact, I just saw her earlier, in that exact same dress.

The Wolf Man didn't kill just anyone.
He killed Taylor Topper.
The Protagonist.
The Final Girl.

6

The Wolf Man Returns

Sebas and I are ushered off to the main office, where we wait for questioning. The school is on lockdown, police searching every corner of the building in case the new Wolf Man is still around. They didn't say that over the PA system, though. Only that there is a "potential danger" on campus and that all teachers should lock their doors and only open them for the police. I guess they don't want to immediately announce that a Wolf Man is back and killed a Satterville High junior. Needless to say, classes are canceled for the rest of the day. We're close enough to finals that I wonder if they'll just cancel them, too.

Which is a thought I can't believe actually crosses my mind right now, when I just saw Taylor Topper's murdered body.

It's hard to wrap my head around. Taylor is *dead*. I feel bad for ever thinking she was maybe involved, that this was all a prank. I thought I was saving Nadia, and then Sebas, but being the hero didn't do anything. A girl was still killed.

And her murderer is out there.

One of the police officers approaches me and Sebas. I almost thought they'd forgotten we were here in all the chaos. "We're going to have you two call a guardian to pick you up. You have your cell phones?" Sebas and I both nod. "Good. Once you've made your arrangements, let us know who will be collecting you and I'll let my buddy know to let them in." We nod again and the officer walks away.

It takes me three tries to unlock my phone. I keep pressing the wrong numbers with shaking hands. Finally, I press Mom's name.

"Mae, todo bien, pero . . ." Sebas's voice fades as my attention is drawn to Mom's.

"CJ? What happened? Are you okay?"

I don't think the school told her anything yet. Mom must know that I'd only call in an emergency. It's also possible that Mr. White reached out to her earlier, even though I told him not to bother her. Shit, he's about to get his counseling schedule filled by me alone.

"There's someone else," I tell her. "He's back and . . . I found the body."

My voice comes out in a choke. She's able to understand enough. She's been preparing for it, after all, even if we hoped that it was over.

"Fuck," Mom says. "*Fuck.* Are you hurt? Are you safe?"

"No and yeah. I'm okay. Just need someone to pick me up."

"I'll be right there."

My chest is tight. If the Wolf Man left the high school, I'm not in danger. At least, not immediate danger. But what if this was only his first stop? What if he goes after my brothers and sister next? "Maybe you should get the twins first. And Orion. Just to be safe. The police are here and I still have to talk to them anyway."

I can almost hear her uncertainty over the phone. "You *swear* you're safe?"

"I swear."

Mom lets out a sigh. "Okay. I'll call Ian. Maybe he can meet you since he lives so close to the high school."

That's not a bad idea. Uncle Ian does have a way of making things feel better. Not that this is a situation that could be made better, but I'll take the comfort anyway.

"Sounds good, I'll be in the office. Tell Uncle Ian to text me when he's here so I can tell the police to let him in."

"Because those assholes have done *so* much to help us."

I know she's thinking about past incidents, like those boys bullying Orion in the bathroom and years of trying to keep journalists and threatening Moon Satter fans away. Mostly, the police suggested we ignore it or move. While leaving Satterville might have made sense, Mom never had the money. Not to mention, there's nowhere else to go. We don't have any family elsewhere. At least in town there's her work, Uncle Ian, the Maedas, and people from Mom's kickboxing gym. Satterville is all any of us have ever known. It was never as easy as just leaving.

I understand why Mom doesn't trust the cops here. I don't think I can either. Even if they do something, it likely won't be enough to keep my family safe.

"Well, I can't exactly refuse questioning. I was in the room with . . ." I have to stop myself from saying *Taylor*. It doesn't sound right. None of this seems right. ". . . the girl he got."

I hear the car engine start. "Shit, sweetie. I'm so, so sorry. I really hoped we'd never have to deal with this again. But I already texted Ian, he's on the way. We'll figure this out. We've been training for this, and the important thing is you weren't hurt. It'll be okay, all right?"

It takes me too long to answer. "Yeah. I know."

Even after hanging up, I can taste the lie lingering on my tongue. There isn't anything about the situation that's okay. Not only is the Satterville Wolf Man back, but the freaky book that was mailed to me yesterday predicted it. Except, because I got involved, the person destined to *stop* the Wolf Man was his first victim.

It's clear from the energy in the front office that no one caught him. And I have no idea who the hell it could even be. The Miller brothers definitely didn't have a third sibling, and they both died before having any vengeful kids. Mom made sure to look into that. Without a blood connection to the first two who wore the mask, this new killer could be anyone.

"Do you need this?"

I turn to Sebas. He's holding up a small trash can. I must look like I'm about to vomit.

"I think I'm good," I say, but I take it anyway. "Thanks."

He gives a little smile. He doesn't seem to smile with his teeth generally. This one is still weak. "I feel like we should talk . . ."

Something tells me the talk is a continuation of his question before. I understand why he wants to know what my deal is, but there's no way I can actually tell him the full story.

Luckily, I don't have to. His eyes widen at something behind me, and I turn to see Nadia walking out of the principal's office. I'm surprised when my shoulders sag with relief. She's still alive. She's okay.

"What are you doing here?" Sebas asks her. His voice dips. "They don't think you killed that girl, do they?"

While it isn't exactly the best way to greet someone given the circumstances, Nadia immediately rolls her eyes and flips him off. They must be close, at least in the way me and Orion are. It would take more than a murder to stop my brother from giving me shit.

"No," Nadia says, almost a little too defensively. "I was with CJ when it probably happened. I can't say I'm sad about it, though . . ."

Nadia and Taylor had a well-known hatred for each other. Back at the end of eighth grade, Nadia confessed she had feelings for Taylor, which Taylor rudely rejected before outing Nadia to basically the entire school. Nadia rightfully never forgave Taylor for it.

Nadia glances over her shoulder, like she's realized that's probably not something she should admit in public. "Like, okay, I wished a lot of bad stuff on her, but little things. Like constantly stepping on Legos or getting massive pimples daily or getting knocked up and moving far away. Not . . . this." Nadia shakes her head, blinking away glassy eyes. "But, uh, one of the school's officers caught me vaping outside, and we saw the guy in the wolf mask run off into the woods." She gives a small, unconvincing smile. "On the bright side, he totally forgot to get me in trouble."

"Why did you go outside?" I ask.

"You said not to follow you." Nadia holds up her hands in defense. "I didn't know what the hell was going on. It's not like I could guess the goddamn Wolf Man was back. But don't worry, I say vape because I have a pen, but it's THC."

I don't know why I'd worry about it being weed or not, but hell, I'd probably want to smoke after dealing with me, too.

"You thought I was in danger and you went to smoke?" Sebas snaps.

"Um, first, I didn't know you were in *danger,* and even if I did, bitch, you'd do the same."

He smiles a little. "Maybe."

Nadia puts her hands on her hips. "If anything, you both should be *thanking* me. If me and the rent-a-cop hadn't seen the killer literally fleeing the crime scene, they might've thought it was one of you."

"I'm not going to thank you. You sent me there." Sebas reaches down to pick up something from next to him. "Here you are, by the way."

It's the birdhouse. Some blood stained the wood, making it legitimately look like a prop from a horror movie, but Nadia doesn't seem to notice. She holds it like a child. "Hell yeah, it looks great. Abuelo would be so proud."

"Cassiopeia Jane Smith?" an officer calls.

Ugh. He says it in the way that definitely makes me not like it. I start to stand.

"Wait," Nadia says. Her voice is low. "Are you going to tell us how you knew something was up?"

My stomach drops. I can't tell them about the book. There's no way they'd believe me, and even if they did, that's just creating a liability. The message on the wall was left for *me*. Nadia and Sebas shouldn't be involved, not when Nadia was so close to being the one wheeled out of here in a body bag. Getting close to me will only put them in more danger, and I've already let them get a little too close for comfort.

I keep my voice even. "I thought I saw someone in a Wolf Man costume, that's why I went to the room. I just thought they were pranking me."

Nadia makes a face. She clearly doesn't believe me. "When? I was with you right before. And how did you know to go to the shop room?" When I don't reply right away, Nadia softens her tone. "C'mon, CJ. Let us help."

I harden my expression. I feel bad about it, especially with how nice both she and Sebas have been to me, but that's all the more reason to shut this down. The Wolf Man is back. He's coming after me. I can't afford to have a new friend or a new crush. I can't afford to trust anyone. Mom's right. We prepared for this by making a plan as a family. The most important thing is keeping each other safe. Protecting my siblings, like I promised Dad.

Everyone else, from this point, has to fend for themselves.

"It was before I ran into you. That's why I was acting weird. Okay? That's the whole story. I thought I saw someone strange, and so when I heard your cousin was alone, I wanted to make sure he was all right. I honestly thought it was a prank. I didn't know it was an actual copycat Wolf Man." I can't look at Sebas. Even meeting Nadia's eyes fills my chest with lead. "But I don't owe you any explanation. There's no big secret. We were in the wrong place at the wrong time. I'm sorry about that, but it's better if we keep our distance."

"Cassiopeia Jane Smith," the officer repeats.

"Sorry, I'm coming." I look back at Sebas and Nadia. "Take care of each other and stay safe."

I don't feel good about it, but I walk away, toward the officer. Neither of them say anything to stop me.

The process of getting my statement taken isn't bad. Nadia was right about them not thinking I killed Taylor, at least. Between town lore, witnesses of the killer fleeing, and the message left on the wall, the police are convinced that Sebas and I are just unfortunate students who thought we were finding a friend's birdhouse and found a friend's body instead.

Nadia and Sebas are gone by the time I'm done with questioning. In their place is another familiar face: Uncle Ian. My ability to keep it together has been quickly deteriorating as the adrenaline wears off, but I have to admit, I do start to feel better when I see him. He's good under pressure, although a big part of that might come from having grown up in Satterville and being on the periphery of both attacks as Dad's longtime best friend. Plus, he can always make me laugh, even if it's in a cringe, dad-humor kind of way.

Which is something he can't get enough of. And might explain why he's always single, despite being objectively handsome. Even now, he's in a T-shirt that has a cat wearing sunglasses and the text "Check Meowt."

I want to make a comment about how embarrassing he is, but instead, I practically tackle him into a hug. Uncle Ian lets it happen, pulling me in tight and not caring that I get some tears and snot on his ridiculous shirt.

"Come on," he says softly, "let's get you home. I have a surprise in the car."

While another surprise is the last thing I want, I follow him. The news of the lockdown must have already spread, because the lot is filling with frantic parents coming to pick up their kids. I don't see any local news vans, so I'm guessing the reason for all this hasn't been released yet, and I don't want to be caught up in that. Besides, while some surprises, like finding one of your classmates murdered in the shop closet, are terrible, others aren't that bad.

Like Uncle Ian's surprise, which meows at me from the passenger seat of his car, the sound carrying through the cracked window.

"Chekov!" I exclaim. "Who's a good boy?"

Chekov paws at the window, like by sheer determination he could open it.

"Thought you could use a little emotional support cat," Uncle Ian says, unlocking the car.

I jump in and immediately pull the tabby into my arms. He purrs happily. Uncle Ian adopted Chekov's Gun not long after Dad died. (Yes, Uncle Ian actually named him that, because he's pretentious as hell.) Even though Chekov doesn't live in our apartment and stays in Uncle Ian's house, he's basically my cat, too.

He's a weird cat. He loves going for drives and has a little pink harness he's more than happy to wear. He pretty much hates everyone outside our family, though, and will growl and snap at people who try to pet him, which is kind of hilarious considering his harness says "Purrfect Little Angel" with a halo and a heart.

I love him.

I lean down toward Chekov and he closes the distance, shoving his nose and mouth into my face for his idea of a kiss. My eyes water a little. Despite everything, he does make me feel a lot better.

"Sometimes I think he likes you more than me," Uncle Ian teases as he starts the car.

"Oh, he definitely does." I scratch Chekov's chin. "Can you blame him?" I keep inhaling the warm cat smell. "I didn't interrupt your work, did I?"

Uncle Ian gives me a look. "There is nothing at my job that would be more important than your safety. Don't even worry about that."

It's nice to hear him say it, especially because Uncle Ian's job actually is important—boring, but important. He's in insurance, so there are a lot of confidential documents with, like, Social Security numbers and medical information and everything. From what he's told us, he handles a lot of the more costly claims, so I'm sure people are constantly calling about expensive payments or accidents or real-life emergencies.

"Thanks," I mumble into Chekov's fur.

Uncle Ian's smile drops after a moment. "How are you holding up? I'm assuming not well, but you know, considering."

I doubt he knows more than what Mom told him, which is just the bare minimum that I told her. I still have to break the news about that freaky-ass message the Wolf Man left, but better to save that for when we get home.

"I'll be okay," I say, not really meaning it. "At least, I will be once we're all together."

Uncle Ian nods. "Exactly. As long as we have each other, we're good."

That's where I need to keep my focus. But anxiety snakes in my gut knowing the killer is still out there.

"Do you think they'll find him before he gets someone else?" I ask quietly.

I don't know why I do. Of course Uncle Ian will say they will.

Uncle Ian's expression is pained. I notice then how red his eyes are. He's probably more torn up about this than he's letting on. Uncle Ian was messed up after losing Dad. I mean, we all were, but knowing there's a new Wolf Man has to be as hard for him as it is for us.

"I hope so . . ." He trails off and swallows. "I think the most we can do is make sure we aren't the someone else."

He's right. Dad was a hero, and it almost killed him the first time and actually killed him the second. I played hero, and Taylor was stabbed to death. Heroes die. Or the people around them do. We have to stick to the plan and save ourselves.

The rest of the drive is tense and quiet, and the state of the apartment isn't all that different when we arrive. Mom wraps me in a hug the second she sees me, and we stand there for a while just holding on as tightly as we can. Orion doesn't say anything, but he doesn't have to. Leo is distracted by a game and Lyra is buried in her book (already a new one from this morning).

"Uncle Ian, are you here to buy us ice cream?" Leo asks, eyes staying glued on his game. Clearly he hasn't forgotten Mom's bribe from this morning.

"Later, bud. I gotta talk with your mom and the big kids for a minute first."

The twins groan while Mom and Uncle Ian sit Orion and me at the kitchen table to talk about what happened. Or most of it, at least. I decide not to tell them anything about *Return to Slasherville.*

I know I made the right choice by the looks on their faces when I tell them about the message the Wolf Man left for me on the storage closet door. It's bad enough that the message confirms I'm a target—they don't need to know just how close to home the killer was. Plus, I'm still not entirely sure what role the book plays in all this. It essentially predicted how and when the first murder would happen—or at least, it was a warning. But now I've changed the script. The book could be completely useless now. I don't even know what the rest of it says, or if there's anything helpful. Before I get anyone else involved, I have to keep reading.

Because I know Mom. Despite all her talk, I know she'll want to rush off and put herself in danger in order to stop the Wolf Man herself. While Mom always makes protecting us a priority, she won't focus on *her* safety.

She'll focus on revenge.

Even though our life-or-death drills emphasize evading and escape—aka living—that's just for us kids. I see the look on her face when Mom trains on a heavy bag. When she took shooting lessons and gun safety classes and bought her shotgun.

Mom will die before she lets the Wolf Man get to us, and I mean that literally. I know that she is prepared to die for us, for Dad. And I can't allow that. I can't lose anyone else. I refuse.

I have to know what the Wolf Man may be planning next so I can keep us all out of it. Which means I can't read the book here.

My eyes trail over to Chekov's Gun, who is pawing at the front door.

"Can I take Chekov out?" I ask.

Uncle Ian and Mom both glare at me. It's possible one of them was in the middle of saying something. I wasn't really paying attention.

"CJ," Mom warns. "You shouldn't be going out alone."

"I won't be alone if I'm with Chekov."

"*Cassiopeia Jane*, now is not the time for attitude."

Ugh. It's not attitude. It's just the way I talk. She should know, she's the one who gave me my sass and humor. But I get it, I do. After all the shit that went down today, of course they'll be on edge.

"I'll just head down the street to Red Page. You have Ms. Maeda's number and I . . . I could use the fresh air and distraction for a minute, okay?" Mom and Uncle Ian look empathetic, but not convinced. "Please?" I add.

The *CJ's been retraumatized* card works, and soon enough, I'm on the street with Chekov's Gun's cat-window backpack around my shoulders. I can feel him adjusting himself in there as he chirps at birds that fly by.

Although I wouldn't admit it to Mom and Uncle Ian, I am a little scared to be walking alone. The panic from this morning stays settled in my stomach, ready to rise at a moment's notice. Thankfully, this walk isn't far at all. Once I reach the end of the street and turn the corner, I'm there. My spooky home away from home, Satterville's own indie bookstore with a specialty in mystery, thriller, horror, and all things frightening.

And the place where I can use this strange book to learn about the new Wolf Man, and more importantly, take in the one thing it got totally right:

CJ Smith is better off as an extra.

7

Handling Horror by the Book

I've been going to Red Page since I was a kid. It opened not long after Dad died, and I've found something comforting about characters that had it just as bad, if not way worse than me. It's not easy to find people my age who get it outside fiction. It's not like we all walk around with signs that advertise our traumas, and I'm hardly the person to try to start some Slasherville Survivor Support Group (although it kind of feels like everyone who'd need it is dead or long gone anyway).

"How are you holding up, Chekov?"

He growls at a woman outside the store.

"Sorry," I mutter to her.

It's not like Chekov has some sixth sense about people that I should heed as a warning. I'm pretty sure the little old lady holding a "Books Are Magic!" tote isn't about to don a wolf mask. Chekov's just a little asshole.

It makes me trust him more. And feel special, too, like I'm a chosen one. (But not in the main-character, my-life-is-doomed-to-be-shit kind of way. Being the chosen one in the horror genre is more of a curse.)

Stepping up to the bright red storefront, I push open the door. There are a few people browsing inside, but it's relatively empty. Fortunately, Slasherfest is essentially this place's Christmas, so business will be booming soon. I step under Ms. Maeda's Horror Holy Trinity (Junji Ito, John Carpenter, and Jordan Peele—yes, she has photos for each of them) and approach her at the checkout counter.

"CJ!" She darts around the counter to pull me into a hug. "And you brought my second-favorite kitty."

She always says that, but it's not like she has a cat. Her first favorite is Jonesy, as in the orange cat from *Alien*. Ms. Maeda is nothing if not consistent with her brand. She's a huge fan of the horror genre, not that you can tell from looks alone. She has on her signature hot pink glasses and always wears brightly colored sweaters over equally cute dresses.

"Hi, Ms. Maeda," I greet her. "How has today been?"

"Not bad. You know it will be wild as the festival gets closer."

"Let me know if you need help."

While I'm not an official Red Page employee, I have been known to help here and there. Ms. Maeda will pay me in food, mostly. She offers cash, but I feel bad, considering the years she's let me read books here without buying.

According to her, if she says one of the Satterville Smith kids recommends a book, it flies off the shelves. So at least that's something.

"Is Hana around?"

"Hana's always around, unfortunately," Hana answers, walking up one of the aisles.

I'd be lying if I said Hana Maeda wasn't my first love. It was totally unrequited, she's ten years older than me, but when I was in middle school, I would wish on nearly every 11:11 that I'd get to marry her.

The crush mostly died over the years, but it didn't make her any less cool.

Her head is shaved and her eyeliner is impossibly perfect, and while she dresses in far more muted colors than her mom, I am in awe of her style. The heeled boots she's currently wearing are practically to die for. Too bad that kind of heel would likely literally kill me. I can barely outrun people in sneakers.

Hana lays her arm around my shoulder. She's way taller than both me and Ms. Maeda at five eleven, so she has to lean down slightly. "Are you okay? We heard a girl died at your school."

"There's another Wolf Man." Might as well put it all out there.

They both have wide eyes. "Oh my God, that's horrible." Ms. Maeda takes my hand in both of hers. "And you know for sure it's a new Wolf Man? Someone actually saw him?"

I nod. "I . . . I did."

She shakes her head, letting out a long breath of air. "I'm sorry, CJ. I can't believe it. That's so . . . shitty."

She lands on the word like she desperately tried to think of something better but couldn't. It's pretty fitting. And she doesn't know the half of it.

"If you need anything, just let us know," Hana says.

"Thanks, I really appreciate it. On the bright side, it will probably be good for business," I joke.

Hana flicks me in the forehead. "Shut up, your family is more important than that." Hana eyes my back. "Now, let Chekov's Gun out. He's my boy."

"He hates you."

"He hates everyone, I relate. Let me see him."

Well, she brought it upon herself. I unzip the window backpack and Chekov's Gun sticks his head out. He hisses immediately at Hana before jumping out and rubbing against Ms. Maeda's legs.

While he doesn't quite get cozy with her, she's one of the very few people that he likes.

"What does my mom have that I don't?" Hana asks him.

Ms. Maeda smiles. "You can't blame him for having good taste."

A customer comes up with a question, so Hana goes off (looking a little rejected) to help them. I sit with Ms. Maeda and Chekov's Gun behind the counter. I probably feel a little too at home here, with all the horror memorabilia, posters, and decorations. You'd think it would bother me, considering there's a whole Ghostface section and *Scream* is practically my biography, but Ms. Maeda and Hana are like family. I've stayed late enough times to have fried chicken and beer (the beer just for them) or go out to the ramen restaurant Ms. Maeda deemed the most authentic (passably, she said, ever the critic) to feel safe in this killer-filled place. Not to mention, horror books were basically my self-help books, since the information in them always felt more applicable to me than positive thinking or learning my love language.

Ms. Maeda looks closely at me. "You need a distraction," she says. She reaches over to grab a book from the counter and places it in my hand. "I just finished this YA horror book, you'll love it."

"Nothing to distract from real monsters like fictional monsters." I put on a smile. "I actually brought something to read today, but I'll start it after."

"No rush." She taps the cover. "But the lead in this one is nonbinary, so I thought of you! They aren't as funny, though."

What a compliment. She knows exactly what to say to get me to do anything she wants. Ms. Maeda and Hana were the first people I came out to, sort of like a practice round before telling my mom. I take the book from Ms. Maeda and flip through the pages.

Maybe I'll like it. Sometimes I feel like a fraud with gender stuff, though. I consider myself gender fluid, or at least under the nonbinary umbrella. I almost feel more like a gender chameleon. I adapt to whatever makes the most sense to me at the time or based on my surroundings. Once I figured that out for myself, I didn't really care how other people saw me. I don't mind if I'm called a girl or a dude or a kid or a creepy bitch. Which makes me feel like I'm almost not genderqueer enough, since a lot of people rightfully *do* care.

But it's hard to care how people perceive you when you'd rather just not be perceived at all. At this point, I'd like to identify as someone who doesn't get brutally murdered by a man in a mask, but generally just claiming the term "queer" feels the most right.

"Thanks, Ms. Maeda. That means a lot." I reach into my pocket. "How much do I owe you?"

She waves me away. "You don't have to pay. It's an early copy so I got it for free from the publisher."

Right. "NOT FOR SALE" is written right across the top. It's been a long day.

"I appreciate it," I say. "Mind if I head to the corner spot to read?"

"You can lie in the middle of the floor and read if you want. Whatever you need." Ms. Maeda's smile is sad as she rubs my back. "Oh, but I am doing a new window display soon and I'd love your help. I'll treat us to fried chicken or something."

"That sounds great."

I walk with Chekov's Gun to the back of the store. Next to the stage area where the occasional event is hosted, there's a little reading nook that no one uses. Aside from me, that is. In part, it might be because of John Doe, the giant stag head hanging precariously by two chains from the ceiling.

John Doe is objectively terrifying. He looks like a décor piece from a murder mansion on a good day, and the person who originally taxidermized him didn't really do a great job of it. His glass eyes look particularly cold and dead, and his lower jaw is half missing, which doesn't help his overall aesthetic but works for the theme of the store.

Besides, grotesque or not, John Doe is part of Satterville history. He was mounted at the Camp Satterville mess hall at its opening, and technically, he saved Dad's life.

The first time.

It was the glare of his unsettling eyes in their flashlights, splashed red with blood, that alerted authorities to investigate the mess hall and find my teenage father, bleeding out underneath John Doe's half-holding-on chin. Without John Doe, I probably wouldn't exist, so we're cool. Ms. Maeda bought him at an auction they held as part of Slasherfest a few years back. Cops had noticed tourists were looting the old campgrounds, and the town figured they might as well sell the "memorabilia" and make some money off it. No one wanted John Doe, though, for obvious reasons. He was looking especially raggedy after nearly thirty years in a decaying building and was barely hanging on to his original mount by then, so Ms. Maeda got him for cheap, hooked him up to some chains, and he's been hanging here ever since.

I sit on the cushioned chair under John Doe's not-so-watchful eyes, Chekov hopping up and first hissing at the dangling stag head before settling onto my lap. I appreciate the comfort, especially since what I'm here to read is the exact opposite of cozy.

The book feels heavy as I pull it out of my bag.

I flip through the pages, to the chapter after the first death, and begin to read.

It's strange to read from Taylor's point of view. I was never close to her, and based on what I know, I'm not sure I would've wanted to be, but it's still so extremely fucked up to be in the head of someone whose dead body I saw earlier that day. It almost makes it seem like she's still alive in some way.

But it's not like she actually wrote this. It's not like it's *her*.

My stomach feels both hollow and tight, like there's a vacuum within me but a little vomit might still escape from it. She's really gone. Just like that. Yet I'm still here, doing what even Dad couldn't: surviving the Wolf Man twice.

Why me? I could have easily been the one to die. Why wasn't I? My breaths threaten to release too quickly and I feel lightheaded, so I try to focus on the words like they are something I'm reading for school. Distant, just a play-by-play of events. While, in the story, the dead girl is Nadia, I try to focus on what happens in general.

In the book, there is a memorial planned for Friday on the Satterville High football field. Taylor and a group of her friends (mostly the popular, partying type) skip the vigil and go off to drink in the wooded area where I first saw the Wolf Man this morning. Max, Taylor's ex-boyfriend, heads off deeper into the woods alone. Worried, Taylor eventually follows him, only to find the Wolf Man standing over his dead body. She narrowly escapes, and the Wolf Man still gets away.

Which means if the killer is following this book, or if it's true in any way, the next death will happen at a memorial on Friday.

Chekov starts to get a little antsy, so I pack up the book and return him to his window backpack. My mind races, though. If there is a memorial this week, the best option would be to just totally avoid it. That should keep my family safe. Mom will probably want to go to support Taylor's family, since if anyone gets it, it's her, but I'm sure I can come up with some reason for us to stay home. The killer still being out there is a pretty damn good one.

It's a plan, at least. While I can't put all my faith in this book, I don't think I can ignore it either. I might not have all the whys—like, if this was the Wolf Man's plan, why the hell did he send it to *me*—but I don't exactly need them.

I'm not trying to play Nancy Drew and figure out who the Wolf Man is, I'm just trying to keep my family alive.

I feel okay about that much as I tell Ms. Maeda and Hana good night and step out of the store.

At least, until I hear a voice behind me.

"We've been waiting for you, CJ."

The Dead Girl Intervenes

My initial panic subsides into confusion when I realize that Nadia is the one who spoke, arms crossed as she gives me a hard stare.

"Don't say it like that, that makes it sound like we were stalking her," Sebas says from next to her. He looks at me apologetically. "Which we were not doing."

I eye the two of them. Neither looks exactly inconspicuous. Nadia is wearing a Pokémon pajama set and Sebas is even worse, looking vaguely sweaty in shorts over spandex pants and a tight shirt with some kind of karate cat printed on it.

"How did you know I was here?" I ask.

He bites his lower lip. "I was training next door and walking by when I saw you in that library."

"Bookstore," Nadia amends.

He rolls his eyes. "Whatever. I wouldn't have mentioned it to you if I knew you would literally Uber here and try to confront her like some maniac." He looks back at me. "I promise this was not my idea."

It's a lot to take in at once. "You were training? For what?"

I'm not sure why that's the first question I land on. Maybe because I associate training with Mom's drills, and from what I remember, the place next door was an insurance company. When I look over, however, it is entirely different. The sign now reads "FAIXA PRETA JIU-JITSU." The window even advertises a special for new students.

Well, I guess that explains the outfit.

"My brother opened a jiu-jitsu gym recently. That's part of the reason why we moved here in the first place. Apparently there's a big demand here to learn self-defense?"

Yeah, that sounds about right.

While I don't exactly know what jiu-jitsu is, I can definitely see Satterville locals wanting to learn martial arts. I don't know how effective that would be against a killer, but like Mom's kickboxing, it probably can't hurt.

"You should come try a class," Sebas continues. "It's very fun and only a little bit like a cult, I promise." He winks at that. I didn't know people could actually look good winking until that moment.

"Wait, hold on," I say. He's too cute. It's distracting me from what is actually going on here. "So you guys stalked me to try and convince me to take a jiu-jitsu class?"

"Again, we weren't stalking you," Nadia says. She takes a step toward me. "Yet. We want answers. Tell us what you know about the Wolf Man."

I look at her blankly. "No."

"Ah-ha! So you admit that you know something, you're just refusing to tell us."

I roll my eyes at her *gotcha* grin. "I'm not admitting anything. There's nothing to tell. I thought I saw something suspicious and it just so happened that I was right. You're welcome for saving your cousin's life, but I don't want anything to do with any of this."

I turn on my heel to walk away, and Sebas gasps.

"Is that a cat?" he asks, voice lined with excitement. "Can I at least say hi? I love cats."

I sigh. He's too handsome. It's not fair. Maybe Nadia needs to ask her questions with an excited smile, because apparently I'm weak to beautiful people showing their teeth. "Fine, but he hates everyone. You've been warned."

Sebas walks up, leaning down to look at Chekov. "Que *lindo*," he says. His voice raises several octaves as he talks to him. "Este gatito es todo guapito y todo bonito." His smile is the biggest I've seen it, and it makes my heart flutter. "Cómo se ll— I mean, what's his name?"

Dammit. Why couldn't Uncle Ian have given the poor cat a normal name? "Um . . . Chekov's Gun? I call him Chekov." I unzip the backpack enough that Chekov can stick his head out. I expect him to growl or even hiss, but shockingly he immediately bumps his head against Sebas's fingers, happily taking the pets. "He's not like this usually," I say. "He's a total dick to most people."

"You've made my day," Sebas says.

"Okay, Chekov is cute," Nadia says, "but that doesn't mean we're going to ignore the fact that you know something about this new Wolf Man, CJ. And since the two of us are kind of involved, I think we deserve to know what that something is. I mean, a girl *died*."

I press my lips together. She's not exactly wrong. In fact, she's more involved than she even realizes, considering she was supposed to be that dead girl. But how the hell am I supposed to explain that? I can't.

"I don't know what you're talking about," I say.

"You have the communication skills of a webcomic male lead," Nadia says with a groan. She throws her hands up. "Do *not* make this shit go on for chapters. I hope you know, if there were people commenting on this exchange, they would all be dragging you and complaining to the author. But I have the patience, Cassiopeia Jane. I have the time. Dedication. Do you know how many daily updates I read? How many romance fantasy stories I loyally follow even though they all have the exact same tropes and concepts? I've waited over one hundred chapters for the couple to simply *blush* while *holding hands*. I can wait until you break. And I will."

I don't even know how to respond to that. Thankfully, Sebas interjects.

"Nadia, can I talk to CJ for a moment?"

Nadia rolls her eyes. "Fine." She looks at her phone without moving.

Sebas, while still petting a purring Chekov, focuses on me.

"First of all, are you okay?" he asks.

I shrug. "Not really."

His smile is anything but happy. "Yeah, me neither. I know Nadia can come on strong, but she's just worried. We're both pretty freaked out, and we want to understand what happened. We want to keep ourselves safe. If you do know something that would help, I just . . . I'd appreciate you telling us."

When he says it like that, it's hard not to relent a little. Nadia and Sebas are family. They're trying to protect each other, just like me and Mom are trying to protect our family. Would it really be so bad if I helped them?

"It's just . . . I don't know . . ."

I can't find the words, and I can tell Sebas is trying to be nice, but there's still disappointment in his eyes. It leaves a bitter, guilty taste on my tongue.

"If you're scared, I get it. I'm scared too. I mean, shit. I literally just packed up my entire life and left my home for a new place. I knew

I'd have to deal with some stressful stuff, but I never would have imagined *this*." He looks a little more vulnerable, eyes almost glassy, before catching himself. "I like you, CJ. And you're right, I probably wouldn't have gotten through this day without you. So let me return the favor. You don't have to carry whatever this is alone. We want to be able to help you. To help each other." He shrugs, expression lightening a little. "Plus, I almost died for a shitty birdhouse. I think you can at least give me some explanation for that."

"The birdhouse is not shitty!" Nadia snaps.

My face heats a little because a part of me almost forgot she was there, but now both of them are watching me, waiting for a response.

I look at Sebas. "I don't understand why you even want to help me. We just met."

Nadia rolls her eyes, stepping forward to pat his shoulder. "That's because Sebas here is, like, the king of insta-love. He falls embarrassingly fast. You saved his life, so I guarantee he's already planning your wedding on Playa Hermosa in Jaco and the names of your future feline children."

Sebas glares at her. "Sea necia!"

"Mae, relax, I'm exaggerating, obviously." Nadia turns to me to mouth, *No, I'm not.*

Sebas mutters something in Spanish before looking back at me. "The point is, we just want to help you and ask you to help us. Be in this together."

I try to swallow my unfamiliar mixture of embarrassment and delight. Sebas is probably right. I should give them something. And considering Nadia seems ready to bother me every day until I do, I might as well get it over with so we can all go back to lying low and staying the hell out of the Wolf Man's way.

"Okay," I say. "We can talk, but not here."

Nadia claps her hands together. “Great, we’ll go to my place.”

I sigh. “Just . . . try to keep an open mind.”

“Oh, we have, like, the most open of minds,” Nadia assures me. “You don’t have to worry about that.”

9

When Major Rewrites Are Needed

Sitting across from me at Nadia's kitchen table, both she and Sebas look at me like I've lost my entire mind.

"What the fuck is that?" Nadia says, eyeing the book I dropped in front of them.

"That," I say, "is what I know."

After leaving Nadia and Sebas to drop off Chekov at home and get permission from Mom to hang out at Nadia's house (her exact words were "I'm just glad you're finally making some friends, there's safety in numbers" like a jerk), I took an Uber to Nadia's place. I was able to delay the inevitable as her dad hooked us up with arroz con leche, but after her parents went to watch TV in another room, I had to spill.

Showing them the book felt like the easiest way to do that.

"I don't get it," Nadia says finally.

I sigh. "Do you know Moon Satter?"

"Everyone knows Moon Satter," Nadia says.

"Everyone knows they're a piece of shit, maybe."

"Hey, you brought them up," Nadia defends. "So . . . what is this?"

I can already tell I'm losing them. But at this point, my only option is to keep going. It's not like I can hide the book and run. They'll have even more questions now than they did before.

"A third Moon Satter book. Or a fake Moon Satter book, I don't know. It was left on my doorstep yesterday. I thought it was some kind of fucked up joke because the story is about the Wolf Man returning and murdering a Satterville High student, but then it actually happened."

Nadia bites her lip. "Couldn't that just be a coincidence, though? It's always high school students that get killed in slashers. And that was the original Wolf Man's whole thing."

I shake my head. "The death happened in the same exact place at the exact same time as it did in the book. And it got other things right, too. Like the bathroom being out of order and me running into Taylor as it was announced. All that happened for real." I force myself to keep looking in their eyes, even though I don't like how their gazes feel. "I know this sounds insane and unbelievable. All I know is this weird book got a freaky amount of today's events right."

"So the manuscript said that Taylor was going to be killed?" Nadia asks.

At that, I have to tear my gaze away. "Not exactly. But almost everything else was the same."

"What did it say, then? Who died?"

I don't answer. Sebas speaks instead.

"This isn't making any sense. You're saying this book predicted the future?"

He's looking at me like I've lost my mind, and I can't blame him. I'm pretty convinced I have, too.

"I'm not saying it's a magic book or anything. I think the killer wrote this or got it from an AI generator or something and is making it come true. Like, it's not that hard to clog a toilet."

It doesn't explain the timing of everything, but there has to be some explanation that doesn't make Moon Satter or whoever wrote this thing into some freaking prophet.

Sebas cracks his knuckles. "I don't know. This seems a little . . . hard to believe."

"I know it is," I say. "I don't know what to believe either."

"Did you read the entire thing?" Nadia asks. "Like, how it ends?"

I shake my head. "Not yet. I was planning on it, but I've only gotten as far as the supposed second murder. In the book, it happens at a memorial on the football field this Friday."

"I didn't hear anything about a memorial . . ."

Immediately as Nadia trails off, her phone buzzes against the table and mine lights up. It's an email notification from my school account.

Candlelight Memorial to Be Held for Satterville High Student Taylor Topper This Friday—Volunteers Needed.

Jesus Christ.

Nadia pales instantly. "What the fuck?" She looks up at me. "How did you know that would happen?"

I point to the book. "I told you. It's in the book. I'm freaking out just as much as you are."

That much isn't a lie. I'm still conflicted over how to feel about this *Return to Slasherville* mess, and the book getting another thing right doesn't exactly make me feel better.

Nadia takes the book and starts reading from the beginning. She immediately makes a face like she bit into a too-sour lemon. "Wait, Taylor is the lead in this?"

I grimace. "That's the one major difference."

"But then who was supposed to die . . . ?" She flips through the pages, skimming, until she lands on the reveal. I don't have to know what part she's reading when it hits her. It's all in her expression. Stunned, confused, scared. "What the fuck?" Her eyes whip up to me. "You swear you didn't write this?"

I shake my head. "No, I promise."

"How do I know you aren't involved?"

"CJ couldn't be involved." Sebas may be a bit confused about the situation, but at least he's still sure of me. "She was with me when the killer was outside."

Nadia glares at him and slams the book down. "Don't defend them because they're pretty. The book fucking says that *I* die."

That lands like a brick. Sebas's mouth falls open. "What?"

Nadia rubs her temples, processing everything. I don't know what to say. I'm having a hard enough time with it all, and I wasn't even the one who was supposed to die.

Nadia looks up at me and lets her hands fall to the table. "That's why you were waiting in the hallway. That's why you called out to me," Nadia says. "You were trying to stop me from going into the shop room, weren't you?"

My voice is quiet when I say, "I still didn't fully believe it, but it didn't seem worth the risk. I thought even if it was some kind of prank, you could've gotten hurt."

"That's why when I said Sebas was in the room, you freaked and ran off."

I nod.

Nadia takes a moment. "Huh. And why did you put yourself in danger to save us?"

"Because you're pretty," I deadpan, stealing her earlier compliment.

She lets out a laugh at that, cutting through some of the tension. "This is fucked up."

"Extremely. Although 'fucked up' kind of feels like the Satterville brand," I say.

"Yeah." Nadia rests her head on her hand. "So, you think that someone took this Moon Satter draft and changed the identities to real people . . ."

"Or they made a fake Moon Satter book based off the first two and edited the details."

"Either way," Nadia continues, "you think someone is using this book as a way to live out their Wolf Man fantasies?"

"Basically."

"But, for some reason, probably your meddling, they killed Taylor Topper instead of me."

I bite my lip. "Yeah."

Nadia laughs. "Take that, bitch," she says.

Sebas gives her a look. "You know she actually died, right?"

"Okay, yes, that part is indeed fucked up and I feel for her family," Nadia defends. "It's not like I wanted her dead. Really. But Taylor Topper was a mean, self-obsessed, homophobic shit stain. I'm not saying people shouldn't be sad for the loss, but I'm saying *I'm* happy that the Latina lesbian lives in this one."

When she puts it that way, I can't argue. There's nothing we can do to help Taylor now, and the Wolf Man is still out there. Like Uncle Ian said, the best thing to do is make sure we're not next.

Maybe Nadia and Sebas can be included in that "we."

"Wait." Sebas looks up. "So I seriously almost died because of your birdhouse? What the fuck, Nadia?"

"It's not like I knew there was a killer there."

I look between them. "So . . . you both actually believe me?"

Nadia shrugs. "I don't know what else to believe, and honestly, I've read enough webcomics where the main character learns they're living in a book that the idea is kind of exciting."

"I think I'm still in shock maybe. And confused definitely," Sebas says, "but I'm along for the ride."

Well. That's unexpected.

"But we still have a problem," Nadia says.

Sebas snorts. "Yeah, the killer is still out there."

Nadia crosses her arms. "Yes, but also the person who was supposed to be the Final Girl is dead. Which means even if the book says how to stop the Wolf Man, Taylor is no longer around to do it."

"Right," I say, "which is why we need to stay out of it."

Nadia laughs. "Um. No. We *need* to make it to the end and stop the killer before they kill us. And since *you* found the body instead of Taylor . . ." Nadia points directly at me, expression hard and serious. "CJ Smith, you need to man the fuck up and be the new Final Girl."

10

But CJ Smith Is No Protagonist

No, no, no, hell to the absolute no.

Nadia is getting this all wrong. I can't be the Final Girl.

"No," I repeat aloud. "My only job here is to avoid being killed and keep my family safe. *This* is how we do that." I point at the book. "The Wolf Man is going to keep killing no matter what. We couldn't stop him today. If anything, we only made ourselves targets. What makes you think it will go any differently on Friday, when this next murder is supposed to happen? The smart thing to do is make sure he doesn't kill us next, not dive right into the line of fire."

Nadia rolls her eyes. "You're getting female-lead syndrome already."

"What?"

"You are falling into a trap of self-doubt while trying to preserve the original story, like every protagonist does whenever a comic uses this trope. Once again: you would be getting roasted in the comments right now. Forget the original story, forget the original female lead, and just fuck the seemingly monstrous but secretly charming Duke of the North already!"

Sebas opens his mouth, clearly not following. "A duke?"

Nadia just waves him off. "It's a romance webcomic thing. Different genre, I know, but bear with me. In this case, instead of fucking the handsome duke, CJ needs to fuck *up* the creepy Wolf Man."

It sounds so easy when she puts it like that. But today proved that it isn't. I'm useless in front of the Wolf Man. Dad was the hero. Me? I was lucky enough to survive by hiding twice. But the killer said it himself: that isn't going to work a third time.

How could I face him for real?

My eyes threaten to burn. Even the thought of the mask has me ready to panic.

"That's not how this works," I say softly. "It's not as easy as rewriting a story."

"Um, absolutely it's as easy as rewriting the story," Nadia says. "The original story sucks. We are going to rewrite it, and it's gonna be more fun, it's gonna be more gay, and best of all? I'm not going to be serial killed by a weirdo wannabe Wolf Man."

It's not like I want to argue with that part, but Nadia is going about this entirely the wrong way. I bite my lip, trying to control my emotions.

"We aren't actually living in some horror story, though," I say. "I mean, it feels that way, yes, but this isn't a magic book. It's some sick fuck who might actually want you dead. You haven't faced the Wolf Man, Nadia. But I have. This isn't a joke, or something a group of ragtag teens can take on. My family has been preparing for this shit for *years*, and the best defense is getting the fuck away. That's what will keep you alive."

Nadia's eyes are hard. "So you just want to let other people die?"

My eyes sting. Of course I don't want other people to die. Thinking of it fills my stomach with a sickening weight. I didn't even like Taylor, but I still wish I could go back in time and save her. But that's the problem. Trying to save someone just makes someone else the target. Dad tried to save us, and he died. I tried to save Nadia, and Taylor died. It doesn't matter what I do. Nadia is right about one thing: this isn't a romance fantasy and there's no guaranteed happy ending.

What I want doesn't matter. It never did.

"I don't have a choice."

"Of course you do. You're the Final Girl!" Nadia yells.

"Do you know what being the Final Girl means?" I ask. My voice comes out harder than I intended, the sounds sharp and jagged. "That other people die! And not just other people —it means that *everyone you love* dies. I'm not going to let that happen. I want us all to make it to the end, and the best way to do that is to stay out of it." I pick up the book. "I'm sorry if you were expecting me to be some kind of hero. I'm not. And even if I was, heroes can't save everyone. I had to learn that the hard way, and it seems like the Wolf Man won't let me forget it." My eyes threaten to overflow, so I look away from them. "I'll let you know what I learn from the book. For now, just focus on saving yourselves. Please." My voice cracks. "Thanks for having me over, but I have to get home."

I don't give either of them time to say anything else, instead making a beeline straight to the front door. Tears are starting to fall, and even if it may be understandable, I don't want to cry in front of Sebas and Nadia. I just want to go home.

"CJ, wait!"

I turn around at Sebas's voice. He stops by my side with a lop-sided smile and holds up keys.

"Do you need a ride?"

While this sort of ruins my embarrassingly dramatic exit, there *is* a killer on the loose, and Nadia's place isn't as close to my apartment as Red Page. I don't need to consider the options long.

"Sure," I say. "Thanks."

I get into the passenger seat of Sebas's brother's car. "I'm kind of sad you had to give your uncle's cat back," Sebas says. "I love him."

I blink. I half expected him to continue the conversation from earlier, or try to convince me to change my mind. It's really nice that he isn't.

"He shockingly loves you," I say.

"Wow. Shockingly?" Sebas holds a hand to his chest. "That hurts."

My face heats up. "Not that you aren't great, just that I'm serious when I say Chekov usually hates people. I can count the number of people he doesn't constantly hiss and growl at on one hand."

Sebas sighs dramatically as he puts on his seat belt. "It's okay, I like him better than me, too."

Now he's just teasing me. "So if the killer comes after us and I have to choose between you and Chekov . . ."

"Then it's been a good run. Tell my father I died with honor."

I snort. "Noted." I shrug. "That might get in the way of our future beach wedding and cat children."

He groans. "Please don't. I'm not that bad."

"Right, we have to get birria first at least."

"At *least*," he says with a smile.

There's a bit of a pause. Keeping up the joke any longer will make it seem like *I'm* way too into him already, and I don't want to be the one to scare him away when not even the Wolf Man did.

Sebas awkwardly rubs his hands together. His fingers have little calluses around the joints, some of them slightly bent like he's broken them in the past. I suppress the desire to take them in mine and see how different they feel. I shouldn't be thinking about how cute he is right now. I'm getting too sidetracked by this new kind of attention, and I need to get my mind straight. Dating is not the focus. Survival is.

Especially with things going off the rails, I can't afford a distraction.

Not even a charming distraction, with that perfectly imperfect smile.

"I'm going to admit, I still don't know what the hell is going on," Sebas starts. "I'm not the smartest person with books and everything, and it all seems weird and a little confusing, but what I do know is that I could've died this afternoon and you saved me. So, thank you."

I don't know how to respond. My heart thumps in my chest.

"I didn't do much . . ."

"You did something." He smiles slightly. "I don't know much about your history or about this Wolf Man thing, but I know you helped me and my cousin, and I don't take that lightly." He slowly, slowly reaches out his hand to mine, fingers warm and tough. My skin feels like it was just plugged in, tingling and buzzing. "If you want to stay out of it, I'll support you. Either way, I'll do whatever I can to protect you. Return the favor."

Something about him being lit by only the moon and the lights on the dash has me hyperaware. The skin he's touching is so sensitive and alive. I don't know why I'm reacting like I've never experienced touch before. Although I guess I haven't, not in this sense.

I've stayed firmly away from any semblance of romance. Hooking up with someone is practically a death sentence in slasher movies. But all that was easier to avoid when it felt like no one wanted anything to do with me.

This is different.

I want to focus on all the details. The bends in his fingers. His dark eyes, this little scar on the corner of his mouth.

Would it be tender if I kissed it?

Maybe it's a trick of the light, but it almost feels like he's thinking it, too. That he wants to lean in, to try and close the distance . . .

"I'm sorry you have to deal with this," I say quickly. "I mean, that this is your introduction to Satterville. I'm sure you miss home a lot now."

He blinks as if coming out of a daze. "Yeah," he says, voice soft. "I do."

He looks away from me. Maybe he could use a bit of a distraction from all the . . . murder stuff. "What do you miss about it?" I ask.

"Aside from the fact that no man in a cheap mask was trying to stab me to death there?"

I can't help but chuckle. "Yeah. Besides that."

Sebas leans back in the seat. "I miss my friends. The lifestyle. You know, more . . ." He looks at me, searching for an explanation. "Pura vida. I miss going to sodas and eating there. I miss actual beaches with nature and *warm* water. I miss my mom." His voice cracks a little at that, and he quickly clears his throat. "But it was my choice to come with Samuel. I love jiu-jitsu and want to make a life out of it. The opportunity to keep learning from my brother and get to teach was too good to pass up. Plus, it's nice to have a dream to follow, you know? But sometimes the sacrifices can feel . . . hard."

I swallow. I can't say I know what it's like to have a dream like that. I've been so caught up in making sure I have a future at all, I've never spent much time thinking about what I want that future to look like. What do I want to do, other than survive? In some ways, the future feels like a foreign language, something I will never be able to fully grasp, a conversation that doesn't apply to me. It's like, everyone else feels like the future is a promise, when I know it could be taken away at any moment.

Especially now, with the Wolf Man back, the idea of dreams for the future seems even more useless. How can I think of what I want when he's out there?

Still. I like to hear Sebas talk about it. I like that he has this dream, this passion. I like that talking to him makes the future feel possible.

"I'm sorry," I finally say, "about the sacrifices."

He smiles. "Está bien. I have my brother and tío and tía and even Nadia here. And there are things I like. It just . . . it doesn't feel like home." He looks away. "That's the good thing about jiu-jitsu, though. No matter where you are, the language is the same. No matter where I am, the mats are like home to me."

I make a face. "I'm still not entirely sure what jiu-jitsu is."

Sebas gives a real laugh at that. "Have you ever seen an MMA fight?"

I nod. "I think so."

"Well, it's like all the parts of that done on the ground. The wrestling. No punches, elbows, or kicks. Mostly chokes and trying to break joints."

"And that's fun?"

"I don't think anyone in this town has the right to judge learning self-defense."

"Well, you got me there." I shrug. "Although most of what I know about self-defense involves getting away, not fighting back."

"Sport jiu-jitsu is different from the self-defense aspect," Sebas says. "It's not about just trying to beat up an attacker. It's about incapacitating them so you *can* safely get away. So it's not really that different."

"Oh," I say. "Maybe I will try it sometime, then."

"I'd like that."

"You've been doing jiu-jitsu for a while?"

"Since I was a kid, yeah. Samuel got me into it. I've always been into sports, and the community was nice. The academy we went to was like a second home. Some of the people there are like my brothers."

There's a long beat of silence. It's clear that he misses that. I'm sure there hasn't been enough time here for the people at his brother's new academy to feel like family. "I don't know what it's like to be homesick or anything. I've only ever been here, really. But . . . well, I do know what it's like to miss someone."

"Yeah?"

My eyes burn. "I lost my dad a few years back."

It almost feels weird to admit. Everyone in town already knows that, plus exactly how it happened. I've never had to *tell* anyone before. It feels vulnerable, but at the same time, kind of empowering. That I get to be the one to say it.

"Shit, CJ, I'm so sorry."

I shake my head, wiping my eyes. "It's fine. I mean, they say it gets easier, but it doesn't. You just keep going because that's all there is to do."

"I understand," he says. "Nadia and I lost our abuelito two years ago, and I still miss him so much. He's the reason why she's so into woodshop. He was a carpenter."

His eyes are glassy and I watch a tear slip out.

"I'm sorry," I tell him. "Even though I know saying that doesn't help."

"I don't know," he says. "I think sharing it does." He wipes his eye. "Better than being angry about it and punching a hole in the wall."

I laugh. "That from experience?"

"Honestly, I hurt my hand more than the wall."

I have to dab my own eye with my sleeve. "Thank you, for listening. And talking. But that's why I can't get involved with this. I can't lose anyone important to me again."

Sebas's voice is soft. "I'm not going to tell you that you have to do anything. Nadia is intense, but if you want to just keep yourself and your family safe, I get it. I'm not going to judge you. Honestly, this is all super weird and new to me."

"I'm not sure this is something anyone can be prepared for, and I've been doing life-and-death playground drills since I was eleven."

Sebas gives me a look. "You've been doing what?"

"It's . . ." I look for the right words.

"Some white people thing?"

I laugh. "Kind of." The end of the phrase expands into a yawn. Guess the day finally caught up with me.

"All right, I think it's time for me to actually take you home," Sebas says.

I type my address into his phone. The ride there is pretty silent, but it's a comfortable one. And in a car, my apartment isn't that far. "It's that gray one on the right," I say when I see it come into view.

He pulls over before looking at me. "Do you want me to walk you in?"

I almost make a comment that it isn't a date, but save myself from blushing at my own joke.

"Nah, but can you wait to drive away until I walk inside?"

"Of course. But you should still text me when you're in your apartment so I know everything is good."

It's not so much the thoughtfulness but the understanding that bad things can happen at home and the willingness to be an escape driver that have me almost swooning. Sebas may not fully understand what's going on, but he at least has some survival skills. That will make things so much easier—I won't have to worry so much about him, hopefully.

"Is this you asking for my number?" I can't help but ask.

"I promise I'll only call to ask you about extending your car warranty three times a day."

"Limit it to two and you got it."

He hands me his phone, and I text myself my own name so both of us have each other's. I pass back his phone but hesitate before getting out of the car.

"Thanks for being so cool about all this, Sebas. I'm not glad you had to end up in a crime scene, but . . . is it okay to say I'm glad you were there with me? That I'm glad you're here in general?"

"Very okay," he says, his smile so wide it shows his braces. "Stay safe."

And that's about as good as it gets for a Satterville goodbye.

11

Cassiopeia and Their Little Stars

My anxiety is high as I sit alone in my room, but for once, it isn't only because of the Wolf Man. It's also because of my own inability to understand normal communication with cute people. Sinking deeper into my pillow, I read the last message I sent for the thirtieth time.

CJ Smith

So formal for someone you were just in a closet with earlier

Sebastián Luis Martínez Arroyo

Please do not save all that

I'll save as Sebas Luis Martínez Arroyo

To be casual

I'll put you as Cute Blond Who Saved My Life

Please God no

Put Cassiopeia Jane before that

???

Tell me you didn't

Guess you'll have to hang out with me to know

:)

Like a date?

Fifteen minutes have already passed, and for someone who has done a lot to desperately survive despite all odds, I actually kind of want to die. Why would I even ask that? I'm so awkward. Sure, Sebas definitely made it seem like he was interested, but I should be playing it cool and keeping a distance, not getting butterflies in my chest and goofily smiling at my phone literally every time he texts.

Sixteen minutes. Still no response. Why wouldn't he respond? Maybe he wasn't actually interested in me and just likes the attention. Maybe we got too serious and emotional in the car and it freaked him out. Maybe I somehow left one of my old self-insert fan fiction stories of me brutally torturing Moon Satter in my backpack and it fell out and he found it and realized what a mess I am.

Okay, the last one is next to impossible, but I'm already overthinking, so even the most outlandish worst-case scenarios are fair game.

Seventeen minutes. Still nothing. This is painful.

Just messing with you

I'm sure I'll see you and Nadia soon

Immediately after sending it, I realize I likely made it two times more embarrassing now. I toss my phone onto the mattress next to me, unable to bear looking at it anymore. That was enough of a distraction. I'm supposed to be reading anyway.

After I got home and deftly avoided Mom's questions, I holed up in my room and made it as far as the third murder, where Taylor's favorite teacher (Mr. Collins, an art teacher I never had because I took the Film Studies elective) is killed in the school library during finals week. It doesn't make me feel great that two more people are scheduled to die, but it shouldn't be hard to avoid staying late once exams are over. Nadia, Sebas, and I should be fine.

The panic pit in my stomach only worsens, though, as I keep reading.

With the amount of pages left in the book, I figured there would be maybe one more murder before Taylor gets around to stopping the asshole. The story seems like it's setting up the final showdown to take place at Slasherfest, which makes sense.

But the Wolf Man goes off the fucking handle, killing *five* more people. *FIVE.* Enough bodies to fill a sedan in one evening. I start speed-reading, skimming the pages to see how Taylor eventually stops him. But it's like pages are missing from the story. I slow down, rereading the same two pages over and over to make sure I'm not missing something. One moment, Taylor is alone at the showdown with the Wolf Man, somewhere downtown during Slasherfest, and then it literally skips ahead to the Wolf Man being dead and Taylor's bloody victory.

Then it ends.

"What the fuck?" I say aloud. "What in the bullshit, poorly paced fuck?"

It doesn't say how she stopped him. Hell, it doesn't even say who the Wolf Man is! Whoever left me this manuscript gave me the major events but censored the actual important part of the story: the big reveal.

I throw the book against the wall. Fuck that book. And fuck Moon Satter.

It's a good thing my only job is to stay out of it. Even if I wanted to go through with Nadia's plan, I couldn't now, not without the book giving us the answers. I check my phone again. Still nothing. I wonder if the Wolf Man is reason enough to get me into witness protection, because after this embarrassing one-sided text chain, I think I need a new identity. I should be sleeping anyway. I *was* tired. But once I saw Sebas's seemingly flirty texts and brushed my teeth and everything, it woke me up entirely.

With a sigh, I finally shut off my lamp and bury half my face into my pillow.

Without the light of my phone, my room is completely dark. My eyes adjust enough to see the various shapes of my dresser and desk and closet (which always has the door open—I considered removing it but couldn't), although being able to make out the edges in the shadows sort of makes everything worse. Especially without my glasses, the blurs can morph into anything. My mind wants to conjure things that aren't there, bracing for a figure to appear in the corner of the room, for a howl to come from outside the door.

Tears prick at my eyes.

He's back. He's back and he's out there. Waiting. While I thankfully didn't see the full extent of the damage to Taylor, red drips into my subconscious. I imagine what it would be like, to feel the cool metal of the blade sink into my skin. What kind of pain was that? What kind of fear? Not just knowing that you could die, but knowing that you would. That you *were*.

My head spins and my senses surge into uncomfortable overdrive. Death has always been around me. It followed Dad until it claimed him. And I was young enough when it happened that death never felt like this faraway thing. It was always there in the distance, snout in the air and howl whistling in the wind.

But I try not to think about it. About not having any consciousness or thought. About *not being*. I can't accept it. I *can't*. No matter how close it follows my family. The idea of death, when it latches on to my mind, is enough to send a wave of panic and dread over me until the room spins and I want to pull at my hair and my mind feels too *alive* for the temporary body it's in.

But not Taylor.

She's dead, just like these seven other people will be.

And I'm alive, worrying about a cute boy texting me back.

What the hell is wrong with me?

Footsteps creak outside my door. My heart picks back up in a panic as my gaze locks onto the wood, bluish gray in the night. I hastily shove my glasses on crooked, but at least my vision is back. Not that it does a ton in the darkness. I don't move my gaze but reach over to the drawer of my nightstand, where I keep my pocketknife. My fingers close around the handle just as the door opens.

Leo and Lyra stumble through the doorway.

"CJ," Lyra whispers, "can we sleep with you?"

I put down the knife, instead turning on the lamp again. A warm glow washes over the room, slicing through the shifting shadows and revealing the pale faces of my little siblings in their dinosaur- and shark-print pajamas. Initial panic rushes up my throat, but the two of them look fine.

"What's wrong?" I ask.

"We're scared," Leo says, tugging on the bottom of his shirt.

I'm really not going to get any sleep tonight. I can't be upset, though. I'm the one who told them to come to me first whenever they have nightmares. Mom is always overworked, so I'd rather my sleep get interrupted than hers.

Plus, it's sometimes nice to not be alone at night.

"Okay," I say. "But remember, if you snore, I'm kicking you out."

Leo shuts the door behind them before they rush onto my twin-size bed like there's actually room for all three of us. Lyra smashes into my side while Leo flops onto the bottom of my bed, pulling the throw blanket around him like a cocoon.

I let them settle before eyeing him.

"Leo, is that comfortable?"

He lets out a light snore. Of course. He could sleep through a tornado. It's hard to believe he was having any trouble sleeping at all. I turn to Lyra, about to ask the same question, only to immediately get the same answer with her eyes closed and her mouth dropped open in sleep.

"If you drool on my pillow, I swear . . ." I mutter, not bothering to finish the thought.

I'm about to take off my glasses again and try to grasp for any strands of comfort I can, but I catch a figure behind the slightly cracked door. My heart leaps in my chest until I focus on him clearly.

"Orion, you dick, you almost gave me a heart attack."

"Sorry," he says.

For a minute, I have some concern that the middle schooler in the doorway is actually an alien or some kind of body snatcher, as there is no way my actual brother would apologize without sprinkling in a swear or insult.

Then I notice the pillow and blanket tucked under his arm.

"Can't sleep?" I ask.

He shakes his head.

"Me neither, come on in."

Orion cautiously steps in, gently shutting the door behind him. Unlike the twins with their excited energy, he sets up his pillow and blanket on the floor next to my side of the bed before making himself comfortable.

"Good night, Orion."

"'Night, CJ."

I place my glasses on my nightstand and shut off the light. We're plunged back into the dark, the room silent aside from the soft sounds of sleep from Leo and Lyra. While my eyes are tired, my mind is moving too fast to doze off.

"Hey, CJ?" Orion's voice rises up from the floor.

"Yeah?" I whisper back.

"Can I tell you something? But you have to promise not to tell Mom?"

"Sure."

"You can't tell anyone, actually."

"Yeah, promise."

There's another pause, the silence stretching like the shadows on the ceiling before I hear his voice again.

"I'm scared, CJ." His voice cracks. "I think I saw him earlier."

I almost disturb the twins with how fast I shoot up, barely managing to stop myself at the last moment. "The Wolf Man? You saw him? Where?"

"Outside school. Right before Mom picked me up." Orion's voice is soft, fear dripping from the sounds. "He was just standing there, at the edge of a group of trees, not moving. I thought maybe my eyes were playing tricks on me at first, but it was him for sure. I know it's hard to tell with the mask, but I swear he was staring at me." I hear him shift in his blanket. "What if he's after us?"

My heart cracks along with his voice. Orion never opens up. He's never vulnerable like this. He's always too cool, too collected, snarky and sassy. I wish I could say something to make him feel better.

But I don't even know what to say to myself to keep from crumbling.

If Orion saw the Wolf Man, that means he left the message for me and then went straight to the middle school to give my brother another message, no words needed. Taylor may have been the one to die, but I was stupid to think we didn't already have targets on our backs.

Orion sniffles, trying to muffle his crying. "I'm tired of being scared. I'm tired of worrying about the Wolf Man while people act like he's some kind of joke. CJ, he's gonna come here. I know it's not the same guy, but it doesn't matter. It's still *him*. He came back for Dad because he survived the first time and now he's gonna get us because we were supposed to die before. He's gonna finish the job."

I twist toward him. "Hey, we weren't *supposed* to die. We made it because Dad protected us."

Orion shakes his head. "He died. The Wolf Man is *back* and he's going to kill us if you don't do anything to stop him."

Shit. Shit shit shit.

Orion's right. Just like Nadia was right. If the Wolf Man is targeting us, and it sure as shit seems like he is now, it won't matter if we avoid the crime scenes from *Return to Slasherville*. He might go after those victims first, but he won't give up. Especially not without the Final Girl around to do anything.

Staying home won't save us.

He killed Dad at home. He'll find us.

Both Orion and I saw him today. The message is loud and clear. We're not extras anymore. We can't be. Which means there's only one way to guarantee our survival.

"You have to protect your brother, okay, Cassie?" I hear my dad say, the panic on his face not visible under the control, the resolution, the love. "You're my strong girl. It'll all be okay. You know this. We planned for this, didn't we?"

It was like he knew back then. I have to protect my brothers and my sister. My mom. My family.

And maybe, by the grace of whatever God exists in this fucked up universe, I actually can.

Tears spill down my cheeks.

Fuck you, Dad. I had to be just like you, huh?

I imagine his laugh. The smile he'd give with one dimple on the left side, just like mine.

I lean over the edge of the bed to face Orion.

"Maybe we were supposed to die then," I say finally. "But we didn't. And you know what that means? Why he's after us?"

He shakes his head.

I smile through the tears I hope he doesn't notice.

"It means we're not just afraid of the Wolf Man," I say. I lean down, closer toward my brother, to the point where I have to grip the mattress to prevent falling. "He's afraid of us, too."

Orion's eyes shine back at mine, bright like a cat's in the darkness. In that moment, I know we both believe it, and I have to hold on to that feeling.

Because, as dangerous and horrible of an idea as it is, I have to be the one to stop the Wolf Man.

12

Main Character Shit

Mom doesn't comment on the fact that all of us are camped out in my room when she wakes us up in the morning, only says that school has been canceled and she's making breakfast. While breakfast wasn't predicted in *Return to Slasherville*, considering my family of extras, school being canceled was.

After getting ready as much as we need to without school, we all gather at the table as Mom finishes making breakfast. She must have gone shopping when I was at the bookstore yesterday, because she went all out. Fried ham and scrambled eggs with cheese melted inside (the only way to eat scrambled eggs, really), fancy bread from the bakery section with butter, plus a side of bacon. She even got apple juice.

Well, I can't plan to defeat a murderer on an empty stomach.

We're all shoveling food onto our plates when Mom speaks. "Listen, kids. I know there's some . . . scary stuff going on, but we're going to be okay. The important thing is that we stay together."

I swallow my first bite of eggs piled on toast. "I love that, but I actually have to go out today."

She glares at me. "That doesn't sound like staying together. Go out where?"

"I'm hanging out with a friend from school," I say vaguely.

It's better to avoid going into too much detail—or any detail, really. If I explain *anything* about what I'm planning, she'll kill me before the Wolf Man has a chance to. Mom lost many of her friends and her husband to this chain of masked murderers. I don't think she'd take too well to the idea of her oldest kid going after the latest addition to the deadly lineage.

Orion looks up from his slice of bacon. "You don't have friends."

Even though everything sounds like an insult the way he says it, he's not *entirely* wrong.

"I do now," I retort. "Where do you think I was yesterday, jerk?" I turn back to Mom. "Besides, I'm gonna be close, just at the new martial arts academy down the street."

Mom actually brightens up at that. "You want to learn self-defense?"

That's . . . actually not a bad excuse. "Yeah," I say. "I'm gonna try out a class and see how it goes. Just in case."

Mom double-checks on her phone that my location is still shared with her. "Okay," she says. "But you have to come right back after and I expect you to tell me all about it."

While I have no intention of actually taking a class, I'm sure I can google enough to convince my mom I got an intro. Either way, I have to hope that Sebas will be at the academy. While I could text him, he still hasn't responded since last night, and I think adding another message on my end would literally take ten years off my life. I could reach out to Nadia first, but after the way I left yesterday, I could use Sebas on my side before I apologize to her.

"Why don't you take Orion to the class?" Mom suggests.

Shit.

Orion glares at Mom. "Ew. No. Not with CJ."

Glad it's me that's the problem and not the martial arts class. I am so close to bringing up how he wasn't too cool to cry in my room last night, but I swallow my annoyance with my cheesy eggs. Maybe it's because of my gender fluidity that Orion will open up to me on rare occasions, but with Mom, all bets are off. He can't help but want to act like the man of the house and protect her. Which means he doesn't want her to know how scared he is.

I can't betray that. Not when I kind of feel the same way.

"Well, if it's a good school, I'll get everyone signed up," Mom says. "I bet Uncle Ian will help pay if it's teaching defense. Maybe he'll want to join, too!"

"Sounds good," I say. "I'll let you know how it goes."

I'm sure it can't hurt to just say it's great and get Sebas's brother some business. Mom's right in saying Uncle Ian would pay—since he doesn't have kids himself and can only treat Chekov so much, he likes to spoil us a little.

Part of me figures it's some guilt over the fact that he's alive and Dad isn't, even though Uncle Ian didn't even go to Camp Satterville. Neither he nor Mom even stepped foot in the camp, but they still knew most of those involved through Dad and school. Grief and guilt can be a weird bitch, but I'll take the help we get because of it. There has to be a silver lining somewhere.

After I finish breakfast and make myself more presentable, I head out. I still don't know for sure if Sebas will be at the academy, but I wouldn't be surprised if Mom checks in on my location, so I have to at least stop in. Besides, if he's not, I can hang out at Red Page next door to catch up on my webcomic updates and try to summon the courage to call him. I give everyone a goodbye and my promise to stay safe, as if it is something I can actually guarantee, and then head out the door.

The walk isn't bad, especially during the day, but without Chekov growling at passersby on my back today, it's a little lonely. Especially when I turn onto the main street and am bombarded with advertisements for Slasherfest. It seems extra fucked up to keep the festival going after a girl was just killed by a copycat, but being problematic has never stopped Satterville before. If anything, Taylor's death will probably just draw in a larger crowd than ever.

I casually fix my hair in the reflection of my phone (which has a notification from Sebas that I'm too scared to look at right before seeing him) and then walk into his brother's gym, Faixa Preta. The majority of the place is made up of large mats on the floor and padding on one wall, with a trail of wooden flooring on the right side that leads to a back section with weights and what look like locker rooms. In the front, a variety of merch hangs over a front desk where a girl who looks to be in her twenties smiles at me.

"Hey! Are you here for the class?"

"Uh . . . I just wanted to try . . ."

While I was going to finish with *to find my friend,* it's clear that her mind fills it in as *jiu-jitsu right now actually.* "Great! The first class is free, and I'm assuming you need a loaner gi, so let me get you set up quickly since it starts in a few minutes. How old are you?"

"Um, seventeen."

"Cool, if you can just get a parent to fill out the form on this QR code . . ." She points to a paper on the desk. "We'll be set. I'll be right back!"

She's gone before I can say anything else. Well, at least this is proof for Mom. I text her the link and get her response almost immediately.

Done. Have fun, love:)

Listen to instructors so you don't get hurt

But also go for it!

Ok mom

Thanks

If anyone is weird with you call me

I'll headkick them before they can even get grips

Sure

As if I even know what that means.

By then, the front desk girl already has the uniform for me, along with a white belt. She hands it all over to me.

"Women's locker room is in the back to the right. Top and pants go on like how you'd expect, but we can help you get the belt on."

I thank her and head to the back. I don't mind the whole women's locker room thing. I know how I present, and it's not that I don't identify as a girl, it's just I don't *only* identify that way. But gender identity is kind of a complex thing, and I don't mind keeping it to myself at times or getting into it more with people who understand. Using spaces meant for cis girls makes sense for me and doesn't make me any less of who I am.

My actual concern is trying to figure out some excuse to get out of this, but with the loaner gi already in my arms, I feel like I'm in too deep. Next thing I know, I'm in the pants and have the jacket on and open over my tank top as I exit the locker room. I hold the belt in my hands. I don't want to embarrass myself by tying it the wrong way.

Maybe this won't be so bad, though. I did tell Mom I'd take the class. Now I don't have to lie about it. Besides, if I'm supposed to be the main character, I've got to do main character shit. Training is totally main character shit. Although I doubt I'll be shockingly good at it on the first try or that time can pass in an intense training montage that has me ready to take on the Wolf Man with my hands alone by the end of it.

"Hello and welcome," a voice says. "This is your first time trying jiu-jitsu?"

I look up to a man with a black belt tied around the waist of his uniform. I don't have to be a martial arts expert to know that's good. He has thick black hair that stops around his chin and a neatly trimmed beard that encircles a familiar smile. Between that and the similar accent, this has to be Sebas's older brother.

My face threatens to heat as I remember my messages and immediately stress over the unopened late response.

I nod. "Uh, yeah. Very first time." I squeeze the belt. "I'm still not totally sure what jiu-jitsu is. Like wrestling, right? My mom wants me to learn self-defense."

"That seems to be a popular reason around here," he says. "But I'm glad you're here. Jiu-jitsu will be good for you. You don't have to be the biggest guy in the room to be the best. Trust me." He smiles wider, gesturing to himself. Sebas's brother seems a bit shorter than him, but definitely stockier and muscley. He's still taller than me, though, probably around five foot six. He holds out his hand. "I'm Professor Samuel. And you?"

"CJ," I say, shaking it.

A spark of recognition lights up in his eyes. I can't help but panic. Does he know about my family?

"CJ! Sebas and Nadia were talking about you. Mi hermanito especially," he says with a wink. My cheeks flare but he continues, "Perfect. He can be your training partner today and show you the ropes." Samuel drops his smile and turns toward the locker room. "SEBAS," he barks. "Come here." His expression is kind and voice softer as he turns back to me. "If anyone makes you feel uncomfortable at all, you let me know, okay? And never feel like you have to train with anyone if you don't want to. Yes?"

I nod. "Yeah, thank you."

He smiles again before stepping off. *"Sebastián Luis!"*

Sebas rushes out of the men's locker room, expression annoyed. "Mae, qué quieres?"

"Help CJ tie her belt."

"CJ?" Sebas looks past his brother and at me. His eyes widen a bit and he almost seems embarrassed, but it disappears behind a smile as he rushes over. "Hey, is everything okay? You didn't text me back."

My face is on fire. "I, uh, I thought I made you uncomfortable last night."

He makes a face. "I'm not easily uncomfortable. In fact, jiu-jitsu has me used to being uncomfortable all the time, so." He scratches the back of his neck. "You didn't look at my message this morning?"

"No, sorry, I'll look at it now . . ." I unlock my phone.

"Wait, I . . ."

> I'm sorry, I fell asleep! But if the date offer is still on the table, I would like that

He doesn't meet my eyes. My heart thumps in my chest.

"I, um . . . I just have to talk to you about something first . . ." I start. People are already lining up for the class. I hold up my belt. "Can you help me with this?"

"Let me just tie it for you now and I'll show you after."

I hand him the belt and he steps closer to me.

"Lift your arms a little?"

I comply and he wraps the belt around my waist, closing the jacket. Even though he's not touching me, I can't help but notice how close he is. My breathing catches as he finishes tying the knot, and I have to look anywhere but his face. Sebas shows me where to stand and I follow everyone in bowing in for the class. As they go through warm-ups, Sebas takes me off to the side so I can learn the movements. He assures me I'm doing great, but I kind of feel like I've never actually used my body in my life.

Definitely not the kind of protagonist who's immediately good at stuff.

The class progresses quickly, and soon Samuel is instructing on a way to escape from something called a closed guard, which seems to mean lying on the ground and wrapping your legs around your training partner.

Which is kind of a sexual position to be in with the guy I maybe sort of definitely have a crush on.

"Am I top or bottom?" I ask Sebas, and immediately pray for a swift death.

"Whatever you want to do first," he responds, totally professionally. "Either way works for me."

This was a horrible idea.

I start bottom.

"Essentially, your guard is your legs," Sebas says. "So you start on your back." He kneels in front of me. "Now, you want your legs around me, like this." He helps me adjust so I have one leg on either side of him, with my ankles crossed behind him. "It seems a little weird at first, but I promise you get used to it."

"That's good, I guess," I say, although I'm not entirely sure I believe him.

"My goal, being on top, is to pass your guard, or get past your legs. Your goal is to keep control by keeping your legs between us. This is called closed guard because I'm closed in with your legs around me."

I try to focus on keeping my ankles crossed, and that sort of makes the awkwardness of the physical closeness disappear.

Mostly.

"Okay . . ." I say, hoping to remember any of what he said.

"Don't worry, it's gonna be overwhelming at first. Just have fun and try your best, and you'll get it eventually."

He slowly takes me through the next move of the day, which involves breaking your partner's guard (opening their legs) and getting past their legs into side control, a position that keeps his body on one side of me, chest pressed to my chest.

Why does so much of this sound so suggestive?

I try to put that out of my mind and concentrate more on the way Sebas talks about the practice. I do like how he explains things. He's clearly excited, more at home. It makes a lot of sense that he followed his brother to an entirely different country for this sport. He's good at it, and he's good at teaching it.

"Basically, you want to be heavy when you're on top, keep that pressure," Sebas finishes explaining.

I need to focus. "Okay."

"Ready to try?"

No. "Sure."

We switch positions so he's on his back and I'm on my knees, in his closed guard. I awkwardly adjust my knee to his butt, pushing down on his leg to break open the guard. He guides me a little as I slide over his leg and stumble into what I think is the side control he just instructed me on.

"That was great!" Sebas says as I lift away from him.

"Seriously?"

"Yeah, for a first attempt, that was really good."

He's probably just being nice, but it still makes me feel happy. We continue drilling, switching off even though he clearly knows this well already. It's a nice distraction, and actually kind of fun, but a lot is weighing on my mind.

Namely, what I actually came here for.

"I need to talk to you and Nadia again," I say quietly as we switch off again. "I think that she was right."

He makes a face. "Well, she'll love to hear that." He pauses his movement to look up at me. "What part, though? Are you saying that you want to go after the werewolf?"

"Wolf Man," I correct. "And yeah. Or, not that I want to, but I have to. If someone doesn't stop him, he'll keep terrorizing the town and hurting people."

"But why does that someone have to be you?"

It's not a bad question, and one that's crossed my own mind quite a few times since I made this decision. "Because he's after my little brother."

"What?" Sebas sits back.

I swallow. "My younger brother Orion saw him too yesterday. I don't think hiding is going to be enough anymore."

Sebas nods. "Okay, then we'll stop this wolf."

"Really?" I ask. "You'll help?"

"Of course." He puts on a teasing grin. "I can't let you go after a killer alone. Your jiu-jitsu's shit."

"You just said I was doing well!"

"Yeah, for day one. Do you know how long it takes to stop being shit?" He pointed to the blue belt around his waist. "I've been training for nearly all my life, and I'll even tap adult blue and purple belts, but I'm still shit. Black belt is like when you stop being shit and start your real jiu-jitsu journey."

"Tap?" I ask.

"Remember how I said if anything hurts and you want the person to stop, you tap on them twice? Getting someone in a submission and having them tap is basically the goal." He bites his lip. "Well, unless it's the serial killer. Then the goal is to break things or make them go unconscious so you can get away. But in class, we always stop immediately when there's a tap and take care of each other." He flicks my belt. "Even the zero-stripe white belts."

I laugh. "Joke's on you because I don't know what the stripes mean."

"They are smaller promotions between belt levels. You'll get there one day if you keep at it," he says. Then frowns. "If the Wolf Man doesn't kill us first, of course."

"Of course." My expression gets a little more serious. "Would it be unfair if I asked if we could hold off on that date until after all this?" He doesn't immediately answer, and I hope my blush passes as being red from the training. "And would it help if I say I'm looking forward to it?"

Sebas smoothly slides right past my guard. "I don't think it's unfair, and that does help."

Samuel gets the attention of the class, telling everyone to grab water and their mouthpieces and get ready to roll. I have no idea what I'll do when that happens, but going with the flow hasn't been all that bad.

Sebas stands first, giving me an adorably awkward smile that shows his braces as he holds out his hand to me.

"And while we will focus on stopping that wolf guy first," he says, "I'm looking forward to it, too."

13

Which Horror Movie Trope Are You?

Sebas texts Nadia after class, and while we shower and change in our respective locker rooms (thankfully I brought a change of clothes in my backpack in case Mom checked), she agrees to meet us at the bubble tea store down the street, Tea Time.

Instead of a normal greeting, Nadia places a hand on my shoulder and looks me right in the eyes. "I'm glad you came to your senses. I'm not in the mood for another protagonist who takes, like, a hundred chapters to stop trying to follow the original story of the fiction they're living in."

"Nadia, we're not *living* in a fiction. Someone is trying to make a fictional story come true," I say to her.

Nadia purses her lips. "Not my preferred option. Satterville gives off strong horror fiction vibes. I've read a few webcomics with this exact trope and it adds up: this is all a horror story."

Sure, I've read some of those webcomics, too. Where the lead is transported into the world of the book or comic they're reading, or they die and end up in that world or, like, hit their head and regain memories that prove they are living in the world of a book. I can see how it'd be fun to think our life is like that.

But this is real life, and it is impossible that we're living in a book.

Now's not the time to pick that fight, though. "As long as we focus on figuring out who potentially wants us dead, believe whatever you want."

It's our turn to order our teas, so Nadia doesn't have a chance to respond.

"Do you think the events will follow the book?" Sebas asks after we step away from the counter. "Even though some things have changed?"

I nod. "At least for now. I finished reading last night, and there are some things we need to go over." I decide now might not be the best time to tell them I don't actually know how the Final Girl is supposed to kill the Wolf Man. "But since the memorial time and location are the same, I don't think there's any reason to believe that they wouldn't keep to the script in that way."

Nadia taps her chin. "Time for a murder board." A group of people near us turn their heads toward Nadia. "Or a storyboard. Both seem to apply in this situation."

"Maybe this isn't the best place to talk about this?" I say, keeping my voice low.

"Good point. We'll go to my house again. I might actually have something that will help."

After grabbing our tea, we head to Sebas's car. He drives, Nadia taking shotgun and me slipping into the back. Nadia opens up her calendar app.

"Okay, so the next death is supposed to happen Friday at the memorial. Remind me again how it goes down?"

While I do have the book with me (I can't leave it at home and risk Mom coming across it), I know the basic details enough to recite the plot by memory. "A bunch of kids will go off into the woods behind the football field to drink. Max goes off by himself, and when Taylor follows him, she sees that the Wolf Man killed him."

"Max? As in Taylor's ex-boyfriend, Max Dolan?"

"Yep."

She makes a note of the event on her phone. I hope she didn't just write something like *Max dies,* considering that might be a little incriminating if anyone ever sees it. It does make sense to focus on the timeline, though.

"And the death after that? When does that happen?"

"First day of finals. Mr. Collins, apparently he's Taylor's favorite teacher. Or was . . ." I bite my lip. "It's supposed to happen in the library."

"The art teacher? Bummer. He's nice." Nadia frowns as she makes the note. "And after that?"

"Five people are killed at Slasherfest."

"Holy shit. *Five?*"

"Yep."

"Damn," Sebas says from the driver's seat. "So, we want to try to stop this guy *before* Slasherfest."

"Ideally, as soon as possible," I agree. "Which means the memorial is our best bet."

After she marks the important dates in her calendar, Nadia makes a weird face. She's either thinking extremely hard or holding in a fart, and based on the sugary drink she got, I wouldn't be surprised if it is a combination of both.

"I'm not sure about one thing . . ." she starts.

Sebas gives her a look as he stops at a light. "Just one?"

"It seems like in the book, the victims were connected to Taylor. Her nemesis, her ex-boyfriend, her favorite teacher . . ."

"At least until Slasherfest," I interject. "Those killings seem more random."

"Okay, sure," Nadia continues, "but is the killer really going to be targeting those same people now? Taylor isn't the Final Girl anymore." She turns around in the passenger seat to look at me. "Especially now that both you and your brother saw the Wolf Man, it might make more sense if he goes after people with a connection to you."

"Yeah, but Taylor wasn't exactly my nemesis," I start, although I know that protest is weak. We weren't fans of each other, and it would be a lot harder to track down and kill my actual nemesis and Smith Enemy #1, Moon Satter, considering no one knows their real identity.

Sebas keeps his eyes on the road as he speaks. "So that would mean the next target might be CJ's ex-boyfriend."

My face heats in the back. "Except I don't have an ex-boyfriend."

"Ex-girlfriend?" Nadia asks.

"No."

"Ex—"

"I don't have any exes," I interrupt. "I've never dated anyone."

I look down at my hands. It shouldn't be embarrassing. I know there are plenty of people who don't have time or desire or opportunity to date in high school. But none of those reasons kept me from dating. More lack of interest from others and the proximity of a masked murderer in my life.

One of those things seems to be changing, but unfortunately, not the one that might actually kill me.

"Huh," Nadia says. "Then who the hell could it be?"

I swallow. I think I'd actually combust into flames if I admitted it now, but what if the killer targets Sebas? Even if there isn't an official term for what we have going on, since it's only been two days, it probably wouldn't be a stretch to notice I'm interested in him. I mean, the Wolf Man knew we were in the closet together.

Nadia must catch my worried glances toward the driver's seat. She sighs. "Sebas won't be the target, you two haven't started dating yet."

Now he seems as embarrassed as I feel.

"Well, if there isn't an exact match, how can we be sure?" I protest.

"I guess it's possible," Nadia says, "but it's just as possible the Wolf Man will still go after Max and try to get back on script for the original story. We don't really know. I wouldn't be too worried, though."

Sebas raises an eyebrow. "Why not?"

"Because you're the Love Interest. If they aren't the killer themself, the Love Interest always gets plot armor."

"Plot armor?" Sebas asks.

"It's, like, a guarantee that a character will survive because of their role in the story," I say from the back before glaring at Nadia. "But this isn't a story. No one has plot armor."

She rolls her eyes. "Sure it isn't." Her sarcastic tone drops and she is fully back to business with her next line of thought. "If we should be worried about anyone in general, it's me. My original role was the Dead Girl and now I've been recast as the Scholar. You know, the friend who knows horror movies and tropes and always talks about it? That's a high-risk role for raising a death flag, don't you think?"

"If this were horror fiction, sure . . ."

"Which it basically *is*," Nadia exclaims. "Or at least, it applies. I mean, come on. The tropes fit. All we need is, like, a Dumbass Cop, a Hunter, and the Harbinger of Doom."

I don't have the heart to admit that my mom is kind of the Hunter.

"What's the doom one?" Sebas asks.

"You know, like the old lady or random drunkard who warns of impending danger."

"Wouldn't that be the book? Or the author, I guess."

Nadia widens her eyes, actually looking proud. "Sebas, you're so right." She turns back to me. "That's another vote for being in a horror story, CJ."

"Come on."

"You can't tell me you never thought it was weird that Satterville looks like a horror movie set." She points at the logo on her plastic tea cup. "Literally every business name tells you exactly what it is. That's kind of strange."

"No, that's just marketing," I say. Clearly, she isn't buying it, so I go for a subject change instead. "Well, since we aren't sure who the next target is, maybe we should focus on who the killer could be?"

Nadia grins.

"Like I was saying before, I have something that might help."

I wasn't expecting much of anything when Nadia said she had a surprise, but I definitely wasn't expecting her to pull out a few poster boards from her closet dedicated to the various Wolf Man slayings. She quickly tapes them on a blank wall of her bedroom. There are article printouts, old newspaper clippings, and photos of key people involved.

"Uh, why do you have all this?" I ask.

"I had to do a project about Slasherfest last year and got pretty in-depth," Nadia explains. "But now I'm glad I didn't throw it all away, as it might give us the whole picture. Just have to make a few additions."

I step forward, closer to the wall. "Where the hell did you even get newspapers?" I ask.

"Dad's a history dork. We were able to track some down."

It's a little overwhelming at first. From the initial Camp Satterville slayings to the connection between the two original Wolf Men (although Nadia did draw penis doodles over their faces, which somehow makes it easier to look at them) to the information on the worst night of my life.

And a picture of Dad.

It's how I remember him. That great smile that makes it so you can barely see his sparkling eyes. Skin that could get a tan in the summer but would immediately grow red in the winter cold. That dimple on his left cheek.

I blink away tears that threaten to fall.

Nadia pulls out her phone and sends some things to her printer, carefully cutting out images and adding them to the wall. I can immediately tell they are for the most recent incident with Taylor.

It is wild to see it all spread out like this. Just how many people were affected by the Wolf Man.

"Seriously?" Sebas snaps. "You add me to the murder board and use *that* picture?"

I twist to where he's looking. Sebas's newly added picture is near mine, which is my yearbook photo from last year. Only instead of a yearbook photo, Sebas's is a printed picture of him in a shark onesie, sticking out his ass.

I snort.

Nadia's picture of herself is a polished photo that looks great. I also notice that the photo she added for Taylor is an objectively bad one, but don't comment on that.

"Are there any ideas on the killer's identity in here?" I ask. "It's not like there was a third Miller brother."

"So they were brothers . . ." Sebas starts, tracing the line between them. "No other siblings? Cousins?"

"No," I say. "No surviving family, far as we all know."

"Why would they do all this? What was the reason?"

Nadia takes that question. "Losers who think not getting laid makes them oppressed." She draws another dick on Brett. "Plus bad parenting, violent tendencies, and boners for Batman saying he is vengeance. I don't know. They were both evil pieces of shit."

That pretty much sums it up.

"You read Moon Satter's books, right?" I ask Nadia. "Was there any mention of their motivation?"

Nadia thinks back. "Actually, there was something about Brett Miller leaving some kind of letter or, like . . . incel manifesto, I don't know exactly." She pulls out *Camp Slasherville* from her bookshelf, and I try not to be too judgmental about the fact that she annotated it. She did have a project, after all. Nadia continues, "It never says what he wrote about, only that he had some weird beliefs. Dad and I tried to find it, but we came up with nothing."

That's annoying. Although it does kind of make sense they wouldn't release the screwed-up ramblings of someone who killed people.

"Maybe we can look into it some more . . ." I start. "Without the family connection, that might be our only lead for finding suspects."

"Luckily, we aren't alone in our search," Nadia says. "Because we don't have that much time on our hands."

Sebas gestures to the board. "Well, clearly you do."

"But there are always people with *more* time who dedicate themselves to ridiculous theories, and I know exactly where to find them." Nadia opens her laptop and gets to a website before turning the screen to Sebas and me.

SLASHERVILLAINS FAN FORUM

I eye her. "Seriously?"

"Hey, no one knows Satterville better than them."

As much as I doubt the accuracy of Moon Satter fans, it's not a bad idea. The forum is probably filled with posts about the recent events, especially with these freaks gearing up for Slasherfest.

"All right." I pull up the website on my phone. "Let's get looking."

There has been a flurry of new posts since Taylor's death, most of which try to uncover the identity of the new Wolf Man. Theories range from the more understandable—Evan Miller had a secret lover out for revenge, along with photos of him and some woman—to the absolutely unhinged—there's some cult of people called The Pack who actually believe they will be reincarnated as wolves if they kill someone. Nothing stands out as a valid lead. I keep scrolling.

I do a search for Brett Miller's letter, even though Nadia said she already looked into it. No one seems to have access to what he actually wrote, and from the comments on this post about it, people have certainly tried. One person even says they applied for an internship at the Satterville Police Department just to see if they could get it. But that's still not the weirdest comment I read.

> **Truecrimejunkie26:** found a source that says it might be in the name of the Creator

Like . . . God? What the hell does that mean? I do a search on the forum, and the words "the Creator" come up a fair amount, but there's no explanation.

"Who's the 'Creator'?" I ask.

"Wait, I just saw something like that, too," Nadia says. "Here: *The Creator will give instructions, just wait*. Spooky."

My most recent search result is something similar. *I am awaiting my calling from the Creator.*

Even the Slashervillains seem confused. The first response under it is, *lol bitch what?*

"Is that the author?" Sebas asks. "Since they created the books."

I scan through a few more comments. "I don't think so. It would make sense, but the Creator is mostly mentioned in threads about Brett's missing manifesto. If Brett had something to do with the Creator, it can't be Moon Satter, because they weren't around when Brett was alive."

"But Moon might know something." Nadia finishes off the rest of her tea and twirls the straw, sitting on the edge of her bed. "Even though they don't use real identities and some stuff is fictionalized, Brett's writing *is* mentioned in *Camp Slasherville*. While it never goes into detail, there's a chance they got information these out-of-towners didn't. We don't know who Moon is, but they could have had an in with the Satterville Police."

It is an unfortunate reminder that Moon is closer to home than I'd like. But Nadia is making a good point. If Moon referenced it in the first book, they might know something about the Wolf Man's motivation. It's a long shot, but that could give us a lead on who the copycat is.

"I guess if we reach out to Moon, we can also ask if they know about *Return to Slasherville.*"

If Moon Satter wanted to stalk me and kill people around me, I sort of feel like they would have done it already, but it doesn't hurt to double-check on their involvement. The creepy manuscript does have their name on it, after all.

"But how are we supposed to get in contact with Moon?" Nadia asks. "They're a famous author."

"Hardly *famous*," I mutter.

"You know what I mean," Nadia says. "I'm sure they get tons of fan mail."

I sigh. "I have an idea on how to get their attention."

"Really? Does it cost anything?"

My stomach already feels sick. "Only my dignity."

CJ's Unsent Email Draft:

To: ronjcunningham@nicedealliterary.com
From: cassiopeiajanesmith@sattervilleschools.org
Subject: Satterville Smith Kid Interview Opp for Moon Satter

Hi Ron,

My name is CJ Smith, and you might know me since your client Moon Satter used my family's trauma for two bullshit books without permission. I hope you didn't know about the lack of permission, but in advance, I'd eat my uncle's cat's shit before signing away my life rights, so you can forget about a movie deal and don't bother asking.

Moon harassed me online in the past about interviews, and while I thought they were a creep at the time, after some soul-searching and counseling, I realized, what better way to tell my story than through Satterville's most exploitative and cringe author? At the very least, in exchange, they can give me their research. Did they get that freak Brett Miller's actual manifesto? As someone actually related to the damn case, I think I deserve to see it.

I was going to inquire about a time in person, as I frequent Red Page books in Satterville and saw that Moon was scheduled to come in for a stock signing on the morning of May 26, but they never arrived. What the fuck was up with that? Super unprofessional, if you ask me.

Anyway, I'm willing to give them a second chance, so feel free to pass along my email and say I'm willing to talk.

Thanks,
CJ

P.S. There's not going to be a third book, is there?

Nadia's Revised Email That Was Sent:

To: ronjcunningham@nicedealliterary.com
From: cassiopeiajanesmith@sattervilleschools.org
Subject: URGENT: Satterville Smith Kid Interview Opp for Moon Satter

Dear Mr. Cunningham,

My name is CJ Smith, and my father, Christian Smith, was a prominent inspiration for your client Moon Satter's work. Moon requested an interview from me in the past, and while I was not prepared at the time to talk about my story, after much soul-searching and therapy, I decided that now is a great time. What better way to do it than with an acclaimed writer and Satterville icon like Moon Satter?

I would love to have a conversation with Moon, not only to tell my side of things, but also to get a bigger picture of my family's history. I would be so appreciative if Moon would be open to sharing their sources with me to better understand the possible reasoning behind the tragic attacks and my connection to them.

I was going to inquire about a time in person, as I frequent Red Page books in Satterville and saw that Moon was scheduled to come in for a stock signing on the morning of May 26, but they never arrived. Did something happen? Are they okay?

If you could please pass along my info to Moon if they are still interested, I'd love to hear from them.

All the best,

CJ Smith

P.S. Is Moon considering a third book? Perhaps I could consult if they are looking into detailing the events of the most recent tragedy. I haven't heard anything official yet, but would love to know if there is something in the works.

14

The Most Toxic Fandom

Apparently, my celebrity is not enough to get an immediate response from Moon Satter's literary agent, listed as the main contact on their website. In fact, it's not even enough to get *any* response, considering two days pass with no word. Now it's the evening before the memorial, and while we have a general game plan for tomorrow night, I don't exactly feel prepared.

But instead of readying myself for the likely confrontation, I'm sitting in the front window of Red Page, arranging Moon Satter's books with other slasher titles and decorating with a variety of red fabric and wolf decals. Maybe it's a little weird that *I'm* helping with a Slasherfest window display, but if anyone is going to make money off my family trauma, I want it to be Ms. Maeda.

"CJ, you really have a skill for this," she says from the counter. "That looks great!"

I eye the wolf mask that I painted on the backdrop, under the words "Red Page Welcomes You to Slasherfest! Read and maybe you'll survive . . ."

It's wordy, but it's also kind of our entire plan.

"Thanks," I say, even though I can't help but notice one of the soulless black circles of the Wolf Man's eyes is bigger than the other. Maybe I should have taken art class.

While the mask is burned into my memory, it's always hard to recall the eyes. In my brain, it's almost like he didn't have eyes at all. Like the human in him was swallowed up by that mask. When he put it on, it wasn't Brett, or Evan, or whatever asshole was donning the mask now. It was greater than any of them, a character that transcended them all. The Satterville Wolf Man.

A symbol of the town, of everything it lost.

Of evil fucking douchebags.

"You don't think it's too on the nose?" I ask Ms. Maeda to distract myself.

"When it comes to Slasherfest, I think on the nose sells," she comments without looking up from her screen.

She's not wrong. Satterville has always seemed like a pretty on-the-nose town.

I pencil in a small penis outline on the Wolf Man painting's nose. It's too faint to notice unless you are up close and personal, but it is a needed finishing touch to a real dickface. Nadia was onto something with this idea.

"Did you notice my addition to John Doe, too?" I ask Ms. Maeda.

This gets her to glance back up. "You're a genius."

It took Hana's help and a ladder, but I carefully pinned a *I Survived Slasherfest* baseball cap in between his antlers.

"You might want to double-check that his chains are still structurally sound," I say. "He seemed to be swaying more than usual."

"Well, he wasn't meant to have a teenager hanging off him," Ms. Maeda responds with a laugh. "As long as no one messes with the chains, it should be fine."

I step back to look at the full window display, when a voice behind me interrupts. "Have we met before? You seem familiar."

I jump, turning around to an unfamiliar face. It's some guy, probably in his twenties. I have no idea if he thinks I'm older and this is some kind of gross pickup line or if he's seen me in the bookstore before. Either way, I don't recognize him.

"I don't think so," I say. "I just have one of those faces."

It's not like I'm the only dark-blond, white teenager in town.

That's when I notice his shirt.

"I Survived Slasherville, OH!"

No one wears that bullshit except for the worst fucking fandom in the world: Slashervillains. Even local fans aren't caught dead in shirts like that. That means this guy traveled in from out of town just to celebrate the anniversary of my dad's almost-death and actual death. He's probably deep in the forums we were digging into and one of the weirdos who comments about the Creator or whatever.

My heart pounds in my chest. Maybe it's unrelated. Maybe I really do look like someone he knows. Maybe he doesn't actually recognize me at all. Just because he's deep in the lore doesn't mean he actually looked up pictures of me and my family.

Then recognition starts to light up his face.

Motherfucker.

"Wait a minute, are you one of those Smith ki—"

"Hey, Mary, great work on the display!" Hana calls, rushing right up to us. She twists toward the guy, crossing her arms and popping one hip. "Can I help you find something, sir?"

I can't help but notice the sass in her voice, but the Slashervillain scum seems too crestfallen at the fact that she called me Mary and not the name of the oldest kid of Christian Smith to notice.

He does answer her question, though. "Do you still have that signed edition of *Welcome to Slasherville* with the sprayed edges? It's the one I'm missing from my collection."

Hana leads him away, and if I wasn't drowning in my own relief, I would've barfed.

How does he have a *collection*? Moon's only got two books out.

"You okay?" Ms. Maeda asks. She steps over to me, eyes behind her glasses filled with concern and maybe even a bit of anger.

I know that if the guy harassed me, Ms. Maeda and Hana would have kicked him out themselves. It isn't often that I'm recognized by out-of-towners, but sometimes the intense fans can put two and two together. I basically look exactly like my dad did as a teen (which, unfortunately, is how he is often portrayed, thanks to *Camp Slasherville*). Add long hair and glasses and it's pretty uncanny.

"I'm fine," I say.

"Are you sure? I know with Slasherfest coming up and now the memorial tomorrow . . ." She shakes her head. "I wouldn't be upset if you want to call it for today."

My adrenaline spikes at the mention of the memorial. "Actually," I start, looking back in the direction Hana led the Slashervillain, "I think I will take off if that's okay."

"Of course," she says. "We'll do chicken next time. And we'll see you at the memorial tomorrow."

"You and Hana are going to the memorial?" I ask, a little surprised.

Ms. Maeda nods. "If we're going to lean into Slasherfest, it's the least we can do."

I don't remember much from Dad's funeral, but I do remember how many people showed. Whether it was out of actual care or to gawk, I'm not sure, but either way, the town does come together in moments like these. Hopefully this will be the last time it needs to.

"Stay safe, okay?" I tell Ms. Maeda.

"You too, CJ." She looks back at the front window and smiles. "And excellent work. Those freaks will love it."

I snort. "Tell Hana I said thanks and bye and I'll see her tomorrow."

"Will do."

As I walk out of the shop, I notice a new email notification on my phone. It's from Moon Satter's agent. I completely pause to take a look.

Hi CJ,

Sorry about the delay, but I'm a little confused. Maybe there was some miscommunication with Red Page? I don't see mention of that online anywhere, and we certainly didn't schedule anything. Moon doesn't do in-person events. I'll reach out about sending signed page inserts again. Even if Moon did contact the store without me knowing, Moon was out of town on a solo writer's retreat in Vermont that day, so they definitely wouldn't have scheduled anything back in Ohio. In terms of a book three, we don't have anything planned. They are actually busy working on an original romantasy project (the pages I've read are stunning, so definitely keep an eye out for updates!), but I'm sure I can convince them to put that manuscript aside since you'd be interested in consulting for a third book!

They will also be thrilled about the interview, and I'm sure they'll be happy to share any sources. They are very detailed in their research, I can assure you! Forwarded your email to them already.

Thanks,
Ron

My chest tightens. Moon didn't write *Return to Slasherville.* I can't imagine their agent not knowing about it if they had, especially since it sounds like he's pretty up-to-date on what Moon is working on. While there's still a chance Moon might not have told their agent everything, I'll have to wait for their response before I can confirm anything. Regardless, it seems like they have a pretty solid alibi for the day Taylor was killed.

With Moon Satter likely not involved and the Creator's identity still unknown, I feel like I'm stuck at square one while the Wolf Man hunting me remains steps ahead.

My skin pricks with the feeling of eyes on me. Panicked, I twist around.

I lock eyes with the Slashervillain from the store, looking right at me. He's not moving, still a good ten feet away, but his unblinking stare sends a chill up my spine. Something tells me if I try to walk home, he'll follow me or try to corner me.

Without much thought, I rush into Faixa Preta. I'm through the door so quickly, I practically barrel into the person walking toward me.

"Whoa, CJ? What's wrong?"

I look up at Sebas, who steadies me. He's standing right next to Samuel, both of them watching me with concern.

"There was some weird guy outside staring at me," I say. "I didn't want to walk home alone while he was there."

At that, Samuel immediately goes from zero to sixty on the intensity scale. His expression is hard and he puffs up a little. With his tensed muscles and cauliflower ear, he fully looks ready to fuck someone up as he heads out the front door. Sebas's jaw is tight, but since his brother is handling it, he stays with me instead.

My hands are shaking, so he cautiously reaches out and takes them in his. His skin is warm and the touch makes my heart flutter.

"Deep breaths," he says. "You're safe now."

The words almost make me tear up. I'm so used to feeling unsafe, to always having to worry. It's nice to have someone assure me that I'm protected. I can almost believe it.

I follow his breathing pattern until my muscles relax slightly.

"Do you know who it was?" Sebas asks.

I shake my head. I still haven't told Sebas everything about my past, and while a lot of it was laid out on Nadia's murder board, I don't *want* to tell him more. Looking at him now, feeling the butterflies that appear every time I'm with him, I don't want to explain Slashervillains or why a stranger would have a sick interest in me. I like that I'm not defined by my past with him. I like that I don't have to be *that Smith kid* with him. I can just be CJ.

Maybe it's only pretend, but when it's just him, it's like that part of me takes a back seat.

I'm not the extra or the Final Girl or the queer kid whose dad was murdered by the town monster. He's not someone who moved into a horror town only to narrowly avoid death within the first few weeks.

We're just two people who want to get to know each other.

It almost makes me feel like I can rewrite my story.

"I think I'm just nervous because of . . . everything going on," I say.

"That makes sense," he starts, but doesn't look convinced.

Samuel walks back in. "I didn't see him, he must have run away." Samuel looks at me with softer eyes. "I'm glad you came in here, though. You never know what people are like. I hear stories."

Yeah, Satterville is full of them.

Samuel is getting ready to start an advanced jiu-jitsu class for people with at least three stripes on their white belts (i.e., not me), so Sebas takes me to a smaller room in the back, where there is a little square mat along with a line of heavy bags hanging from the ceiling.

"There's no class in here now," he says. "We can chill."

I look down at my clothes. I dressed in joggers and a tight-fitting top I didn't mind getting paint on while I did the bookstore display. They wouldn't be bad to move in.

"Can you show me some more techniques?" I ask.

He smiles enough to show his braces. "Already hooked, huh?"

"Something like that." I bite my lip. "I wouldn't mind feeling a little stronger right now."

His jaw twitches, but he keeps that smile. "Come on."

I take off my shoes and socks before following him onto the mat. It doesn't feel like a legitimate class with only the two of us. Excited nerves tickle my chest. The mats are cool beneath my bare feet. I hop a little on them in an attempt to warm up.

"Is there anything specific you want to learn?" Sebas asks.

I shake my head. "I still don't know anything."

"You'll feel like that for a while." He teases, "I still sometimes feel that way." He sits on the mats. "How about we go over arm bar basics?"

I join him on the mat. Sebas gently takes my arm.

"Arm bars are joint locks, so what we are doing is attacking the elbow joint. Basically, you're bending it the wrong way, forcing the joint in the direction it normally doesn't go, so with enough leverage, the arm will snap." His face is excited but serious. "In training, I want you to go really slow with these locks and tap early when someone gets you in one. Against creepy guys and Wolf Men, go hard and snap that shit with no remorse."

I laugh, but he doesn't. I think he's totally serious.

Sebas shows how to trap an arm between your legs, their thumb pointing up and their elbow above your knees, so when you pinch your legs together, move your hips up, and pull the arm down toward your chest, it would theoretically snap. Of course, we tap right away, not getting close to the real-life breaking point. He takes time to explain each small movement, and a few times I have to ask him to repeat or clarify, not because I'm not paying attention but because it's a little easy to get lost in the passion of his voice. I feel like I could happily listen to him talk about ways to break people's joints for hours.

But he does actually expect me to try the technique, so with his help, I get through it a few times. It's hard to remember all the little details—especially when we start from the mount position (which is basically exactly as it sounds) and transition to an arm bar—but he assures me those things get ironed out with practice.

I'm so concentrated on getting it right that I'm barely thinking at all, or aware of time flying by, until Samuel comes in with a big spray-bottle kind of backpack and a mop.

"I have to clean the mats again?" Sebas asks.

Samuel shrugs. "These white belts don't volunteer like they used to."

"I can help," I offer. "Since you basically gave me a free private lesson."

Sebas gives me a teasing smile. "Who said anything about it being free?"

"Save your flirting for after the mats are clean," Samuel says, handing Sebas both the spray and the mop. "Nothing cute about ringworm. And give CJ a ride home." He walks into the other room.

I take the mop from Sebas. It doesn't take a belt promotion to know how to use that.

"You sure you don't mind?" he asks.

"Nah, it's cool. After all, you're teaching me how to break the arms of bad guys."

He starts spraying the mats, waving the hose back and forth to get the cleaning solution spread evenly. I follow with the mop.

"You're a good teacher. Would you ever want to open a gym like your brother?" I ask.

"No way," Sebas laughs. "I love jiu-jitsu, but I don't want to deal with the business side of things. If I keep coaching, I'd rather just stay with Samuel."

"I guess that makes sense."

He shrugs. "Yeah. What can I say? I'm not good at math and my brother pays well."

I mop faster, trying to keep up with his spraying. "Well, I'm sorry for not paying, but I appreciate you training with me."

"For you, anytime." Sebas smiles. "And now you're a little more prepared for tomorrow."

Tomorrow. Fuck. That had completely left my mind. I squeeze the handle of the mop.

"You really think we'll be okay?"

"Creo que sí. You have me." He stops spraying the mats for a moment, to look at me. "But I need you to promise me one thing."

He seems very serious, so I meet his gaze. "What is it?"

"If I get stabbed, don't take me to a hospital here. Let me bleed out on the plane back to Costa Rica, because that will still be cheaper than United States health care."

I laugh. "How long is the flight?"

"Like six, seven hours. I'll risk it."

I mull it over. "If it's not fatal and you can reasonably survive on a six- or seven-hour flight, I'll consider it."

"Good enough for me."

"Although, new pitch: maybe don't get stabbed."

"Wow, wish I thought of that."

I stop mopping for a moment. While stopping the Wolf Man seems like something we have to do, the danger of it is really hitting me. What am I supposed to do if something actually happens to Nadia or Sebas?

"Are you sure you want to do this?" I ask. "The Wolf Man is after me. You can still stay out of it. Keep yourself safe. I mean . . . we basically just met."

"Yeah, but from the moment we did meet, I thought you were beautiful, and I'm happy to do stupid things for beautiful people." He seems a little embarrassed, but still serious, unlike me, who is blushing. "And Nadia's my cousin, yeah, but she's like a sister to me. An annoying sister, yes, but I love her. If the Wolf Man wanted her dead, I'm not just going to let that go."

I guess that makes sense. "I get that, it's just . . ."

Finished spraying, he steps closer to me. "What I'm trying to say is I'm not just doing this for you. I'm doing this to keep my family safe, too." He smiles slightly. "Hopefully impressing you is just a bonus."

I can't help but notice how close he is. How cute he looks. How I know I won't, but I still imagine what it would be like to get closer.

"So, we got this?" I ask instead.

"Of course we got this. I keep telling you, I've always been lucky."

Luck was never something I could rely on, but maybe he has a point.

I have him, and that alone is making me feel better.

15

Do You Like Scary Movies?

I've only been friends with Nadia and friends(?) with Sebas for a few days now, which is why it is incredibly awkward that I have to introduce them to my entire family. Literally my entire family. Mom wanted to go to the memorial to show support, so Uncle Ian came over to help wrangle the twins.

"Are you CJ's boyfriend?" Lyra asks Sebas once he sits at the table.

"No, but . . ."

"Are you CJ's girlfriend?" Leo asks Nadia.

"I'm not dating anyone," I snap. "Now stop interrogating my friends."

Both twins frown at me. Orion rolls his eyes from the couch. "Do you really think anyone would want to date CJ? They're a complete d—"

"Do we have everything?" Mom asks, stepping into the living room.

Her timing is perfect in terms of saving Orion from a potential slap from me. I try to take deep breaths and be the bigger person, even though the little shit is already taller than me. I know the only reason he's mad is because Mom agreed I could go off with my friends at the memorial while he was ordered to stay with her, Uncle Ian, and the kids.

"It's a memorial," Nadia starts. "Do you have to bring anything?"

Oh, this sweet, naive child who has no idea what my fucked up family is like.

"Let's do a backpack check," Uncle Ian suggests.

Dutifully, all of us Smith kids unzip our respective backpacks and look inside.

"Portable charger?" Mom asks.

"Check."

"Emergency phone or phones?"

"Check."

"Water?"

"Check."

"Orion and CJ only: pepper spray and pocketknives?"

"Check."

"When do we get knives?" Leo whines.

Mom chooses to ignore him. "Flashlights?"

"Check."

"Good." She double-checks Leo's and Lyra's wrists, each wearing a band with her number on it in case they get separated.

To Sebas and Nadia's credit, they don't look at us like we're absolutely batshit.

"Great, let me just get these cupcakes into the car," Mom says. Along with being chronically prepared and a bit of a badass, she also makes great cupcakes. Mom's a shit cook, but her baking is truly next-level.

I don't necessarily think cupcakes are appropriate food for a memorial, but no one is going to complain about free desserts.

Besides, not a single person will be able to say anything about what is grief-appropriate to Mom. She's lost more to the Satterville Wolf Man than anyone.

Anyone left, at least.

Sebas gets up from his chair. "I can help."

Mom smiles and hands him two boxes. "Perfect, I want to ask you about the kids jiu-jitsu program. How early can they start learning submissions? Because I think the twins will be great . . ."

She continues on as the two of them walk out of the apartment.

Immediately, Uncle Ian turns to Nadia. Today, he's ruining his good looks with "formal wear," a black sweater with a goose printed on it. "So, CJ totally likes him, right?"

"Obviously," Orion says with an eye roll.

"Definitely," Nadia confirms.

My face heats. "Shut up."

"I think you two are cute together," Uncle Ian says. "I like that he can teach you self-defense, and come on, who can resist an accent like that?'

"Go to hell, Uncle Ian."

He shrugs. "I've always wanted to move somewhere warm."

"Do I have a cute accent, Uncle Ian?" Lyra asks.

He boops her nose. "Only the cutest."

I grab Nadia's arm. "We're going to my room to get sweaters."

She doesn't protest as I lead her into my bedroom and close the door behind us. Even if we're leaving soon, I can use the few minutes away from my family. I can only imagine the embarrassment my mom is being with Sebas right now.

No. I have to focus. The events of tonight are more important.

"I like your family," Nadia says.

"Don't," I groan. "Did you bring something to defend yourself?"

"My cousin?"

I roll my eyes. I won't give up the knife I got from Dad, but I take the spare I keep in my nightstand and hand it to her. "In case you get separated, I want you to have something." I try to keep my voice hard. "I'm gonna need that back at the end of the night, though."

"You got it." Nadia sits at the edge of the bed, twirling the closed knife around in her fingers. "Do you think you're going to be okay? If you see him?"

"Obviously not," I admit, "but I'm not going to be okay either way, so might as well stick to the plan, yeah?"

She gives a weak smile. "Your family is so good under pressure."

"We kind of were raised on emergency preparedness."

Nadia laughs a little, but her expression grows somber. "Sebas is, too, though. And he wasn't raised like that, not exactly. But, I . . . I know I make a lot of jokes and don't seem to take things seriously, but I am. This, at least. It's just . . . I'm not as used to this kind of thing."

I give her a look. "I don't think anyone is."

"That's rich coming from the gay whose family does *emergency preparedness drills.*" She has me there. Nadia sighs, flopping onto my bed. "I feel like I'm the worst person to have in this kind of scenario. My family always makes fun of me for being oblivious and too much in my own head. And I know I'm like that. I don't pay attention to things. I'm usually daydreaming or escaping into webcomics and pretending to be all these main characters who are more interesting than me. Like you."

I lie down next to her, shaking my head. "I'm not the main character, Nadia, we're all our own main characters."

"Not in this story, Final Girl."

I turn my head toward her, the right side sinking into my comforter. Her dark brown eyes are glassy and her nose is a touch pink.

It sort of hits me right then that I've never been close to anyone like this. I haven't had friends come over and open up to me before. My chest tightens with both worry (do I even know how to comfort her?) and warmth (I'm someone she's going to for comfort!). It's a new, exciting territory. Someone I care about, who has similar interests and worries. Someone to share life with.

I'm far too embarrassed to admit it, but I kind of feel like I love her. I don't know why falling in love is so often reserved for feelings that are romantic or sexual. I don't have the same growing feelings for Nadia that I do for Sebas, but damn is she a lovable person.

"If you aren't interesting, it's because interesting isn't enough for you," I say. "You are dynamic. You are a pop culture genius. You are *hilarious*. You are a hot geek, which is always the best type of person. You're easily the coolest friend I have."

She's tearing up, but still manages to get in a jab. "Aren't I, like, your only friend?"

"Shut up," I laugh. "But yeah. Fine. You're easily the coolest person I know."

Nadia is quiet for a moment. "Can I tell you something? You have to promise not to tell Sebas."

I mime crossing my heart and zipping my lips shut.

"When I thought about how I was supposed to be the first to die—really thought about it, I mean—I honestly thought it made sense. I've never been a main character kind of person. I'm mostly just an observer, responding to whatever happens around me. It's like . . . how can you be a main character when you aren't even in control of your own story?"

I don't know what to say. But I know what she means. I've rarely felt in control of my life. I've always felt at the mercy of the Wolf Man, unable to escape that shadow. If anything, that feeling has only gotten worse. Nadia continues.

"Sebas and Samuel don't get it. They're so easygoing, they got to grow up with all the pura vida vibes, always sure of themselves. I'm the one who's always left out, not tica enough with my dad's side, not Italian enough with my mom's. Too shy and bookish for both." She snorts, tears leaking. "Hell, I wasn't even the main character in my own fucking coming-out story. Taylor took that from me."

Now I'm tearing up, too. I reach out and grab her hand.

"I'm sorry, Nadia. I've always been an odd one out, too. Maybe that's why we found each other."

"Thanks to some psycho fanfic writer?"

I roll my eyes. "I like to think I would have accidentally seen you reading gay smut webcomics even without the Wolf Man." I press my lips together. "Actually, I'm sure of it. Because it isn't the circumstances or the Wolf Man coming back or us as doomed extras or accidental heroes causing it. I am *choosing* to be your best friend because I like you."

"I'll choose you, too, Pikachu." She laughs. "Can I tell you something I never got to actually tell anyone the way I wanted?"

I nod. "Of course. Even if I'd pick Eevee over Pikachu any day."

Nadia leans in closer. "Don't tell my husbandos, but I'm a huge fucking lesbian."

I squeeze her hand. "Thanks for sharing that. I'm a genderqueer bisexual."

It's a much better coming-out story, despite everything.

"I'm so glad I didn't die. That I get to have you on my side, CJ." My chest feels warm and I'm also crying, until she slightly ruins it by adding: "Thanks for letting Taylor die instead of me."

"I didn't *let* her die—"

"It's okay, I'm not judging. Us queers have to stick together, right?" She shrugs. "Well, us queers and Sebas. But it's not like

Latino boys constantly survive horror stories either. All of Moon Satter's original Final Girls were cis, straight, and white." Nadia looks back at me. "No offense to your dad."

"Well, he wasn't exactly the Final Girl," I say. "He was half-dead the first time and full-dead the second. I get your point, though." I pause. "It's still so weird that you basically know my dad because of those damn books."

It's not like I wrote them, but it still feels so personal. Almost like knowing half the town read my diary. The thoughts weren't mine, and I know the fictional version of myself is barely in *Welcome to Slasherville*, but it still feels so unnerving and strange.

"I hate to break it to you, but I think basically everyone knows your dad," Nadia says. "He's arguably the best character, the audiobooks are great, and *Camp Slasherville* is literally on the ninth grade summer reading list."

"Which is so fucked up," we say at the same time.

It causes us both to laugh. Nadia leans her head against my shoulder. Feeling her there and her palm in mine are both so nice. Comfortable. I like being able to touch someone and not have to worry about the butterflies, only enjoy the warmth. Nadia and I might both be queer, but we're just friends, and that's a dynamic I've never had before.

I like it a lot.

I lean back into her.

"I'm sorry you had to go through that shit," Nadia says. "I mean, you were just a kid."

"Nadia, we're still kind of just kids."

"Well, at least we can drive."

"I can't. I don't have a license."

"You gay stereotype." She twists against me. "Neither do I."

For some reason, that feels like the funniest thing in the world and we both burst out laughing. It takes me a good two minutes just to catch my breath.

"Thanks, though. It does kind of suck." I blink. I can't believe I'm actually crying. "And thanks for believing me and sticking around to help."

"It might be a gamble to be a supporting character in this scenario, but hey, I'm already living on borrowed time." She pulls away enough to meet my eyes. "Still, let's kill this damn wolf to be safe."

Before I can respond, my phone lights up. It's Sebas calling.

Did they drop the cupcakes or something? Or is everyone ready to go? It seems kind of weird that he would call instead of Mom or Uncle Ian. Unless they're just making him do it to embarrass me further.

"Hello?"

"Hi, Cassie."

It isn't Sebas's voice. My blood chills.

"That's not my name."

Only Dad called me Cassie. No one else can. No one else *does.*

"Cassie, Cassie, Cassie, Cassie, Cassie," the voice repeats with a laugh.

My hand shakes. "Where's Sebas?"

The voice loses all traces of humor. "In danger. Just like your mom, and your uncle, and your little rodent siblings. You see how easily I can get to you, Cassie Jane? Do you see how easily I can take everything from you?" The voice grows louder, speaking in a growl. "So stay out of this, you little bitch." It laughs again. "And save me a cupcake. Chocolate's my favorite."

The line goes dead.

I run out of the room, ignoring Uncle Ian, Orion, and the twins, and rush straight out of the apartment building to the lot. I nearly knock Mom over, who stops me when she sees my tears. I quickly check her over. She seems fine.

"CJ? What happened?"

"Where's Sebas?"

Mom points back to the car. "Looking for his phone. He must have dropped it as we were loading the boxes."

I follow her gesture, where Sebas is kneeling next to the car, checking underneath. Relief washes over me when I see he's okay, and a part of me quickly notices that he has a really cute butt for a guy, but the somewhat rational and terrified side of me suppresses that.

"Sebas?" I call.

He looks up. "Everything okay?"

"Just come back inside for a second," I say.

Although he and Mom both look confused, they follow me back toward the front of the apartment.

"Hey, Sebastián . . ." my mom starts. "You got an iPhone?"

"Yeah."

"Well, I think I found it."

She points to the base of the door, where the phone is neatly placed over a piece of paper that has a drawing of the Satterville Wolf Man, an exact copy of the one I painted at Red Page.

Only this is drawn with what looks a lot like fresh blood.

16

Real Main Characters Make Bad Decisions

Uncle Ian wanted to call the police. Mom wanted to kick someone in the face. Sebas liked that idea and offered to follow up with a Berimbolo to heel hook (whatever the hell that means). Nadia wanted to analyze the drawing. Orion said it sucked. The twins, having no idea what was going on, wanted ice cream.

Somehow, we landed on reporting it to the apartment building security to handle and going to the memorial anyway. Safety in numbers or something like that.

I think it's a bad idea.

Clearly the Wolf Man knows what we're up to, that we're trying to stop him. But I'm trying to be a main character for once, and not just any main character, a *Final Girl.* Final Girls don't use logic. They investigate the weird shit, they go back for the debatably charming, possibly creepy dude they just met. They do the exact opposite of what any extra with common sense would want them to do. And, above all, they never let threats from the killer stop them.

Not for long anyway.

The fact that going to the memorial is a bad idea means it's the right one. Besides, it's all part of the plan. And if I like anything, it's a plan.

Still, aside from Leo and Lyra singing TV show theme songs, the car is awkwardly quiet. The drive feels impossibly long, in part because Lyra is on my lap so Uncle Ian could fit with us. I could have gone with Sebas and Nadia, but since I'll be with them during the memorial and I don't know how things will go down, I wanted to spend a little more time with my family.

Lyra farts on my leg.

"Sorry," she says.

I hug her tightly, trying not to breathe in. "It's okay."

Leo giggles, letting out a huge fart himself.

I shove him. "Come on, that one wasn't an accident."

"It also won't be an accident when I punch you all," Orion snaps, frantically rolling down the window. "Seriously, what have you two been eating?"

I really hope I don't die tonight and have this as my last memory. As we approach the parking lot outside the football field where the memorial is set to take place, I can already see that it's packed. We're a little early, maybe pushing it to be on time, but there are already hundreds of people scattered across the football field, lighting candles in Taylor's honor. I don't think everyone here is a Satterville local, though, based on the amount of people already visibly taking pictures and videos. The fact that we are exactly one week away from Slasherfest probably has something to do with the big turnout.

"At least there are a lot of people . . ." Mom starts, although her heart doesn't seem in it.

A lot of people means a crowd to hide in.

Which can be just as good for the Wolf Man as it is for us. Although, if the killer is following the story, they're probably planning on luring the target away from the crowd anyway.

"You should have made more cupcakes," Uncle Ian comments.

Based on Mom's glare, I half expect him to be the next dead body.

Sebas parks right next to us, in an open spot way off in the corner of the second lot, so we all get out of the cars together. We help Mom carry her bakery boxes while Uncle Ian controls the twins, but once we get inside and grab our candles, I split off with Sebas and Nadia.

"Where was it that Max and his friends wandered off?"

"The wooded area," I say. "Down by that little stream."

"Because of course. There's a killer on the loose, why not go off alone to drink in the woods? Who can honestly think that's a good idea?"

I frown. "Popular kids in a horror story."

Nadia bites her lip. "Well, you got me there."

"CJ!"

I twist toward the voice, Sebas and Nadia getting a few steps ahead before they realize I stopped. It's Mr. White, holding his already lit candle. While it makes sense for Satterville faculty to be in attendance, it's almost weird to see him outside of the guidance office.

"Hi, Mr. White," I say.

"I'm glad I ran into you. How are you holding up?" he asks, voice low.

I shrug. "I'm doing okay."

"I'm a little surprised you're here," he admits. He seems on edge, almost squirmy. "It's not safe for you."

That's a weird thing to say. My heart pounds.

"What do you mean by that?" I snap. Has he seen the Wolf Man? Is he here already?

Mr. White's eyes immediately soften, his free hand going up in some kind of apologetic gesture. "Only that, given what happened the other day and everything going on, I'm a little worried it might trigger a panic attack."

Oh. He isn't warning me about the Wolf Man. He's worried about me.

"I'll be okay," I say. "I appreciate you looking out, though."

A sort of awkward moment passes. I glance back at Sebas and Nadia, but the two of them are talking.

"Um. Well. I'll see you," I tell Mr. White.

"Just one moment . . . Are you sure everything's all right?" Mr. White asks. "I know finals are coming up, and with everything going on, we can talk about getting you extra time or potentially a retake."

I might have to take him up on that, but I don't want to deal with this now.

"Um, cool, yeah."

"It's just terrible this has to be happening again," he says. "Especially so close to Slasherfest."

Doesn't he have someone else to talk to? I look to Nadia and Sebas for a save, but they've stepped far enough away that they don't notice my discomfort. Something about Mr. White seems off. It's rare for him to seem frazzled, but I guess all this brings up bad memories for him, too—he started working at Satterville High back when my parents and Uncle Ian went there, so he's been around for it all. But I don't have a lot of time to chat.

That's when I see Peyton and Bethany, walking by with stuffed drawstring bags. It's hard to miss them with the Febreze-covering-weed smell. I try to get their attention with my eyes, to no avail. I think back to my last conversation with Peyton and the assurance he gave me.

As Mr. White goes on about how terrible it all is, I let out a desperate meow.

Peyton perks up, immediately looking toward me and nodding with some kind of understanding. He yanks Bethany over. "Mr. White! We're sad and in danger of using drugs to deal with our grief, please help." Peyton gives me a wink as Mr. White focuses on them and allows me to escape.

Guess he really did learn from his pet therapist mom.

My stomach feels a bit tight, but it's probably just from the weirdness of this day. It's not like anyone knows how to act at a memorial with a killer on the loose.

"What was that about?" Sebas asks.

"Peyton sensed the anxiety in my meow."

He looks at me blankly. "Is that some kind of Ohio slang?"

I shake my head. "No. It's nothing. Mr. White's my guidance counselor. Just trying to give . . . too much guidance, I guess. Some lunch friends saved me."

"Let's focus on finding Max, since he's the only lead we have," Nadia says, back to business. She gives a teasing smile. "Unless you think Mr. White is a DILF and therefore a potential victim."

I fake barf. "I hate you."

"I mean, you like Sebas, I can't trust your taste."

"Shut up, Nadia," Sebas and I say together, sounding equally embarrassed.

The crowd is lessening as we walk farther down the football field and closer to the wooded area behind it.

Sebas has a thick hoodie on and at least one layer underneath, but he's visibly shivering.

"Cold?" I ask.

He gives me a helpless look. "Isn't it almost summer?"

I grimace. "The whole four seasons thing is kind of a myth in Northern Ohio. We basically have two seasons: cold and construction."

Sebas groans. "I'm not built for this."

"Does it not get cold in Costa Rica?"

"It's literally a rainforest, CJ," Nadia says. "Of course it doesn't get cold." She sighs, looking at Sebas. "That's the US education system for you."

I jokingly hit my shoulder into hers, but she's also not *wrong*.

Sebas gives an easy smile. "It's okay, you can come and visit sometime. Actually feel warm ocean water. Learn some geography, even."

"I'll have you know I've never felt *any* ocean water."

"Really?" Nadia asks. "Have you only flown to landlocked places?"

Now I feel a little embarrassed. I put my hands in my own hoodie pockets. "I've never been on a plane?"

Not exactly easy for Mom to plan family vacations as a single parent with four kids. Even with Uncle Ian helping, she doesn't like taking that much time off work. And it isn't like we have family anywhere else. Mom lost both her parents, the rest of her family are people she never met in Italy, and Dad's family . . .

The ones who are left don't talk to us. Even before his death, they were basically strangers. So it really is just us and Uncle Ian.

Nadia looks a little shocked, almost like she hasn't considered the fact that there are people who haven't traveled like that.

"I also don't know how to ride a bike," I admit. "My Achilles' heel is transportation."

That addition gets Sebas, too. He shakes his head. "Well, that you should learn."

"Why? It's not like I'll be outrunning the Wolf Man and conveniently have a getaway bike appear as my only hope. I think I'm good."

Although I sort of regret saying that, because these things always come back to haunt protagonists in the movies.

At this point, we've reached the edge of the woods. The noise and the probably fake tears from the memorial start to fade behind us as we slip into the trees. We have flashlights, so we blow out our candles, making sure they're completely extinguished before leaving them on the dirt.

We keep our voices quiet, steps light, and eyes alert as we make our way down to the stream. New voices cut through the near silence. I can make out laughter and the sound of Max speaking.

Guess the book got that part right, too. I bite my lip. Or the killer made the plan themself. Which might mean it's a Satterville student.

Like actual creeps ourselves, the three of us stick to the shadows and behind trees to take in the scene. It's not a huge group of people, just about fifteen or so, few enough to not draw a ton of attention from everyone back at the football field. Someone lit a small fire, which dances in the center of the group, casting oranges and yellows over their shadowed faces. Most of them have cans of beer, but there are also some flasks being passed around.

"So, who are we watching?" Sebas whispers.

I sort of forgot that he's new to town and doesn't know people yet. Satterville's not huge, but not small either, so it's not exactly an everyone-knows-everyone kind of place anyway.

"Technically, everyone. Teens going off in the woods is a major potential murder trigger. But the tall, blond guy in the jersey is the victim in the book," I say.

Sebas makes a face. "Isn't he *cold*?"

"Shut *up*," Nadia whispers. "We're supposed to be looking out for weird shit."

"I'm doing that, too."

"You're going to get us caught."

"You're talking more than me!"

I gently hit them both, cutting off their whisper-fight. Melody, a senior girl who I don't know well, is pulling on Max's hand and leading him back toward the trees.

"They're going off alone. We have to follow them," Nadia says. She's already on the move.

I know she's right and I should follow, but my attention is grabbed by my phone lighting up. It's a string of texts from Hana.

hey! Mom's with your mom passing out cupcakes wya?

wait is that you going into the WOODS? At NIGHT?

hold up

i'm coming

Shit. I really don't want to explain what we're doing here to Hana. I look around, but don't spot her yet. She shouldn't have come by herself, it's dangerous for her to—

Wait.

Hana. My first crush.

No. Oh fuck, no.

I turn to Sebas. "Get Nadia. It's not Max. I have to go."

"I don't think we should split up," he starts, looking between me and his cousin, who's all but disappeared into the darkness.

"She needs you," I say, remembering our conversation in my room earlier. "I think I know who's in danger. I'm going after them. But you can't leave Nadia alone, just in case."

He doesn't seem convinced, but Nadia is family, so he backs up, ready to follow after her. Maybe it's the desperation in my voice that does it.

"Be safe," he says.

Then he turns, slowly disappearing into the trees.

I take out my flashlight, holding it in my elbow pit, and my knife, keeping it tight in my grip. I start running back in the direction we came, but I'm calling Hana at the same time with my free hand. Each ring sends a pain through my stomach.

Please pick up please pick up please pick up.

"Hey there—"

"Hana, where are you? You need to get out of the woods *now*—"

"Leave a message and I'll probably text you back."

My stomach drops to the dirt. No. Fuck. Why isn't she answering? I'm already freaking out, and then I hear it.

A sharp scream that's abruptly cut off.

My blood runs entirely cold.

I dart to the right, in the direction of the shout. And there's Hana.

Slumped on the ground, blood dripping onto the dirt, hands gripping the knife that's sunk into her torso.

My heart stops. I think I scream.

I look up. At him. The Wolf Man.

Standing over her.

And looking right back at me.

17

Fight or Flight or Unfortunately Freeze

"Hana!" The name escapes from my lips, rough and desperate.

She looks up at me. At the same time, the Wolf Man pulls the knife from her, blood spilling. No. *No.* Her hands clutch at the wound, shirt drenched in that deep red. But she's alive. There's still a chance. I have to give her time to get away.

My heart pounds in my throat and my hand shakes around my small knife. I know they say size doesn't matter, but the comparison between the two weapons doesn't make me feel better about the situation, especially because I don't *really* know how to use it and the Wolf Man's blade is already dripping with Hana's blood.

My mind is disoriented, filled with panic and horror. I know I should be stepping in, trying to save Hana, but my feet stay frozen.

I don't understand why I'm reacting like this. I *prepared* for this.

I remind myself to move forward again, but my legs are stiff, heavy, hard as stone. I feel like my soul isn't attached correctly to my body, so as much as my brain moves, everything else refuses to listen.

Hana is still there, grunting as she tries to back away and get to her feet. Blood drips from around her fingers.

So much blood.

Red staining my socks. My feet. Dad's blood. Metallic and thick. The same that ran through my veins. So easy to spill out. Red all over the floor. The tang of piss. The cartoonish, unsettling mask. Red all over my hands.

No. No, not my hands. My feet. My legs. Dad's hands. The killer's hands.

My mind is crashing, sounds and scents and hopeless feelings flashing by my eyes like an old projector film. I'm shutting down, I can feel it. I can't move, I can't breathe.

I can't breathe, I can't breathe, I can't breathe.

The Wolf Man howls and lunges toward Hana.

I don't know if it's the howl that snaps me out of it, awakening some hidden willpower inside me, or pure desperation, but the world seems to speed up and takes me with it. I'm charging into the Wolf Man, pushing him against the tree so he can't get to Hana.

"Go!" I scream. "Get help!"

She doesn't have a choice. Jaw tense and sweat bubbling up on her face, Hana stumbles off toward the field. And I'm shoved. Hard.

The wind rushes out of me as my body slams into the dirt. My glasses fly off my face, and I can't hear where they hit.

Shit.

It hurts. But it's the pain of being alive. It's decidedly not the pain of being brutally stabbed or getting my throat slit. It's the pain of it not being over yet.

And, somehow, that small chance allows me to scramble to my feet. My vision isn't great without lenses, but the Wolf Man is close enough to see his movements. He's already lifting the large knife, ready to swing and deliver a blow. If I try to attack, there's a big risk of getting caught in the exchange.

I find my footing and run away from the direction Hana went. She has to make it. I can't lead him back to her.

The knife stays in my hand, and while my breath comes too quickly and my back aches, I try to dart my way through the trees. I can't see where the fire is. I can't see anyone. It's hard enough to see the trees and avoid running into them. Sebas and Nadia went off in the other direction.

"Help!" I scream anyway.

Someone has to hear that, right?

I'm yanked back by my hair, making my eyes sting. My butt hits the ground as the Wolf Man pulls me closer, fingers entangled with the dark-blond strands. My scalp burns as he pulls back, dragging me across the ground toward him. Twigs and rocks pinch and cut my legs, dirt staining the fabric of my pants.

I fumble my knife above my head, desperate, and cut. The Wolf Man pulls away, nearly half my hair in his fist. I remember Sebas's drill of technical lifts from jiu-jitsu and get to my feet smoothly, holding out the knife toward the Wolf Man.

The dark eyes watch me.

My hand trembles.

The Wolf Man leaps forward to grab my wrist, slicing toward me with the knife. I bend my arm to break the grip and dodge, using the momentum to trip him.

I need to get away. Run as fast as I can.

But I see the Wolf Man on the ground and I have an opening. A chance to use my knife. Somehow, I feel like I know the exact sensation of pushing the blade into flesh, watching the blood bubble up and out from the surface.

I'm dizzy. I sway on my own feet.

Hands stained in red. Dripping. Mixed with tears as they splattered across pale cheeks under wide eyes.

A voice. Saying, "It's okay, it's okay, it's okay." Meaning, "I'm sorry, I'm sorry, I'm sorry, I'm so, so sorry . . ."

Dad. Dad. Dad, come back, come back, please, please, please, you promised.

The next thing I know, a hand grips my ankle and yanks hard. I drop heavy, my quick breaths escaping me altogether.

The Wolf Man looms over me.

"I expected more from Christian Smith's kid," he growls.

He raises the knife, a clear threat. I know I should move, should fight, but I can't.

It's over.

I failed.

I won't be able to protect Orion. Leo, Lyra, Mom. Satterville will see more blood and it's all because I'm not good enough. I can only hope that Hana is okay. That I become the second victim in her place.

Turns out I'm not the Final Girl.

I never was. Moon Satter and their impersonator both knew that, and deep down, I do, too.

Unfortunately, I'm too much like Dad in the worst way.

I wonder how much dying hurts. How quickly it goes black. Where my consciousness will slip away to . . .

Will you be there, Dad? Will I at least be able to see you? To hug you? To laugh about how I didn't just get your looks, but your tendency to self-sacrifice? Can I finally thank you for the knife and apologize for not being able to use it better?

Will you forgive me?

My eyes close as I brace to find out.

The pain doesn't come. Instead, there's a loud, cracking *bang* and a gush splatters over my face, my shirt, wet and warm. The smell is all too familiar.

Is that my blood? Why doesn't it hurt?

I open my eyes. The Wolf Man is still, chest blossoming with red, a gnarly hole in the center, revealing bits of bodily sinew around the edges.

He falls forward, slowly. I catch a blurry glimpse of what's behind him: the short, familiar figure of my mom, and what looks like a shotgun poised in her arms.

"You messed with the wrong fucking family again, bastard," she says.

And the dying, crumbling Wolf Man knocks me back into the tree, my head smacking against the tough bark.

18

The End

My brain isn't working right. The back of my head hurts like a bitch, but when my mom helps me up, everything is blurry. More than the usual amount without my glasses. I can see her lips moving, but I don't hear what she says. Any sounds I'm able to make out are incomprehensible. My ears are ringing.

More people approach. Maybe there are sirens. Maybe there are screams.

I black out.

Another hand on my arm, talking to me. It's Sebas. His eyes are wild with worry.

"What?" I say. "You're not making any sense."

He looks at me in a way that makes it seem like I'm the one not making any sense. Did I forget English or something?

I'm scared. The world is rushing around me and my brain can't keep up. Something's wrong with me. My eyes dip to the ground, where the Wolf Man lies dead. His blood and tissue are splattered on me. Or is it mine? Maybe my brain is leaking and that's why everything is so confusing.

I start crying at the thought.

I think Sebas consoles me, a hand on my shoulder, but he doesn't let me move. Hard eyes tell me not to stand, I think. To just stay still.

More lights, stretching out like diamonds. Falling stars. Maybe this isn't a story. Maybe I am an alien in space, a visitor in time. I am Cassiopeia, returned to the constellations. I am . . .

Fuck, my head.

I'm slipping out again.

"Can you follow my finger? Don't move your head, just your eyes."

"What?"

The paramedic repeats himself. I follow his finger. Where the hell are my glasses?

"What's your name?"

I don't respond right away, not because I *forgot* but because I'm trying to take in my surroundings. I'm sitting in the back of an ambulance. The medic is in front of me. He looks nice. But when the hell did I get here?

Panic rushes over me. "Where's Hana?"

"She's alive," the paramedic says. "She's getting help. What's your name?"

"CJ Smith," I snap. I don't mean to sound so annoyed. I'm just frustrated at myself, really. I need to focus with the Wolf Man right over there so I can figure out who was behind this.

Who almost killed me.

Holy shit, I almost died.

But Hana's alive. Thank God. She's alive.

The medic gets my attention again, and I try my best to follow every instruction and respond to each question, but even after I do I don't entirely remember what I just said. It all passes so quickly, a scatter of scenes and melting lights and questions and—

"Is everyone else okay?" I ask.

The paramedic nods. "Everyone else is okay, CJ. Let's focus on you."

I can't believe everyone is okay. Well, Hana was stabbed, but she's *alive*. And I'm alive. It doesn't even make sense. Everything's okay? I mean, Mom blew through the chest of the Wolf Man. I don't think he can pull through from that.

"Where did she even get a damn shotgun?" I ask.

"Focus, CJ," the paramedic suggests calmly.

I guess I also talked to the cops afterward, but I still don't feel like myself. Everything is off. I'm a stranger in my own body, and not in some gender way, but in a way that makes me feel distant from my own life.

I almost died.

I almost *died*.

Again. For real.

I hardly feel human or alive at all until my mom is able to put her arms around me and pull me into a tight hug. She's lifted enough weights and punched enough pads to be strong enough to hold me together, and my world finally stops falling out from under my feet. She's okay. Uncle Ian is with Orion, Leo, and Lyra. They're all okay. I even glimpse Sebas and Nadia, talking to a police officer. They're okay, too. Hana's alive.

That's what matters.

It's a crushing relief, and I know I should be happy.

I cry into Mom's shoulder.

"Shhhh, baby," she says, stroking my dirty, matted, much shorter hair. "It's okay. It's over. It's over, love, it's all over."

It's over. It's over. It's over.

Once again, the Wolf Man is dead.

The story is finished. Rewritten. No one else had to die.

I feel like laughing. Like crying. I think I do both. Mom holds me tighter, laughing and crying along with me.

We did it. *We fucking did it.*

And it's over.

19

. . . Or Is It?

Something's not right.

That's how I feel in the days following our victory. I can't put my finger on why, and it seems like I'm the only person feeling that way. Mom and Uncle Ian are immediately back to business as usual. *Ding-dong, the Wolf Man's dead, so rest your head, till the next copycat* or whatever. Mom went the whole nine yards, taking a day off work (she doesn't even do that on birthdays) and getting fancy donuts delivered for breakfast. I was half-shocked she didn't have them draw a dead wolf on the box.

I want everything to be over. I want it to be that easy.

But then I saw the report.

They had mentioned the new Wolf Man's name the night of the incident. Drew Dunning. A name that didn't mean anything to me.

But I recognized his face. Drew Dunning was the Slashervillain at Red Page, the one who said I looked familiar. Either Ms. Maeda or Hana reported that, too, and within a day or so, the story came together.

A crazed fan wanted to continue the Wolf Man legacy by finishing what the previous one couldn't. Taylor was probably a mistake (another white blond girl), and Hana was a reason to get closer to me before the killer could end my life and then, likely, Orion's.

The only ones who survived the last Wolf Man.

I mean, that shit writes itself.

Apparently, Drew wasn't even from Satterville. He drove in from outside Pittsburgh, which no one found weird because it just added to the overall opinion that he was a sick freak who was far too invested in the fictional books.

Moon Satter even put out a statement.

I am deeply saddened by the horrific death of Taylor Topper and the attempted murder of Hana Maeda. While I believe telling the stories of the Satterville mass murders was important, I am absolutely aghast that anyone would read my books and glorify the work of the real-life evil individuals who caused so much harm. I am, and have always been, on the side of the victims and always aimed to share their stories with respect.

While I had no contact with or awareness of Mr. Dunning and his plan, I am glad that he is no longer a threat to the Satterville community. I know my fan base is a wonderful group of readers who would equally condemn the actions of Mr. Dunning, and I will cover all funeral costs for Miss Topper and medical bills for Miss Maeda.

I would also like to extend my deepest condolences to Cassiopeia Jane and the rest of the Smith family, who have had their lives upended once again. I hope the physical wounds heal quickly, and for the sake of the emotional wounds, I ask with all my sincerity that everyone give this family the space and peace to begin to heal.

All the best,
Moon Satter

I've read it approximately twenty-five times since they dropped it yesterday morning, and drafted and deleted maybe thirty different responses with varying degrees of rage.

Needless to say, it's now June 2, three days since everything happened, and I haven't left my room aside from necessary appointments like my MRI and new glasses (a gift from Uncle Ian), visiting Hana and Ms. Maeda at the hospital (Hana recovered enough to refuse any kind of apology from me and instead tried to convince me to sneak her fried chicken), and a few meals with my family. Shockingly, even Peyton and Bethany stopped by to drop off a study guide Bethany made for finals and a joint Peyton rolled. Mom found and took the joint, even though it would have been helpful for my post-concussion headaches.

Sebas and Nadia tried to come by, but I didn't want to see them just yet.

I want to be happy. I want to believe everything turned out okay.

I'm not ready to face the truth.

Nadia and Sebas should know as well as I do that the official story of Drew Dunning driving across state lines with the sole intention of murdering me doesn't actually make sense.

Because it doesn't explain the book.

Even if Drew Dunning wrote it, there's no clear reason why he went off script. And if I really was the target, why did he leave me the book? Just to mess with my head and make me think I was safe because I was an extra? When Nadia didn't make it to the woodshop room, did he decide to get Taylor instead because, in the end, it didn't matter who died first? Because he was only building up to my murder?

Even the little details don't add up. How would Drew Dunning have gotten into the girls' bathroom at school unnoticed to block the toilets? How would he know that I would run into Taylor during the announcement? How would he—a grown-ass adult man who knew no one in town—have organized a senior bonfire outside Taylor's memorial to match the book?

And when I inadvertently started rewriting the story, even if that made him adjust the plan, how would Drew Dunning know Hana Maeda was my first crush and the only person who could be comparable to an ex?

He couldn't.

It doesn't make sense.

I've been thinking about it for days now, and the wall behind my bed is starting to look a lot like the poster boards in Nadia's room. Only I don't have a printer, so it's all Post-it notes with my own frantic scribble.

The Slashervillain forums blew up after the news broke, and I've been combing through them obsessively, even making my own account to track the speculation.

Days of reading posts and getting notifications of new comments. Days of trying to get any additional information about Drew Dunning.

Then, finally, SlasherSlut4 comes through.

SlasherSlut4: hey Slashervillains. Just wanted to update on this thread because I know everyone is trying to look into Drew Dunning. Don't ask me how much time I spent on this but I think this is his tag: BirchHowl9.

HorrorGirrrrl: wtf is that warrior cats bullshit

BigBootyJake: no way he's a warrior cats fan, they furries not murderers, great fandom

xxstegosaurusxx: BigBootyJake you're a fucking idiot

BigBootyJake: warrior cats fan, are we?

xxstegosaurusxx: that's beside the point.

Windclan02: leave warrior cats out of your whore mouth

Okay, the rest of the comments are going nowhere. I click on the profile of BirchHowl9. There's nothing in the bio to make it clear that it's Drew Dunning. I find his Instagram, which seems to be his only public social media. Most of his pictures are in front of trees. I scroll through the descriptions: *yellow birch looks great this time of year.*

Well, shit. I think SlasherSlut4 is right.

I go back to the forum, where I look through BirchHowl9's posts and comments. Most of it is pretty normal. Fan theories, excitement over Slasherfest, questions about places to eat in Satterville. But one stops me.

BirchHowl9: I am looking into the Creator and everything makes sense now

My heart thumps in my chest. The Creator again. Whatever the Creator is, it has something to do with getting people to don that bloody mask.

I keep scrolling a little more, but I don't get very far before my phone rings. I'm ready to ignore it, but it's Uncle Ian's name appearing across the screen. I answer and put him on speaker.

"Hey, kiddo. What are you up to?"

I don't think I should tell him that I'm deep into Slashervillain fan forums looking for theories about the guy who just tried to kill me. Although that might get Uncle Ian to try and convince Mom to let me have that joint.

"Studying," I say.

"You seriously still have to take finals? That's bullshit."

"You're telling me." Unfortunately, the studying I've been doing won't get me very far with my exams. "I wish I could bring Chekov as my emotional support cat."

"The 'cat chewed up my exam' excuse would go over great, I'm sure." Uncle Ian laughs a little through the speaker. "When does your last test tomorrow end? Maybe we can pick you up."

"Should be at two ten. I can text you."

"New glasses working out okay?"

At their mention, I push them up on the bridge of my nose. "Might have to tighten them a little, but honestly, it's fine. I appreciate you getting them."

"I mean, you need to *see*, CJ. It's not like I bought you a BMW for fun."

"Still. I could have been forced to get something cheap that looked terrible."

"Come on, kid, you've always pulled off lenses. You'd look great no matter what. You get that from me."

I roll my eyes even though he can't see them. "You know you aren't my uncle by blood, right?"

"Sure, but you wouldn't be nearly as charming without my influence. That's, like, fifty percent of looks. You can thank your dad for the rest."

Both of us are silent for a moment.

"I really miss him, Uncle Ian."

"Me too, CJ. More than I can even say."

I rub my eyes. "I just want this all to be over."

"It is over. They got the guy." A beat. "Well, your mom did."

I bite my lip. "Everyone thought it was over when Brett Miller died, didn't they? I'm sure you thought it was over with Evan. How are we supposed to believe it's over now?"

Uncle Ian is silent for a moment. I hear his long inhale on the line before he finally speaks. "I guess it doesn't matter whether or not it's over forever. What matters is that it's over for now and that we can be there for each other. As a family. No matter what, we'll figure it out. Okay?"

"Okay." I swallow. "I should get back to studying. I'll talk to you tomorrow, okay?"

"See you then."

I end the call. Maybe Uncle Ian is right, even if he doesn't know why. The important thing is sticking together and moving forward. I haven't been all that great about being there for my family and friends after everything, but maybe I can make up for that by starting to figure some shit out.

I return to my spot on Drew's posts.

BirchHowl9: Slashervillain Confession: I have to skip over some of the death scenes in the books! I'm pretty squeamish. While I'm okay with blood (mostly), I can't deal with all the gore. Just shows how descriptive Moon Satter is though!

The fucking killer is *squeamish*? I'd maybe believe it if Hana had been the only victim—since the stab wound wasn't fatal, one could argue there was some hesitation or uncertainty. But not with Taylor. That was brutal. Even without seeing the full extent of her injuries, I could tell that much.

I'm not sure why Drew Dunning would lie like this on a nearly anonymous post, months before the murder and attempted murder happened. Unless he was trying to preemptively cover his tracks in some way by saying that, because someone with a fear of gore wouldn't have killed Taylor like that. Not unless he got someone else to do the dirty work for him.

A chill passes over me.

Maybe he wasn't working alone.

That would explain some of the holes in the story. Someone was helping him, someone who knows me, knows Satterville. Someone else who also knows about the Creator and Brett Miller's message.

Drew Dunning may have been the man behind the mask, but he wasn't behind everything.

I can't ignore this any longer. This isn't just another piece of the puzzle. It might be another Wolf Man. And if that's the case, we're all still in danger.

I have to tell Nadia and Sebas.

I rub my eyes. Maybe getting out will do me some good. Much more of this and I might become a Slashervillain by default. I can't imagine anything worse.

I type out my text before I can change my mind.

Hey, Sebas. Are you and Nadia busy today?

No, we're free. Are you okay? How are you doing?

Well I can see again so that's nice

But I have to talk to you about something important

What is it?

I'll tell you in person

If that's okay

Can you come to my apartment?

Samuel's making dinner

I'm not sure I'll be great company for dinner. Even Orion's been walking on eggshells around me, and he's the last person to be considerate of feelings. But I need to talk to Nadia and Sebas. I need to know if I'm losing it or not.

And maybe I'd feel a little better seeing them.

When can I be there?

20

If Not Moon Satter, Who's the Real Freak?

It's not a date. Nadia and Sebas's brother will both be there, so it's definitely not a date and I don't have to freak out. I mean, even if it was a date, it can't be worse than taking on a serial killer and basically losing. But it's not a date. So it's fine.

I curse myself for reading so many horror and mystery books and not taking the time to check out many romances. This is totally out of my element. How am I supposed to even know how to prepare?

I'm feeling more femme today, but like, comfort femme, so I go with jeans and a pink sweater, plus my off-brand Doc Martens. Most of my attire is pretty feminine, because it's what I think I look best in. I used to worry about everyone probably thinking I'm cis, but I've come to terms with my identity not having to match my presentation.

For the most part. There's definitely some imposter syndrome that creeps up here and there, but it seems like everyone deals with that.

At least my outfit mostly covers all my scrapes and bruises, which have morphed into a sickly yellow-brown. The color looks even more horrific and noticeable on my white skin, like body horror pop art.

Nervously, I pull at my sleeves. But it's fine. It's just dinner. Even worse, it's dinner to talk about the Wolf Man. Can't get less romantic than that.

I grab my bag with all the usual necessities and head out of my room. Leo doodles animals that pop up on the nature documentary playing on TV as Lyra reads a book next to him. Mom's prepping dinner in the kitchen. Sloppy joes. Thank God I'm not eating here for once. Our food is always a rotation of the same three or four bargain dinners, and Manwich is my least favorite one.

"Leaving?"

"Yeah, Sebas should be here soon . . ."

My phone buzzes with his arrival message.

"Or now."

Mom walks over to kiss my cheek. Her eyes are hard as they meet mine. "Be careful, and call me if anything happens, okay? Anything."

I nod. I've heard her say this, or something similar, a million times before, but it feels different now. It's not like Mom had to prove herself to me—she's always been my hero—but she literally saved my life the other day. Maybe that was my big mistake. I thought I could handle everything on my own, but I couldn't. It takes everything in me not to fall into her arms and start crying again.

"Promise."

I'm already walking outside toward where Sebas parked when I notice an email notification. From Moon Satter.

I stop in my tracks. Even though I know Sebas can see me, I can't help myself and I read through the email.

Hi CJ,

I received the email you sent my agent, and while I am thrilled to hear from you, I am horrified by what recently took place in town. I wish I could have done something to stop it, but it all came as a complete shock to me. To hear this while I was away at a writing retreat was heartbreaking. If I had been home, maybe I could have seen the signs . . . I am just so, so sorry for what you went through.

I know you reached out about an interview and even potentially consulting on a future book, but I think given the recent events, it is far too soon for any of that. Take the time to rest and heal. I am honored that you would trust me with your story, but the time to tell it should be on your terms.

That being said, I am of course happy to share my research with you as mentioned in your email. While you shouldn't pressure yourself to look at it now, I've put together the files and notes and have them linked below. Now that this is over, maybe these can provide some type of closure to you and your family.

Let me know if there is anything else you need from me. I am happy to help in any way I can.

All the very best,
Moon Satter

"CJ?" Sebas calls, window rolled down.

It's his voice that snaps me out of my head. I don't know what I was expecting, but it definitely wasn't that. Moon Satter is helping me. I don't know how in-depth the research is, but it isn't something I want to face alone. Once I'm with both Sebas and Nadia, we can see if there's anything helpful.

I'm not saying I forgive Moon Satter or anything, but I'm definitely not above accepting their help.

I finally make my way to Sebas's car. "Sorry," I say as I get in. "I, uh, I got an email from Moon Satter."

His eyebrow lifts. "The writer? Really? Is that what you wanted to talk about?"

"Not really, we'll get into that. I just got the email now." I swallow. "Moon actually sent me their research. We can go through it later."

Sebas gives me a long look. "You still want to do that?"

I bite my lip. Right. Because, at least aloud, we're still operating on the belief that everything is over.

"I need to," I say.

I don't want to get into it without Nadia.

Sebas puts on a smile. "Then that's what we'll do. But after we eat. For now, focus on the amazing free food you're about to have."

I smile back, and I hope it looks like my heart is in it.

"By the way," he adds, "I really like the new hair and glasses."

I run my hand over the back of my now bob. There was only so much they could do to cover my shitty, desperate knife cut. There's probably still a good chunk of my hair sitting on the forest floor, lost along with my old glasses. "Yeah?"

"You look great."

I look away to hide my blush. "Thanks."

We reach the apartment that Sebas and his brother rent, although it's more of a condo or townhouse or whatever. It's connected to other units, but they have a front door and what looks like an upstairs, which is cool.

"Nice place," I say.

"I did nothing to contribute," Sebas admits, "but it is right down the street from Tío's, which my parents like."

I didn't realize it initially, but the street does look familiar. That has to be nice, to have family so close. Or, really, any extended family at all. I can technically walk to Uncle Ian's, but that's it. Maybe it's because I'm already used to chaos and sharing with three little siblings, but I've always liked the idea of a big family. Like where you even have reunions and everything. At the very least, people to see on the holidays.

I love my family, but it sometimes feels small.

As Sebas unlocks the front door, we're immediately greeted by an amazing smell. Samuel is in front of the stove but turns as we enter. Nadia runs up and practically tackles me with a hug.

"Are you okay?" Nadia asks. "It's been forever."

"It's been a few days," I say.

She frowns. "Do you know how many comics we could have discussed in that time? I have talking points for you on recent updates with illegal cliffhangers."

Samuel takes a moment to interject. "We're just glad to see you now, walking around. Cómo estás?"

I smile. "I'm glad to still be walking around."

"And once you finish healing up, I'll see you back on the mats, verdad?"

"I'll try."

"Don't feel pressured," Sebas says, shooting his brother a glare.

"No, it's okay," I assure him. "After everything, I think training might help."

It's hard not to feel so weak, so helpless, over what happened. I'm clearly not cut out to be a hero, but if I go all in and learn self-defense, maybe I can at least take some of my strength back.

"Ah, muy bien," Samuel says. "After a few months of training, you'll be a problem, I can tell."

"That's a good thing," Sebas clarifies.

"A great thing. But first, food." Samuel starts plating four dishes. "I wanted to give you a real tico experience, so this is what we call casado. You got beef, rice, beans, plátanos, picadillo, ensalada, everything you could possibly want, right?"

"Sounds like it."

"It's great," Nadia assures me.

Not that I'm worried. I'm already salivating at the smell.

We all sit at the table, Nadia rushing to take the seat next to me and sticking her tongue out at Sebas. It makes me laugh. When Samuel places the plates in front of us, I almost forget about everything else. It all looks delicious, especially considering the alternative was Manwich on ninety-nine-cent buns. Tasting it proves even better. Everything is so incredible, it's hard to decide what I want to save for the last bite, usually reserved for my favorite. I decide on the plantains.

"I've only had plantain chips before," I admit.

Sebas makes a face. "Then you haven't had plátanos."

He's not wrong. Soft and sweet, the way Samuel cooked them is a million times better than anything out of a bag.

"Thank you so much for cooking," I tell Samuel.

He smiles. "Pura vida."

I tilt my head. "I've heard you all use that, but what does it mean?"

"Technically, it means 'pure life,'" Sebas starts. "But in Costa Rica, 'pura vida' is more than just a phrase. It's like the whole lifestyle, you know? And it goes for everything. Whatever you want to say, really. Hello, thank you, amazing—pura vida."

"Cool," I say. "Pura vida. Because the food is seriously amazing."

"It's shit compared to Mom's," Sebas says.

"Of course it is, you asshole." Samuel pushes Sebas.

"It's great compared to my mom's, though," Nadia says.

Samuel puffs up, but Sebas rolls his eyes. "That's because your mom is a gringa."

"Yeah, but she's Italian," Nadia defends. "So, like, a gringa picante. She can use seasoning, at least." Nadia takes another bite. "Honestly, it's better than Dad's cooking, too. Although I've only seen him make gallo pinto a few times."

Samuel ignores them both. "Anyway, CJ, I appreciate you coming. I'll cook for you whenever. Better yet, next time don't bring this guy." He points to his brother.

"Can I come?" Nadia asks.

"Of course," Samuel says.

Sebas rolls his eyes. "I still live here."

His brother scoffs. "And I'm the one paying for it."

Sebas turns to me. "Only because Dad paid for, like, his entire gym."

"I'll pay him back, what of it?" Samuel rolls his eyes, looking at me like I'm in on the joke. "You don't happen to be looking for another roommate at home?"

I laugh. "No space. I have three younger siblings."

"Tres?!" Samuel makes a mocking sign of the cross. "En esta economía? It's hard enough with one."

"They're not so bad." I frown. "Well, maybe my middle brother, Orion, but he grows on you."

He'd be so annoyed with me for saying that. Not that I care. He's usually annoyed with me regardless.

"They're great," Nadia says. "I wish I had siblings."

"You can take Orion," I tease.

At this point, I'm already done with my plate, and feeling better than I have for days—honestly longer. Probably since before all this *Return to Slasherville* stuff started. Being around people like this, having a meal as if anything were normal . . . It's nice. Almost like a real taste of the typical teenage things I could've had this whole time if not for the Wolf Men and Moon Satter.

I really, really like it.

Of course, the flavor sours upon remembering what I have to talk to Sebas and Nadia about.

Fortunately, once dinner is over, Samuel leaves the three of us to talk. I update Nadia on the Moon Satter news first.

"Did you already open the files?" she asks.

"No, I literally got them in the car ride over."

Nadia puts a hand over her heart. "Aw, babe. And you waited for me?"

"Yeah, but we should look now, right?"

"Email it to me, I'll get my laptop."

With the larger screen of Nadia's computer, we open the files that Moon Satter sent over. If I can give them one compliment, it's that they definitely did their research. The folder is filled with different articles, news clippings, even what looks like blacked-out police reports. I have no idea how Moon got their hands on all this, but I can almost respect them for it.

Almost.

"Wait. What's that one? 'Brett Miller letter.'" Nadia points at the screen. "That has to be the letter referenced in the book!"

I open it. My eyes immediately widen. I feel like "letter" shouldn't be used to describe a fifty-page document of single-spaced, stream-of-conscious ramblings and doodles. Moon left a handwritten note on the top of the document, which they must have printed and scanned:

Brett Miller manifesto, found in his bedroom day after murder, details belief that he is living in a simulation(?) and is controlled by some sort of higher being

"What the hell . . . ?" I begin.

It's hard to make a lot of sense of the beginning of Brett's writing, especially since it is all in his scratchy, shitty penmanship.

> that is what people here don't understand. none of it matters none of them matters because we are not real none of this is real none of this none of this none of this there is no will there is no will there is only a role to play and I have known what my role is I have always known because it is what the Creator wants and I look forward to the day when I can become who I was meant to be and escape from this fiction from this facade no one is real no one is real none of it matters that's the thing when it's fake when it doesn't MATTER then you can do anything you can play any role you can be any person even if it means they'll think of you as the villain it doesn't matter IT DOESN'T MATTER BECAUSE NONE OF IT IS REAL

Jesus Christ. I have to stop reading. I can't believe Moon actually pored through fifty pages of this. I feel like it would make anyone lose their mind a little.

"So . . . Brett Miller believed he was living in a simulation," I start. "One that is run by the Creator."

"Like aliens?" Sebas asks.

Nadia shakes her head. "Not aliens. Not a simulation, either. It's like what I've been saying all along. Miller believed we're living in a horror story. That this is fiction."

Sebas makes a face. "That's your takeaway?"

Nadia jumps off the chair and lands on her feet. "*Think* about it. How would Drew Dunning have predicted all the things he wrote in that manuscript? Because this is all just a story!"

"It's not just a story," I protest. "I mean, we're real people. With thoughts and emotions and inner lives."

"Okay, what character in a story doesn't have those things?"

"Regardless, Drew didn't predict things," I add. "He probably used Taylor's social media and stalked us and *made* things happen. There's no magic or fiction involved. That's literally impossible."

Nadia lifts her hands. "Think of all the potential universes out there. All the possibilities and the unknown. Is it really impossible that we're living in a horror fiction story? You know what else sounds impossible? The fact that we are on a rock hurtling across an infinite universe that is growing. It is infinite, but *growing*? I mean, what the fuck? And everything has to end, right? Us, the sun, the universe. But it's infinite. Time is infinite. So how can it end? What's outside of everything?"

Sebas rubs his head. "I'm not high enough for this."

"My *point*," Nadia continues, "is that being alive is impossible. The world is impossible. So is it really that ridiculous to consider that our entire universe is just a story to someone else?"

My brain is struggling to keep up with her, and in part, might be refusing outright because thinking about all that too hard will likely give me a panic attack.

"But Drew Dunning is in this universe . . ." I start, searching for the flaw in her logic. "Or, was."

Nadia purses her lips, thinking for a moment. "But what if this started because Brett Miller knew someone from a different one? Or got a peek into the other one and put it in his evil manifesto?"

"Are you really trying to agree with a murderous dead guy?"

"He was clearly in the wrong," Nadia defends. "I'm just saying, there has to be some reason he held these beliefs. If we figure that out, we might be able to stop it from happening again. In order to do that, I want to be open to the possibility. That doesn't mean I'm full-on subscribing to his cult. The man was way evil and unhinged."

Sebas looks between me and Nadia. "Isn't this all kind of irrelevant? All of these guys are dead."

I take a deep breath. "That's actually what I wanted to talk about, before Moon sent this over. I . . . I don't think Drew Dunning was working alone. I think there's still a killer out there."

The entire mood of the room shifts, crashing to an uncomfortable and stunned silence. Neither Nadia nor Sebas seems to know what to say.

Finally, Nadia speaks. "Why do you think that? The book didn't have two killers, did it?"

"Technically, no," I admit, "but the book also never revealed the Wolf Man's identity at all, so anything is a possibility. I've been digging around that Slashervillain forum, and someone found Drew Dunning's account. Not only did he talk about being squeamish, but he also posted about awaiting his Creator. If this new info on Drew tells us anything, it's that the Wolf Men all followed this belief in the Creator. But Drew Dunning wasn't the only one who posted about it, remember? There could be more people involved. I mean, think about it. How would Drew Dunning, someone who isn't even from Satterville, know all the information in the book?"

Nadia and Sebas share a look. The fact that they aren't arguing tells me that things already weren't fully adding up for them either.

"That makes sense," Sebas says slowly. "But how are we supposed to know who it is? We don't even know who the Creator is."

"Well, we still have a lot of research to dig through." I look back at the screen. "I don't think I can read this bullshit, though."

"I'll do it," Nadia says.

I give her a look. "You aren't going to get too into it, are you?"

Nadia rolls her eyes. "I can question reality and not develop a bloodlust, thanks."

"Okay, okay." I push the laptop toward her. I also access the folder on my phone, starting from the bottom, while Sebas goes back to the Slashervillain forum on his and jots down the usernames of anyone who might have even referenced the Creator.

I open a document that was put together by Moon, just titled "Rachel Miller Interview."

Call with Mrs. Miller (mother of Brett and Evan):

- **Brett kept to himself, didn't mention his ideas a lot to her**

- **She only learned about most of it in manifesto, which she couldn't read entirely, said "it didn't seem like the words of my son. But those actions didn't seem like him either. I realized I didn't know my sons. I never knew them"**

- **Apparently the only person he discussed things (including his belief system) with was his school-appointed guidance counselor, a new hire named Geoffrey White. In his writings, Brett wrote that this figure was supportive of his beliefs and ideas—the only person to really understand**

  » **Geoffrey White has declined interview request**

My heart pounds in my chest, and bile rises in my throat. Mr. White was Brett Miller's guidance counselor? And, according to the killer himself, someone who supported his ideas and beliefs.

Drew Dunning didn't make sense as the killer because he wouldn't have the knowledge or means required to change the details in *Return to Slasherville.* Because he wasn't a local. He wasn't involved.

Someone who would have all that?

Mr. White.

My fucking guidance counselor.

21

An Ode for Those with Second-Lead Syndrome

It's horrifying. It disgusts me. But it also makes sense.

Mr. White knows about my childhood crush on Hana Maeda. No one would question him at school, since interacting with students is literally his job. He has the access. He knows everything.

I told him.

Almost everything, anyway.

My stomach twists uncomfortably. I can't believe I went to him after spotting the Wolf Man. He knew all about it—might have even had his own mask and knife stored in his desk drawer. Of course the police didn't find anyone—he probably pointed them in the wrong direction. I can't believe he's been talking to me all these years and never thought to mention he was also the counselor for the fucking guy who nearly killed my father after butchering his friends.

He was probably using me from the beginning.

"It's Mr. White," I finally say aloud. My tongue stumbles over the strange feel of the words.

"Wait, the guidance counselor?" Nadia asks. "What, why?"

I all but shove my phone over to her. "Guess who he was assigned to when he first started at Satterville High."

Nadia's eyes widen as she reads, Sebas looking at the screen over her shoulder. He makes a face. "Isn't that the teacher who stopped you at the memorial?"

I really feel like throwing up now. "Yeah. He even said he was surprised I came, because it 'wasn't safe for me.' Made it seem like he was concerned about my mental health, but it was probably a thinly veiled threat."

I can't believe I barely thought twice about it. I can't believe I trusted him so blindly this entire time.

"He could also believe in the Creator, the ideas of Brett Miller. It says in the notes that he agreed with everything Brett told him," I say. "That's why he's doing all this. Did you see anything else in Brett's ramblings, Nadia?"

"Kind of. I don't think the Creator has an identity," Nadia starts, looking back at her laptop. "It's not a person instructing Brett or anything. It's more like a god, the being controlling the simulation, according to Brett. But, CJ. His writings are dark and intense. People following him might not even care who the Creator is, not when Brett left this behind after dying, like some kind of fucked up messiah."

"So, Brett believed in some fake higher being he called the Creator. But he was the one who started it all. The simulation beliefs. The Wolf Man. The killings." I hold my head. "He essentially became the Creator himself by making it all come true. And Mr. White was apparently his fucking best friend."

"We should talk to this guy," Sebas says. "Mr. White. We can get information out of him."

I don't know how I'm going to face him, but Sebas is right. Even if I'm wrong and Mr. White wasn't also donning a Wolf Man mask, he has to have answers that we don't.

"We can confront his ass," Nadia says. "How about tomorrow, after school?"

There's a little part of me that's unsure about confronting him directly—especially if Mr. White actually played a part in Taylor's murder. But I *have* to know. I trusted him. Whether or not he's guilty, he's sure as shit not innocent for keeping his Brett Miller connection from me these past few years.

My hands shake with how angry I am. Drew almost killed Hana and he almost killed me. This is long past personal, and I can't wait around hoping someone will find answers. Not if the answer is so close to home.

"Okay," I say. "We have to be smart about it, though. Someone should stand guard outside, ready to get help. We'll go in recording and we definitely won't go in entirely unarmed. We don't know how dangerous he is."

"No one should confront him alone," Sebas adds. He looks at me. "Wait for me after your last final. We'll do this together."

He doesn't have to worry about that. It's honestly bad enough I have to deal with Mr. White at all after this total freaking betrayal. I'm angry, yeah, but it also makes me feel stupid and vulnerable. I can't imagine trying to face him alone. Hell no.

We all saw how CJ-doing-stuff-themself went with Drew Dunning. If it weren't for my mom, I'd be dead. Some fucking Final Girl I am. Nadia was wrong about that much. I'm still no Protagonist. We're just the only ones who know enough to end this.

"Promise," I say. "I should probably get going, though. So Mom doesn't worry."

And for some more last-minute cramming.

"I'll drive you," Sebas says.

I wave him off. "It's okay. I'll call a ride, you're already home."

"I'll walk you out, then," he says.

That, I don't argue with. After I hug Nadia, Sebas walks me outside. The air is wonderfully warm tonight, hugging my skin.

"Thanks for doing this," I say.

He gives me a look. "It's literally outside the door, no need for thanks."

"No. For dealing with this murder stuff. Again. I still feel bad I got you involved in the first place."

"Don't. We talked about that." He gives a soft smile, revealing his front braces. "Besides, there's no one I'd rather fight a murderer with."

"That's a big mistake. Samuel and my mom are both much better options."

"Fine. Then there's no one I'd rather make a big mistake with."

I laugh. "Are you trying to get us killed?"

"No, your mom and my brother can always save us."

"They aren't coming tomorrow."

"We can call them if it ends up being a big mistake."

"Oh, I'm sure it will be."

"Then can I interest you in what you might think is another big mistake?"

"And what's that?"

He gestures to himself. "This guy."

It's then that I realize how close he is. Standing right in front of me. His face is barely inches from mine and, wow, it looks great in this lighting. My heart flutters with nerves and giddiness, and it's like I'm more aware of my skin and the molecules in the air against it.

How easy it would be to remove that distance.

"I've been making mistakes all my life anyway."

But it doesn't feel like a mistake when I stand on my tiptoes to press my lips to his. It feels soft and warm and has my chest tingling and buzzing. It doesn't feel like a mistake when he brushes my chin-length hair just behind my ear and kisses me back.

It feels easy. Right. For maybe the first time in a while, it feels safe. I feel safe.

And a giddy, bubbly kind of happy that tastes surprisingly sweet.

"Oh, come on."

The two of us break apart, turning toward the open door to see Nadia standing with her arms crossed.

"My Casanova Cousin and Bisexual Brutus, going behind my back."

"What the hell are you talking about?" Sebas asks.

"You don't understand. This is bad for me!" Nadia says.

"Why?" I ask cautiously. "You didn't seem against it . . ."

"I'm not against you two being together," Nadia amends. "I've been building that ship from day one, trust. What I'm against is you doing it with a potential killer out there. Now Sebas has cemented his Leading Man plot armor. No writer of a somewhat silly slasher would piss off the readers by killing the Love Interest."

"Nadia, first of all, once again: we aren't in a movie," Sebas says. "Second, I do not understand why this has anything to do with you."

"Because I'm tired of being the weak link, the one in the most danger! The lesbian friend doesn't get plot armor. If anything, we give off death flags, and I'm *not* having that knockoff Dr. Phil axe me!" She paces on the porch, hand tapping her chin. "There's only one thing to do now. I have to establish myself as the only person who can surpass the male lead as a fan favorite. The Second Lead."

"I don't know why I bother asking, I always end up more confused," Sebas says.

Nadia ignores him, pushing him away so she can take my hands instead. "CJ. You know, I've just now noticed how beautiful your brown eyes are. And how cute your glasses are. And how you have . . ." She tilts her head. "Lips like rosy, plump apples. And I fucking love apples. Forget my cousin, date me instead."

What a way to woo someone.

"Nadia, I know you don't feel that way about me."

"We don't have to feel it, CJ. *They* do."

"Who are they?"

"The *gays*! The sapphic audience! Obviously." She lets out a puff of air, turning away from me. "Their second-lead syndrome is going to keep my ass alive. Sure, the story tried to kill the queer Latina once, but that was before I got any screen time. The audience *has* to love me now. If I'm Second Lead, those femslash fanfic writers will revolt if I die. I can get my own personal plot armor. Finally."

I think of all the ways to argue with her, because there are many. There's no audience, for one thing, unless she includes a confused Sebas. Not to mention, none of us have any plot armor. We just got lucky or had people like Mom close by. Pretending to like me isn't going to keep her alive. Preparation will.

But I also know it probably won't matter what I say. And as long as she stays cautious, it doesn't really hurt either way. Besides, the distraction is kind of helping.

"Okay," I say, drawing out the last syllable. "You can be the Second Lead."

Nadia smiles and winks before turning back to Sebas. "Don't worry, the Second Lead never wins in the end. It's actually annoying sometimes."

He rubs his temples. "Okay, sure."

There's a moment of silence, which feels a bit too loud. Whatever romantic moment Sebas and I had is now deader than the first three Wolf Men, and all of Nadia's second-lead survival plan has my mind thinking about the potential fourth.

My phone buzzes.

Oh, thank God.

"My ride's about here," I say.

"Buenas noches," Sebas says. He looks like he wants to get closer, but I guess decides against it given the presence of the glaring Second Lead. "Be safe."

"I'll try." I smile at them both. "Although, tomorrow, we will be decidedly unsafe."

Nadia shrugs. "Well, someone's got to kill this damn wolf for good."

And I tell myself it can be us that does it.

22

Too Close for Comfort

My finals were not great, but I don't think they were needs-a-summer-retake not great. At least, I hope not. Whether or not Mr. White is an evil Wolf Man who wants me dead, he did apparently get my teachers to take pity on me and offer that option, considering I almost died at Taylor's memorial.

Taking tests is already anxiety-inducing, and it certainly didn't help that I also had to worry about confronting said evil (but on-top-of-it) guidance counselor. Despite that, I finished my last test a bit early, so I went to sit outside to wait for Nadia and Sebas.

I'm reading a comic Nadia suggested (mostly so she could talk to me about it) when my phone lights up with a call from Uncle Ian. I pick it up.

"Uncle Ian?" I ask. "You good?"

"Yeah, all good. You didn't forget we made plans for me to pick you up, did you?"

Oh shit. I did completely forget.

"Um . . . no."

That's when I see his car turn into the far end of the parking lot. "Oh my gosh, you *did*," he gasps over the phone. "Chekov, they don't love us anymore."

"Don't even joke about that, I'll always love Chekov."

"Ouch."

"But . . . I may have accidentally made other plans."

"Cassiopeia Jane Smith! And to think I brought you an emotional support cat."

At this point, Uncle Ian pulls up in front of me, Chekov's Gun in his harness on the passenger seat. Uncle Ian smiles at me, but it's weak. He looks a little worse for wear, to be honest. His skin is pale, his eyes bloodshot, and there are even wrinkles in his "Feline Good" T-shirt. He normally keeps all his shirts, especially the pun ones, crisp.

Maybe he's taking my run-in with the Wolf Man worse than I thought. I don't need to imagine the memories it brings up for him.

Uncle Ian rolls down the window. "So what are these plans that make you too cool to hang out with your uncle and his son?"

"Oh, um, I'm just meeting up with some friends," I say.

His face falls. "Well, I guess Chekov and I will just have to go, then."

"No, no!" I quickly get into the car, grabbing Chekov's Gun. He licks my chin with his scratchy tongue. "I can wait for them here. Still get some emotional support cat time in."

This gets Uncle Ian to smile. "Well, at least it wasn't a total waste. Still need to adjust those glasses? I was going to take you today, but seeing as you no longer care about me . . ."

"Shut up."

"I guess we'll have to go another time."

I roll my eyes before giving him a real smile. I hug Chekov. "I do appreciate you always being here to help, though."

"Anytime, kid. Anything you need." Uncle Ian's eyes look a little teary. "I'm just so glad you're okay. You know, you and your siblings mean everything to me."

Tears prick my eyes, too, but I try to hide it. "Come on, Uncle Ian. You need to find a woman and have some kids of your own."

He holds up his hands. "Hey, I've still got time."

I make a face. "Do you? You're, like, so old."

He rolls his eyes. "Come on. Besides, I clearly already have a son of my own." He gestures to Chekov's Gun in my lap.

Chekov meows. I guess I'll give him that.

"And I don't need—" Uncle Ian is interrupted by his own phone ringing. "Sorry, one sec." I can't make out the voice on the other end, but Ian's expression immediately falls. "Okay, be right there." Uncle Ian pockets his phone and looks at me. "Huge work emergency. I really have to go. Would you mind taking Chekov? He hasn't been out today, and I'm not sure I'll have time to stop at home."

"Sure," I say, already reaching for his backpack on the back seat.

Guess Chekov will join the murderer confrontation.

"Thank you so much, CJ." He examines my face. "Are you sure you'll be okay?"

"Yeah, Sebas will be here in a minute."

This causes Uncle Ian to throw on his biggest shit-eating grin. "Oh, *Sebastián* is the one you're meeting with, huh?"

It's not like he could possibly guess that I had my first-ever kiss last night, but I still find myself blushing.

"Do we need to have the talk?" he teases.

I cringe. "I already had it with Mom. She brought out both a banana and a peach. I didn't eat fruit for a month."

"That's your mom, bisexual ally and a little too intense about everything."

He's not wrong.

"Don't you have to go to work?" I ask.

"You're more important," he says easily, but then looks at his phone. "But, shit. I do. I owe you one for this!"

"Expensive dinner."

"Deal!"

I get out of the car along with Chekov in his backpack, waving to Uncle Ian as he drives out of the lot and onto the street.

The final bell rings inside, so I head back through the main office to find Nadia and Sebas. While I'm probably not allowed to have a cat on campus, no one seems to notice the little head peeking out in the crowd of everyone leaving.

With last period over, the hallways are clearing out quickly, so it's easy to find Sebas and Nadia.

Sebas lets out a delighted grunt upon seeing Chekov, immediately rushing to kiss his little head. Chekov purrs happily.

"Nice to see you, too," I say.

"Cats will always come first," Sebas says. "But you, Cassiopeia, are the closest of seconds."

"That's probably the highest compliment he can give," Nadia says.

"I'm honored. Truly."

Nadia looks between me and Chekov. "Why do you have the cat, though?"

"Long story. Let's just go to the guidance office and get this over with."

As much as I'm trying to appear calm, collected, and in control as we walk down the long, echoing hallway (how did I not notice how creepy the entire school is until now?), on the inside, I'm anything but. It's all panic and nerves and dread. On top of the strange combination of anger, sadness, and disbelief that Mr. White is involved, I have this odd, nagging feeling that I'm forgetting something important.

My heart is nearly in my throat when we reach his office. Fortunately, the door is unlocked.

Unfortunately, he's not there.

"Shit," I say. "Where is he?"

"He'd lock the office if he went home, right?" Nadia asks.

"Maybe he left a note or something in case a student came by . . ." I start searching through the office. I pause at Happy. The silly little dinosaur, with his stitched-on smile, looks right at me. I wish I could pull him in for a hug right now. It's not his fault his owner sucks.

"I think he went to the library," Sebas says.

"Why do you say that?"

He points to Mr. White's open desktop. "There's a notification that says he has a meeting in the library."

My blood runs cold. That's what I was forgetting. Shit. Shit shit shit.

"The next murder," I say. "Now's when the next murder is supposed to happen. *In the library.* He must be after Mr. Collins. Or a teacher I have!"

I don't have to say anything else. It doesn't matter who the target is, only that there is another one. We all start running. Chekov's Gun hisses on my back, but I keep going anyway. My heart pounds so hard it feels like it's going to burst out of me *Alien*-style.

The library is a ghost town.

Technically, it's closed. The door has a sign and everything. Which is a little weird, since it normally stays open a bit later for kids to study.

It's strange to see it so empty. The lights have been turned off, the fading afternoon sun giving the room a hazy glow. As we step inside, I look at Nadia and Sebas and hold a finger up to my lips. While my instinct is to call out for someone, the last thing I want to do is alert Mr. White to our presence.

Keeping my steps light, I walk through the bookcases to the left. It's sort of like a maze in here, and unless you're over six feet, it's impossible to see over the shelves. While I've always thought it was cool to have such an extensive school library, I'm kind of hating it now.

Chekov's Gun stays silent. That has to mean he doesn't see anyone either, since he'd be hissing or growling if he did. In some ways, it's like another set of eyes.

Then the corner of my eye catches movement. A shadow passing between the cracks of stacked books. My lips part but I don't let out a breath. A low whistle sounds from the other side of the shelf, right next to me.

The hair on my arms stands on end. My heart stops.

Chekov lets out a little meow.

I look over, past the tops of the books and into the dark holes of a wolf mask. Just a glimpse of it is visible, but enough to send my entire body into a jumping panic.

He's back.

Or, rather, he's still here.

Being right never felt so shitty.

"Is that blood?" Nadia whispers, oblivious to what I'm seeing.

The Wolf Man rushes off in the direction of the entrance.

"He's here!" I yell, although Nadia and Sebas have caught on to his quick movements now.

From behind me, Sebas turns to chase after him.

"Wait!" I reach out to snatch the back of his shirt. "Don't. It's dangerous."

His dark eyes meet mine. "You had to face him last time, I'll take this one." His fingers brush the edge of my skin, my nerves tingling. "I'll be okay. I promise."

Before I can argue that those kinds of promises can't always be kept, he's off. And I have no choice. I have to keep moving. I turn toward where Nadia is still pointing. At the end of the aisle, in the direction the Wolf Man came from, there is a dark stain in the carpet.

We both rush over, turning the corner. Only, what I'm seeing doesn't make sense.

It's Mr. White, sprawled out on the floor, surrounded by a dark stain, the carpet soaked. Blood. A large cut is sliced across his throat, so deep his head falls back and there are hints of pinkish matter and white bone.

"Holy shit," Nadia says. She dry heaves. "Oh God. He's dead. He's so dead." More heaving. "Oh God, that's his *spine.* Motherfucker."

I want to comfort her but it's like I'm not even in my body. My consciousness is floating over a thrashing sea of stress and emotion. The sea is a storm but my mind remains calm, distant, somehow staying above the surface by being not quite attached to the world.

Mr. White may have known Brett Miller, but he wasn't a killer. When Brett thought he believed him, it wasn't because Mr. White joined his cult. It was probably just because he was trying to do his freaking job.

He was innocent and now he's dead. Because of me.

My eyes burn but I don't feel any tears fall. I'm still stranded on choppy waters. Chekov licks the back of my neck, but the scratchy, barbed tongue might as well be touching stone.

"I'm calling 911," Nadia chokes.

Below the surface, my consciousness calls for Sebas. Wonders why he isn't back, worries, worries, worries, but it can't quite reach the dull raft of my mind.

Time passes. I don't know how much. Everything is bright, loud, ringing, far away.

Hands are on me, leading me and Chekov out of the way. Paramedics cover the gruesome sight of Mr. White's body, but the image sears in my mind before the waves wash it away. The raft dips below the surface, enough that I feel the water lapping over my ears. It covers the sound, so when people are talking, I can barely hear them through the pressure.

I'm blinking away visions of red, Nadia holding on to my arm, when I see him. Sebas is next to a paramedic near the library entrance, sitting on the floor. He looks okay. He's alive. I open my mouth to say something, but I'm not sure the words come out right. Or at all. There's so much pressure in my ears, everything is so, so bright.

He turns to me, looks up.

Before I can blink, Sebas is on his feet, at my side, pulling me into a hug. Chekov meows from my back, but I lean into Sebas, smelling the floral laundry detergent of his shirt, and I'm slowly, slowly able to break the surface. But this time, instead of maintaining calm over the thrashing waves, the water spills from my eyes.

"It's okay," he says. "We're okay."

Chekov lets out a more disgruntled mew. I pull away from Sebas and slip the backpack off, taking out Chekov, still in his leashed harness. He just sits on the floor, unaware of the horrors he's surrounded by.

I find my voice finally. "What happened?"

"The Wolf Man got away. I caught up to him but couldn't do much when he had a knife, but I think I hurt his knee. He was stumbling a bit when he escaped," Sebas says.

I focus so much on the comforting sound of his voice, I almost forget to take in the meaning. A moment too long passes before my brain catches up.

"It's okay," I say. "But Mr. White . . ."

I trail off, looking in the direction of the door. I don't say it, but it's obvious enough. Sebas saw the covered body.

While we broke the hug, I don't let go of Sebas's hands. I feel like without them, I'll go floating away.

Because we were wrong.

We were wrong and another person died.

There is another Wolf Man still out there and we have no idea who he is.

I think of those black-hole eyes behind the mask, looking right at me. Knowing. Threatening.

Telling me that there's nothing I can do to change the story. That I'm no Final Girl, and I'm definitely no hero.

I'm a failure. An extra.

Nothing more than prey.

23

CJ's Intervention

Since Samuel was teaching a class and Nadia's parents were both at work, Mom got in contact with them to pick us all up from school. With the school mostly empty, it will take a minute for word to get out about what happened, but it won't be long before every news station reports on how there's yet another Wolf Man, and Satterville High still seems to be the main target.

Or, more likely, they'll say that CJ Smith seems to be the main target.

I'm not sure they'd be wrong on that.

While Mom signs us all out from the main office and gets the go-ahead to leave, I quickly call Uncle Ian.

He picks up on the first ring.

"Mom tell you what happened?" I ask.

"I think? It was frantic. Something about there being a second one at your school."

"Yeah." I swallow. "I just wanted to say I'm okay and, more importantly, so is Chekov. He's currently cuddling up with Sebas and hissing at the secretary."

Uncle Ian laughs. "I'm glad you're all okay. That's the important thing." After a pause on the line, he speaks again. "I'm so sorry, CJ. I should have stayed."

My heart pangs at the way his voice holds emotion. He's crying. I can't help myself. I start crying again, too. I can't even tell him all of it. That I suspected Mr. White when, if I had thought about the book for even a second, I could have figured out he'd be the next target. The next kill was originally supposed to be Taylor's favorite teacher—a favorite guidance counselor isn't far off. I could have saved him.

Guilt and shock and horror nestle in my gut. But I can't say that.

"You couldn't have known," I say instead.

"I should've been there for you anyway. I'm so sorry. It's scary, and terrible, and you shouldn't have to be dealing with any of this. But as long as we're all alive, we'll get through it, okay?"

I wipe my eyes. Mom's walking back toward me. "Okay. We'll talk soon, we're heading home."

"Love you, kid."

I sniffle. "Love you too, old man."

We have to pick up the twins on the way back, which means Lyra sitting on my lap again. I honestly don't mind. With Sebas riding shotgun, it's nice to have some sort of human contact. Even if she keeps adjusting her ponytail and nearly whipping my glasses off my face. Sebas has Chekov in the front, who happily purrs in his lap.

Fortunately, with a car more packed than it should be, the ride is short, and we all pile out and head up to the apartment. Orion will be coming home on the bus soon, so it's definitely a full house until Nadia and Sebas leave. Chekov seems slightly annoyed that he's not back home yet, but we do have a travel litter box for him at our place, which he immediately uses.

Mom gets the twins set in front of the TV and pulls out some pop and snacks from the fridge before sitting Sebas, Nadia, and me at the table. With her at the head, it sort of feels like an interrogation.

"Now," Mom says carefully. "Are you all going to explain what happened? What were you even doing at school still?"

Right. While it is easy enough to say that the Wolf Man is following me, it doesn't make sense that I didn't go home right after finals.

I start to open my mouth, but she cuts me off. "I know something is going on. So I'm going to need you to tell the truth."

Sebas and Nadia both look at me helplessly. Of course they want me to take the lead. It's my mom. But what am I supposed to say? I don't have any excuses worked out, and I'm just so tired. It feels like no matter how much I try, there is some messed up force (in the mask of a wolf) waiting to take me down. I'll never be safe.

I just want to catch a damn break for once. Mom's the hero. She should handle it.

"I was sent a fake Moon Satter book starring a new Wolf Man and we think the killer is using it as a guideline and essentially bringing his story to life, so we've been trying to beat him and stop the deaths. But we failed. Every time."

Mom's expression is hard. Unreadable.

Nadia leans forward in her chair, voice light. "Technically, we're not sure if the killer is following the book or if we're just actually living inside a horror story. I'm more partial to the second, honestly."

I ignore Nadia and reach into my bag to pull out the manuscript and set it on the table.

Mom doesn't say anything. Instead, she slowly starts examining *Return to Slasherville,* flipping through the pages. Her eyes widen at some moments, she frowns at others. I feel like years pass before she looks up, eyeing the three of us.

"So . . . Nadia got involved because she was supposed to die, but Taylor did instead?"

We all nod.

"And Sebas?"

"Wrong place, wrong time, bad cousin kind of situation," he says. "I almost died, but CJ saved me."

"I didn't save him," I say quickly. "We hid in the closet and the killer left."

Mom carefully considers this, not seeming shocked about the closet detail, at least.

"I can't believe this," she says.

My heart drops. Of course she can't. Who would?

"Why wouldn't you *tell* me?" Mom continues. "This is the kind of thing I've spent years preparing for."

I'm a gaping goldfish. Even Nadia and Sebas look surprised. While I wasn't expecting my mom to disown me or anything, I was definitely not expecting this response either.

"You believe me?" I ask.

Mom shrugs. "I mean, I don't know what to believe anymore. But I know there is another Wolf Man, and if one of them was stupid enough to give us a guide on how to stop him, well, I don't think we can let that go to waste, can we?"

"There's a problem with that." I sink into the chair. "The book doesn't say who this other Wolf Man is or how to stop him."

Mom sighs. "Cassiopeia Jane, we don't need to know *that.* How do you think you stop him? Throw him a tea party and ask for a reconsideration of values? No. You kill him. Doesn't matter how. We already know what it takes to kill a Wolf Man." She throws on a big, wicked smile. "Same thing as any other man. All I need is the time and the place."

"Slasherfest," Nadia answers for me. "It all goes down during Slasherfest. The Wolf Man is going to kill more people there."

"Only if he gets to them before we get to him," Mom mutters. She clasps her hands together. "Finally, a Slasherfest I can actually enjoy." Before anyone can get another word in, she's already opening the closet. "See, honey, this is why you have to get adults involved. I know you kids think you can handle everything yourselves . . ." She takes out a few flashlights. "But you're just *kids*. You shouldn't have to do everything. It's all the fucking people my age, sitting on their asses, saying the next generations will save the world." She also pulls out flares from a box on the top shelf. "Makes you think you have to be a literal superhero, when your brains aren't even fully developed. And that's if you haven't already lost all faith in the future, which, like, would be fair." Mom taps the top of her double-locked shotgun case. "We'll be good. We have two days to fully prepare."

I blink at her. Maybe she knows me a little too well. "We?"

"Well, you won't have to do much. The important thing for you kids is to keep alert and stay out of trouble." She winks. "And worst case, you'll lead that damn Wolf Man right to me."

Samuel comes to get Sebas and Nadia, leaving me to help Mom with prepping for a combination of dinner and the ultimate demise of the serial killer tormenting us all. By the time 10:00 p.m. hits, I'm already beat, half sleeping on the couch after all the effort it took to get the twins to bed.

My phone dings with a good night message from Sebas. Despite everything, I can still smile. I can't help it, in fact. Mom steps into the room, sharpening one of her blades as she gives me a teasing look.

"So, how's it going with Sebas?" Mom asks.

My cheeks flush. Am I really that obvious? "Good," I say. "Great. I like him a lot."

She eyes me, pointing the knife in my direction. "Do we have to have a sex talk again?"

"No, that's covered."

"Oh, it better be covered."

"Mom, stop, we're not even there yet, please." I wave her away. She remains unfazed, back to sharpening the knife.

She admires the blade before setting it on the coffee table to join me on the couch. "I just want you to be safe, kid. It's kind of my job to make sure you don't get hurt. But you're going to keep growing up and doing big things, and I won't always be around to protect you. I mean, we thought your dad would always be here to protect us, and life happened." Mom's glassy eyes match mine. She takes a shaky breath. "All I can do is try to guide you, try to prepare you, best that I can. But I'm still going to let you go out, live your life, fall in love, and yeah, probably make some mistakes. Just know that whatever I can't protect you from, I'll be here to love the heck out of you through it. That's one thing I *can* promise you. And I know your dad is still doing the same from wherever he is now."

I pull her into a hug. I want to be stronger, I want to be braver, but damn, sometimes I just want to feel like a little kid again and let my mom take care of me. No matter what she can or can't promise, in her arms, it's like everything will be okay. Even without Dad being here.

Not that that makes it any less hard. That we don't have him around when going through all this. Not only because he dealt with the Wolf Man twice, but because . . . I just wish he got to be around. To join Uncle Ian in embarrassing me. To tell me I swear too much. To encourage me when I try jiu-jitsu and be overly proud and supportive when I eventually get my first stripe.

There's so much I wish he got to be here for. So much I wish I could experience with him. So much I wish I could talk to him about.

"I never got to tell Dad, you know," I say. "About all the gay stuff."

Mom rubs her hand in circles on my back. "I know, baby, and that sucks. But honestly, I think he had an idea."

I pull away from her slightly, enough to look at her face. "Seriously?"

"He knew you better than anyone," Mom says. She makes a face. "Plus, you made yourself a literal harem of Disney wives. For some reason, the only men included were Li Shang from *Mulan* and Hades from *Hercules*, which, love, is a *choice*. If anything, he'd be more surprised that you're a monogamist."

I laugh, before looking thoughtful. "You know, I stand by the Hades thing."

She laughs before changing the subject. "Have you talked to Sebas about it?"

I shrug. "Not outright. I'm sure Nadia mentioned something and, like, I have my pronouns on my socials and everything, but . . . I guess I'm a little worried about it. On one hand, it might be easier for him to accept because I still don't mind she/her pronouns and I don't want to physically transition. On the other, I'm worried those things make me look like I'm just trying to say I'm under the genderqueer umbrella because it's more acceptable now or I want to feel special or some shit."

It wouldn't exactly be the first time I heard it. That I'm just hopping on the nonbinary train because it's some kind of trend that I would somehow benefit from. It's not like Sebas would think any of those things, but it's hard not to stress about the *what if*s.

"I know that's not the case," Mom says, "but even if it was, who gives a fuck?"

I stare at her. "Mom."

"I'm serious. Cis people change themselves all the time for bullshit reasons. Their names, their hair color, their hobbies. They'll get tattoos and plastic surgery and all sorts of things, and you can't tell me none of them are doing it to feel better or special or because a certain thing is in style. Why should queer people need to have some noble, desperate reason to do the things people are *already* doing just because they feel like it?" Mom takes my hand in hers. "CJ, you don't need to prove anything. You can tell me you're demigirl and two weeks later realize you actually are more genderfluid or genderflux because—I'm sorry, love, I'll have to actually look up the difference again—or maybe you realize you're actually just a girl. Or just a boy. I don't give a shit. I love you for being CJ. And if you want to change your name, I'll love you for being that name. I love you because you are my child, and whatever journey you have to go through to find your happiness is not the ever-loving goddamn fucking business of *anybody* else."

"Language, Mom," I tease.

"I pay the rent, I make the rules," she says, rolling her eyes. Then she smiles. "Besides, even if you did make some drastic change you later decided wasn't quite right, well, that's kind of life. Do you think I could just unbirth you when I realized what a little shit you'd grown up to be?" She flicks my nose and I try to bite her finger.

"I learned it from you."

"Oh, I know. I love it." Mom strokes my hair. "The point is, we all die one day and then nothing matters, so do whatever makes you happy, as long as you aren't hurting others or putting yourself in danger. Whatever language you want to use to define yourself is yours because, let's be real, language is all made up anyway and the worms that devour your rotting corpse won't care."

I pull away from her. "Wow, Mom. Have you ever considered a career in motivational speaking?"

"I had to kill a murderer, like, four days ago, Cassiopeia Jane. Sue me for being a little jaded at this point."

I sniffle. That sort of unintentionally took me back to the events of today. "I thought Mr. White was the killer. That's why we stayed after school. Apparently, he was Brett Miller's guidance counselor, so I thought maybe he was carrying on his legacy or something."

Mom bites her lip. "I can see why you'd make that connection. But I don't think he actually was all that close to Brett. Counselors don't really get to pick their students."

"That makes sense *now*. But I didn't think about it. I didn't even pay attention to what the book said, and that's why he died. It's my fault."

"Oh, honey, no," Mom says, pulling me into her chest. "None of this is your fault."

"It is," I say. "It's because I'm such a shit Final Girl."

Mom gives me a strange look. "What?" I open my mouth to explain, but she stops me with her hand. "You're not a shit Final Girl, because you're *more* than a Final Girl. You don't have to do this alone, CJ. You don't have to take on all the responsibility for everyone and everything."

I shrug. "I was technically born the oldest daughter, so."

Mom chuckles, shaking her head. "Look, love. You went through some horrible things. In the past, last Friday, today. You've dealt with way more than any teenager should have to. So I'm not saying to just get over it. Of course your feelings are going to be a hot mess." She wipes my cheek with her thumb. "But know that it will get better and we will get past this. As . . . a whole-ass Final Family."

I laugh. "You think we'll be okay Friday?"

Mom puts her arm back around me, leaning her head on my shoulder. "I don't know anything for sure, but I think so. I don't believe in any god, or Moon Satter as some kind of fantasy fucking prophet, but if there's one thing I do have faith in, it's this family."

"So you'll let me come, then?"

Both Mom and I turn in the direction of the hallway, where Orion stands. His eyes are rimmed in red, but he's standing tall.

"Come where?" Mom asks, feigning ignorance.

"To Slasherfest. To help stop the Wolf Man." Orion crosses his arms. "I heard everything, and I'm going, too."

Damn. I forgot how quiet he can be. That's so embarrassing. Not only because of what he overheard, but knowing that I really will never beat him in the stealth games.

"Absolutely not," Mom says. "You're too young."

"Are you kidding me?" Orion snaps. "You just said we're a Final Family! Am I not part of the family?"

Mom crosses her arms, too. "The twins are, too, but you don't expect me to arm them and send them off to face the Wolf Man, now, do you? No, you three will stay with Uncle Ian."

"I'm not a baby like the twins!"

Neither of them look like they want to let up. I gently grab Mom's shoulder.

"Mom, he should come with us."

"Don't start with this, CJ, you're lucky I'm even letting *you* go to Slasherfest."

"The Wolf Man is after him, too!" My voice cuts through the room, almost echoing on the walls. I didn't mean for it to be such a harsh reminder, but I have to keep going. "Mom, Orion and I made it together that night. I may be the main target, but I'm not the only one. If the Wolf Man wants to finish what Evan Miller couldn't, that means he's after both me and Orion. We don't want to give him a reason to go after Uncle Ian and the twins, so it's better we all stick together."

There's a long pause as Orion smiles at me. Mom looks between us.

"Ugh. I hate when you two use your logic against me. How did I end up with three of my kids getting their father's booksmarts?"

Poor Leo. Although, she's not wrong.

Mom points at Orion. "You are going to listen to everything I say without question. You understand?"

"Yeah, yeah," Orion answers, grinning. "You say jump, I say how high."

"No!" Mom snaps. "I say jump, you *jump*." She sighs, holding her arms out so both of us come toward her. She pulls Orion in with her right arm and me with the left, both of us leaning our heads against her. "I love you kids. And I'm going to protect you and it's all going to be fine."

"Not if we protect you first," Orion mutters.

"We don't have a great track record defeating Satterville Wolf Men," I say.

Orion gives me a strange look before finally speaking. "Yeah, but things change."

I don't know what to say about that. Maybe he's right. Things change. Just because I didn't succeed before doesn't mean I can't this time. Especially with my family actually on my side.

I smile. Maybe that's something I should have realized from the beginning.

But what matters is now. And despite my guilt, and my grief, and my freezing fear, I feel it deep within me.

I have faith in this family, too.

24

Protagonists with Daddy Issues

While I know black belts aren't built in a day, or anywhere close to it, I still feel better about taking another jiu-jitsu class the evening before my likely face-off with a serial killer. Sure, one class isn't going to make a difference when it comes to defending myself, but it's one more class than I'd have otherwise, and at this point, I'll take what I can get. Besides, it's better than sitting alone with my thoughts, which are pretty messed up at the moment.

It also helps that Sebas is taking the class as well, and we partner up without having to say anything or have those moments of awkward eye contact across the mats (which is difficult, considering I have to take off my glasses while training and can only see the general blob shape of people). Samuel's technique of the day is a rear naked choke, which seems fairly practical.

"What do you do for defense?" I ask Sebas as he gets in position to drill.

"Tap," he says from behind me.

"No, like in a real-life scenario."

"Die."

I turn around to glare at him. "The whole point is trying *not* to die tomorrow."

"I don't think the Wolf Man trains," he says. "So you probably won't have to worry about defense for technical rear naked chokes. And I don't know any knife defense aside from try not to get stabbed, which you have been good at so far."

I frown, even though he's really close and really cute and it's hard not to want to slightly ignore technique and all my worries and just kiss him.

"Okay, but I have to know defense for this sport, which is what we are in class for."

"Well, in that case, let's switch."

I move around to sit at Sebas's back, clasping my arms around him—one over his left shoulder and one under his right armpit—with my chest to his back. His legs are extended, and I tuck my toes into the pits of his knees to get what are called "hooks" in.

"Whenever someone has your back, you immediately want to defend against the choking arm," he says, pointing to my hand that's over his shoulder. "Once you get this around my neck, I'm already in trouble. So the idea is to prevent that. To escape from a back take, there are a few things you can do, but since you are totally new to all of this and will likely remember nothing . . ."

"Correct, thank you."

"Just try to focus on getting your back on the mat. Tuck your chin, fight the choking arm, back on the mat." He demonstrates as he speaks. "Once you get that much, we can go from there."

We work on both the start of the escape and the choke itself, and while Sebas tells me I'm doing great and gives instructions, it feels like time passes too quickly and it's already time to roll before I'm able to do it well.

Of course, I'm too new to actually know how to roll, so mostly the people I partner with stay on their backs and tell me to try and pass their guard (or get past their legs). It's a lot harder than it sounds, especially considering they actually know some technique and I am coming in with what feels like one working brain cell and minimal cardio.

But it's fun, and even better, it's a distraction.

After class ends and we all line up and bow out, I head right over to Sebas, starting to untie my belt.

"Wanna stretch with me?" he asks, mouthguard out.

I shrug. "Sure."

After changing out of our gis, we get back onto the mats, and he leads me in a series of stretches that feel necessary for my muscles but unnecessary in the way they reveal how not flexible I am.

"How are you feeling?" Sebas asks.

I eye the mats, trying to breathe into the stretch. "Like my crotch is going to rip."

He laughs. "I meant more emotionally. About everything."

"Oh, I'm feeling even worse about that."

"Which is saying something. We can switch sides."

Ugh. It's not the end of it. I reluctantly switch to the opposite side and get as far as I can with the stretch.

"I don't know how to feel, honestly. Mom's pretty on top of it at home, but it also makes being in the apartment . . . a little intense."

"Your mom gives off that vibe, yes."

I snort. "Yeah, *Return to Slasherville*'s biggest mistake was not making her the Final Girl from the beginning. How is *she* supposed to just be an extra?"

His eyes meet mine. "How are *you* supposed to just be an extra?"

"I mean, CJ Smith is like peak-extra energy as a name."

"Maybe, but CJ Smith is not peak-extra energy as a person," he counters. "You're smart, funny, beautiful . . ."

"Have just the right amount of daddy issues to be a lead . . ."

He rolls his eyes. "And you can't take a compliment. Very leading lady of you."

We both break out of the stretch, just sitting next to each other.

I smile, even though my heart is still beating a little faster from his compliment. But the conversation I had with Mom is weighing on me. I know Sebas likes me, so it's weird that he doesn't know a big part of me. I want him to. "Did Nadia tell you about what kind of queer I am?"

He shakes his head. "I figured it was the kind that was still interested in me, and honestly, that's what I cared about."

I laugh, but I'm nervous. He's not going to want to break up with me, is he? I mean, technically I don't know if it is breaking up because we didn't, like, fully establish that we're *dating*, but . . .

"I'm bisexual, but also nonbinary. Or, I don't know. Maybe like girl asterisk. Like I find comfort in the idea of a gender spectrum, and I don't mind being referred to as a girl but I also don't need to be limited by that. Like, 'they' pronouns feel right, too. And it makes me happy to be called a dude or a bro as much as it does to be called a girl. Like, I want to be both a short king and a tough queen. Or like, I'm three cats in a trench coat and one is a butch lesbian, one is a gay twink, and one is just tired." I frown. I can tell I'm losing him. "Does any of that make sense?"

Sebas bites his lip. "To me, personally? Not exactly, no." He leans into me and gives a soft smile. "But that doesn't mean I don't respect it. If you are happy, I don't care how many . . . gay cats make up your identity. I like *you*."

"I don't actually identify as a cat or anything, I'm just trying to explain myself and, I think, failing at it miserably."

He laughs. "It's okay. I'm happy you can be open with me. And, anyway, you know I love cats."

"That's what I like about you most," I tease. "And I'm happy you don't hate me."

"That would be pretty hard to do."

"Oh, I'm sure you could find a way."

He rolls his eyes again. Then, with a smirk, he gently and jokingly takes my ankle. "Are you sure you want that? When I can leg lock you?"

"People said you aren't supposed to leg lock white belts!" I protest, reaching for his arm.

His legs are around mine, keeping it in place, but his grip is so relaxed I know I'm not in any danger.

"If you leg lock me after I come out to you, that's homophobic."

"If I don't leg lock you just because you're queer, isn't *that* homophobic?"

"I think the only non-homophobic option is to teach me how to leg lock *you*."

He lets go of me entirely, gently patting my hand. "When you get your blue belt."

"Fine." I take his hand. "Thanks, though. For being cool about all this and not being weird about dating a queer person."

"CJ, I would never feel weird about dating a queer person." He rubs his thumb over my hand before making a face. "I mean, I'm a little embarrassed about dating a zero-stripe *white belt*, but . . ."

I lunge forward, encircling my arms around his neck in our move of the day before he lets out a joking squeal and then taps. I let go and he looks at me with those sparkling eyes.

"Save it for the bedroom, Cassiopeia, this is a family-friendly academy."

I flip him off and he gives me his best smile.

"Do you need a ride home?" he asks.

I am hoping this is an invitation to make out in his car because, even while sweaty and in his rash guard, Sebas looks unbearably cute. He does make for a great distraction from the anxiety and dread that have essentially taken permanent residence in my gut.

I'm about to answer when Samuel walks into the room, his hand jokingly covering his eyes. "Put your pants back on, kids. I'm here."

"Fuck off," Sebas groans.

Samuel drops his hand. "It's so boring to clean in silence. Sebas, can I use your phone to put on music?"

"Sure."

Samuel takes Sebas's phone from the side and connects it to the speaker. Instead of music initially playing, it's part of an audiobook. At least, it sounds like one, but it's in Spanish.

"Don't tell me you're listening to this again," Samuel says.

"Listening to what?" I ask.

"Samuel—" Sebas starts.

"That Moon Satter book," Samuel says. "*Campamento Slasherville.* Sebas was obsessed with that one. Tía brought us the books and got him the audiobooks when they last visited. I swear, this kid barely reads, but he can probably recite half the book. I almost thought he only agreed to move here so he could track down the author."

Samuel laughs, but I can't join in. Because what he's saying doesn't make any sense. Sebas said he never read the books, didn't he? He said that he didn't know anything about the Wolf Man, about Slasherville. Hell, he was calling it a werewolf for like a full day.

So what Samuel is saying doesn't add up.

Unless his little brother is actually a freaking liar.

"I gotta go," I say quickly.

I step off the mats, put on my shoes, and walk right out of the academy.

"CJ, wait!"

Sebas comes after me, catching up right outside the front doors of the gym. I twist on my heel to face him.

"You said you never read the books."

"I didn't say that, exactly. And I listened to them, so—"

"You acted like you'd never even *heard* of them. Or the Wolf Man. Like you didn't even know why they call this fucking place Slasherville."

His face falls. "I'm sorry."

I almost wish he would deny it, tell me Samuel was confused, that it was another horror series he was obsessed with. I thought there was one person who was honest with me, the real me, not just a surviving Smith kid, but I was wrong. If Sebas already knew the story, then he knew who I was. My eyes burn.

"Why did you lie?" I ask. "Are you another fucking Slashervillain? Were you trying to get close to me so I'd introduce you to Moon fucking Satter or something?"

Sebas gently steps closer to me. "That's not it at all. I really, really like you. And I like the books, too, but I didn't connect them to the real people. I mean, it was always just fiction."

"Not to me." My voice cracks. That's how it's always been, hasn't it? My life is just a story to everyone. My pain, my trauma—it's barely a footnote. Plenty of people in Satterville have read the books, but they were here when the killings happened. It's town history, so they at least know it's real, and not just some faraway story.

"Fuck, you're right. I'm sorry. That was the wrong thing to say." Sebas sighs. "It's just . . . after my abuelo died, Tía said I should read the first book. That there were some real things in there about grief that helped her and maybe it would help me. And it did. Say what you want about Moon Satter, but there's a lot of real emotion in those books. It . . . it seemed like they understood, they got it."

I let out a bitter laugh. "Now you're defending Moon Satter?"

"Come on, CJ. They helped us, they gave us their research—"

"Only because they probably felt bad about ruining my life!"

Sebas can't understand. His family history wasn't sensationalized into some fictional series. He can't know what it's like to have your dad's deathiversary marked by a fucked up festival where the killers get more attention than the people they murdered. He didn't unwillingly become some kind of true-crime celebrity when he was a kid. He never had to walk into school knowing every single person was whispering about him, avoiding him as if murder were something you could catch.

If it had just been one news report among a million others, the Wolf Man would be a thing of legend, lost to time. But Moon Satter had to make it larger than life. Sensationalize the brutal reality and tie it up in a bloody bow for everyone to fawn over. Without them, there wouldn't have been a Drew Dunning, or whoever is still out there. Without Moon, Taylor and Mr. White would be alive and Hana would've never been hurt. Sending their research doesn't make up for any of that.

Sebas swallows. "I'm not trying to defend what they did. I didn't realize when I first read it that they wrote the story without asking those involved first. That's bullshit. I just . . . I wanted to explain why I liked it."

"That doesn't explain why you lied," I press.

"It just . . . it seemed like you didn't want to get into it. Like you didn't want to be seen as that person. So I acted like I didn't know." His eyes gaze right into mine. "I can't pretend I know what it's like to go through what you did, but I know you are more than the bad things that happened to you. So much more. I knew that from the start, and I knew I wanted to get to know what all that beautiful more is."

I want to just accept that. To let it go. But there's a part of me that can't. I take a step away from him, my hand at the pocket where I keep my knife.

"I'll give you one chance to answer this, and you better be honest. Are you involved with . . . with the Wolf Men?"

His face cracks. "CJ, you really have to ask that?"

"I do," I choke out.

His eyes are glassy. "Of course I'm not involved. I know I was wrong to lie about the book, but I only did it because I like you. You didn't tell me everything when we first met either, but I trusted you from the moment you told me to get in that closet. I would have thought you'd trust me, too." He wipes at his eyes. "The only reason I'm even reading the book again is because I thought maybe it could help. I know Nadia is better at that kind of stuff, but I wanted to try and see if I could find anything."

The hurt in his voice feels worse than any lingering pain in that moment. I didn't mean to accuse him, not really. Because he's right. He's done nothing but help, no questions asked. But it's just so jarring and confusing to learn he lied. Doubt and distrust crept in and took over before I could even question them. I always thought that's how you survived, that distrust, but that doesn't seem right anymore. I don't know how to explain it, my annoying, confusing, conflicting emotions.

So I say nothing.

His lip trembles. "I'll still help tomorrow." He sniffles, trying to keep composure. "Can you get home safe?"

I nod.

He swallows, a tear dropping down his face. "Call me if anything happens, okay?"

"Okay," I say without meaning it.

Finally, he turns away and walks back inside.

I stand frozen to the spot. I don't know what to do with myself. I'm upset Sebas lied, but I'm also upset at myself for being upset. But can he blame me for reacting with a little distrust?

I think of his face when I asked. Maybe he can. He's been there for me since the moment he met me, putting himself in danger. Nadia too. And yet even after everything we've been through together, I can't do the same for them. I'm so selfish. Worse. I'm a fucking toxin.

I keep living while so many other people have to die.

More tears stream down my cheeks and I wipe them on my sleeve. It's moments like these where I just want my dad. Mom is truly the best, but he was always the emotional one, the one who'd cry at cat videos and movies. The one who would make me laugh through the tears. Dad always made things okay, and without him I don't know how to believe it will be. It definitely doesn't feel that way now.

I wish he was here so badly. I have pictures and videos and memories and stories from Mom and Uncle Ian, but it's never enough. I want more of him, but the only other piece of him left seems to be in that fucking book. I sniffle. What is it about *Camp Slasherville* that people like so much? It's hard to believe it holds some profound understanding of grief. Can it really be that authentic? That helpful?

Is there even a chance that it got Dad right?

I hate that I need to know, but I do.

I walk into Red Page. Ms. Maeda is at the counter. Her eyes widen when she sees me. "What happened?"

I shake my head. "Nothing. It's fine. How's Hana doing?"

Ms. Maeda smiles. "She's recovering well. She'll get to come home soon. She keeps asking for beer, though, like she's not on pain meds."

I snort. "I'll visit again soon, either there or your house."

"She'd like that."

"How are you? With all this?" Yet another example of how selfish I am—I never even asked until now.

Ms. Maeda's lips thin into a line. "It feels a little different. To be honest, I wanted to close the store through Slasherfest, but Hana wouldn't let me. She said if she had to be stabbed by the Satterville Wolf Man, we sure as hell better make a killing off it."

I can't hide my chuckle. "Sounds like her. But let me know if either of you need anything. My family probably gets it better than anyone."

"Thanks, CJ." Ms. Maeda dabs at the corner of her eye. "Now, are you here to make me cry or will you actually buy something?"

I take a deep breath. "I was just hoping to get one thing."

"No problem, hun. I'm just finishing closing up."

I walk over to the display where the copies always are and snatch one. I place it on the counter, and Ms. Maeda's mouth drops.

"Are you sure?" she asks, like this is a clear sign I've hit rock bottom.

It probably is.

I nod, sliding cash onto the counter as she rings up (with her employee discount) a copy of *Camp Slasherville.*

I cried more in the shower at home, which helped. It would have been a nice moment of pathetic alone time if Lyra hadn't bust through the door because she had to pee.

There really is no privacy in this place.

While Mom is in full preparation mode for the Wolf Man confrontation tomorrow—silver bullets and everything, like it isn't just a normal person in a shitty mask—I retreat to my room and take out *Camp Slasherville.*

I start to read.

While I knew what to expect in terms of plot, I didn't exactly know what to expect in terms of reading experience. All these years, I thought that I would hate it. That reading it would just piss me off and make me feel like absolute shit.

But as I get further and further into the book, that's not exactly it.

Don't get me wrong, Moon Satter is no Stephen King or anything. I doubt they'll be getting craft awards anytime soon. And it still is pretty fucked up that they took an actual true-crime story from their supposed hometown and changed the names to make it fiction and profit off it without getting permission from the actual people involved.

But the book is . . . entertaining.

Even though I knew Dad (or at least, his character, Jonathan) was a pretty big part of the book, I figured Moon Satter would have written him as a one-dimensional supporting character. Or someone who didn't seem like Dad at all. That's not the case, though. Jonathan's a fleshed-out, realistic portrayal, and not just that, but arguably the best character. A teen boy who had big dreams for the future, even though he was a total simp for his girlfriend (aka Mom. They really both said one and done when it came to finding love) and got along with everyone due to his friendly demeanor and funny personality.

I find myself rooting for him, laughing with him, feeling like I actually got to learn a little more about him.

I did cringe and gag at one scene about him referring to getting to third base with Mom (look, I know it happened, but I don't want to *read* about it), but aside from that, and other characters commenting on his good looks (like, I'm kind of proud but also, gross, he's my *dad*), it's actually sort of nice.

At least, before all the Wolf Man stuff.

It is a little easier to read all the suspense and horror of that night and the gruesome near-killing of my dad knowing that he made it to the end of this one. When I get to the part where they find him thanks to their flashlights revealing blood on the bright stag eyes and it's revealed he survived, tears are flowing. But somehow, I also don't feel so alone anymore.

Sebas was right. Hidden under the sensationalist horror, there's something raw and emotional. Something that makes it feel like Moon Satter gets it.

I hug the book to my chest.

"I still fucking hate you, Moon Satter," I whisper to myself. "But thanks."

From how I remember Dad, at least, it seems like the trashy writer didn't do Christian Smith all that bad. The little details were there, from the massive dimple that he passed down to me to the way he'd walk with his arms a *little* too forward. It almost felt like they understood the way he could always tell a joke no matter how bad things were, and sometimes, it would be the worst joke you'd ever heard but his delivery would still have you laughing until you couldn't breathe. It seemed to capture the way that he could completely convince you that everything would be okay, even in the worst scenarios. Even in the face of death.

He was written with a different name, a different hair and eye color, but he was my dad. In some way, he's still alive between the pages of that book. Like he's not really gone. He's not really lost. He's just somewhere else. And maybe this is a way that I can get a little piece of him back when I need him.

To remember that no matter what happens, I'm not alone.

Maybe that's a message I needed.

"Hey, Dad," I whisper, not particularly looking at anything. "If you are watching and not reincarnated into a hero or a villainess or slime, do you think you can send a little bit of Final Girl energy and luck my way?"

I wipe my eyes.

Before turning off the light, I adjust my rating of *Camp Slasherville* to three stars.

I'll take all the good vibes I can get.

25

Lead Characters *Can* Communicate

On the morning of Slasherfest, tents are set up and Satterville is busy with preparations. I have to follow suit, and that starts with me standing outside Sebas's place, holding a random bouquet of flowers I bought off the street on the way here.

I knock on the door. Fortunately, Sebas opens it.

He looks surprised to see me, but not angry. That's something.

He eyes the flowers, eyes widening. "Did someone die?"

"What? No." I hold them out to him. "They're for you. I need to apologize and I was trying to be nice."

"Pura vida." He takes them with a smile. "That is nice. I've never gotten flowers before."

"For future reference, I personally prefer gifts I can eat," I say.

He perks up. "So there is a future?"

"If we don't die tonight, I hope so. Can I come in?"

"Oh, yeah, of course." Sebas steps out of the way and lets me take a seat at the table before joining me. "So . . ."

"So, I read *Camp Slasherville* . . . and I'm only going to say this once, but I get it. You were right. I've had this hate for Moon Satter for so long that hearing you talk about the books like that made me upset. But I don't think I'm angry at Moon Satter. Well, I am, but I'm not mad at them for writing the events so much as I'm mad that they happened. And I'm so sorry I took that out on you." I squeeze my fingers together, forcing myself to continue. "I get why you didn't tell me the truth. And while it was shitty to lie, a part of me is glad you did, because if I knew that you knew who I was, I probably wouldn't have been able to open up to you so quickly. Or probably at all." I pull on my sleeve, unable to keep my hands still. "And I'm sorry I questioned you. I know you aren't involved. I know how much you love Nadia and that you'd never do that to her. Or now to me. I wasn't being fair and I'm sorry."

Sebas shakes his head. "I should've been honest. I can see how bad that all looked. *I'm* sorry."

"Well, we can start being honest now." I swallow. "You promise me you're not keeping anything else from me?"

"I promise," he says.

I glance back up at him. "I also wanted to say that you're not the only one who got feelings too quickly, and with everything coming up tonight . . . I kind of need you, Sebas."

He reaches his hand out over the table to take mine. "Well, you have me." His expression is slightly embarrassed. "It's also way too cute to hear you say my name with your accent."

Now I'm blushing. "Stop or I'll call you Seb."

He cringes. "Don't even joke." It's then that he spots the books I've brought with me. "I'm assuming you also want to talk about tonight with Nadia?"

I nod. "If she's free."

"She's always free," Sebas says. "I'll text her." He shoots off a message before standing. Sebas walks around the table and crouches next to me. "But, before she gets here . . . can I have a kiss?"

As if my face wasn't hot enough. Still, I'm not going to argue. I lean down so I can softly press my lips to his. I'm buzzing when I pull away. But then he kisses me. Again. Two more times. He keeps adding light kisses until he's grinning and I'm giggling and we're so close we're touching, but it just feels natural.

The sound of the front door has us jumping apart, though.

Nadia rolls her eyes. "I know you two are together, you don't have to act like you're hiding it."

"I don't want to make my Second Lead uncomfortable," I tease. "Even if she doesn't actually have feelings for me."

Nadia grins. "Thank you." She walks right in, pushing Sebas away to pull the closest chair right next to me, and sits. "Now, what's up?"

Sebas rolls his eyes but takes a seat across the table, and I push forward my copy of *Camp Slasherville*. "So, I actually read this last night."

"Are you okay?" Nadia asks.

I nod. "It wasn't as bad as I thought. I actually . . . I really liked Dad's character."

She nods. "Not to be weird, but your dad is total husband material in that book."

"That is weird," Sebas answers, "and you're a lesbian."

Nadia waves him off. "Yes, I'm a lesbian, but I still have husbands. They're just my two-dimensional faves, okay? Plus, I have eyes. CJ's dad was a DILF."

I frown. "Nadia."

"Don't even get me started on Mrs. Smith. Absolute Mommy."

"Okay, I'm going to ignore that and continue." I turn to them. "I guess it got me kind of sentimental, while also being a reminder of how dangerous this is. We don't know exactly who we're dealing with tonight, and I want to thank both of you for facing this with me. I might have taken you two for granted a little, but I promise, I'll protect you."

Nadia's eyes are already watering. "I did not sign up to cry this early. But you don't have to protect us. We're all going to protect each other, right?"

I smile. "Right."

She pulls both of us into a group hug.

"Oh, by the way, I finished the Wolf Man manifesto," Nadia says. "I'm going to be real, it's a lot of repetition and just unhinged thoughts. But toward the end, Brett does say something about the Creator coming to him in a dream and giving him the plan to attack the camp."

"Did he say anything that could help us? What did he say the Creator looked like?"

Nadia made a face. "It's obviously bullshit to convince people of some higher power when the actual Creator is him. Like, full biblical *be not afraid* angel nonsense. Apparently, there was no visible face, just a bunch of hands with weirdly twitching fingers . . . I'm telling you, this is some creepy-ass shit."

She opens up the document, getting to a specific entry.

now I know my calling, what I must do, what must be done
it is the world of the Creator
and on the sixth
the sheep will bleed

"Oh, wow, hate this," I say. It's a somewhat joking tone to hide from the hollow, unsettling feeling resting in my bones. Do we really know what we're getting into?

"It sounds like some kind of religious cult," Sebas says. "This is why I'm atheist."

"I don't know . . ." I start. "But either way, it's going to be dangerous. Are you two absolutely sure you want to come tonight? I won't blame you if you don't."

Nadia links her arm in mine. "You can't get rid of us that easy. I'm still your only friend."

"You're my most annoying friend," I say lovingly.

"Also your least."

Sebas laughs, taking my free hand in his. "The point is, we're in this together."

And tonight, one way or another, we're learning the truth.

I have to head home to help Mom watch the kids as she does her own preparations for Slasherfest. I am pretty positive it involves target practice, but I don't ask questions. However she needs to prepare, I'm fine with it. Leo and Lyra are both passed out in front of the TV, so it's just Orion and me awake when there's a knock on the door.

"Get that," Orion says.

"Why should I . . . ?" My question stops when I see his hands trembling, clutched around his Nintendo Switch. He's scared, even if he'll never admit it. "Okay."

I feel the weight of my pocketknife, even though I doubt the Wolf Man would *knock*. He certainly didn't when he broke into our old house.

I open the door with the chain still on, but it's Uncle Ian on the other side.

"Hey, kid," he greets me.

"You look like shit."

It's true. He's even more worn out than the last time I saw him.

"My current work project is killing me," he says. "You wouldn't believe how much I had to do before the deadline today. But it's finally done." He holds up a bag so I can see it through the crack in the door. "And I brought lunch."

That's an easy invite in, as if he even needed one.

"This is why I love you," I say, undoing the lock and fully opening the door.

Uncle Ian splurged on a whole spread of sushi, and it's so good, I would almost be okay with it being my last meal. Almost. Leo and Lyra wake up for food only to return right back to their spots on the couch. So Uncle Ian focuses on Orion and me.

"How are you both holding up?" he asks.

Orion shrugs.

"S'okay," I mumble.

Uncle Ian nods. "I just . . . I want to be here for you both today. I know I'm going to be watching the twins while your mom heads out with you, but I want you both to know that you aren't alone." His eyes are glassy. "I know you had to do it on your own last time, but I promised your dad I would protect you, and I'm going to keep that promise." He looks between us. "You're going to be okay. I swear."

Orion sniffles. "You sure?"

Uncle Ian laughs. "Well, I can't predict the future, but I'll do everything in my power to make sure I'm right."

Almost like we planned it, both of us rush into Uncle Ian for a hug. He laughs, pulling us both in tight. He's not Dad, he never tried to be, but he does have that same skill of making it seem like he knows what he's talking about. I'm so glad he's here.

Because Uncle Ian is already right. This isn't the same as last time, where Orion and I had to hide in the closet and only watch things unfold.

This time, we aren't alone.

26

Welcome to Slasherfest

It's a little strange driving to Slasherfest in Mom's car since it's only at the end of our street, but it's way stranger that the trunk of the car is stocked with a shotgun, knives, and flares. I have Dad's pocketknife as usual, Sebas and Nada have collapsible knives of their own, and Orion, wearing his Satterville Middle baseball sweatshirt, not-so-inconspicuously has a baseball bat attached to his backpack.

I'm glad Uncle Ian has Chekov and the twins. They're still too young for Slasherfest, especially at night. Even if it wasn't haunted by an actual murderer. From our parking spot, I can already see the boozy blood bags and graphic Slasherville T-shirts for sale.

The festival just started but it's already packed, buzzing with people walking up and down the closed main streets, checking out the different shops and booths and wearing Slasherfest apparel and even knockoff Wolf Man masks.

Which is a bit of a fucking problem when we're here to find the actual Wolf Man. Seeing those masks, pushed up over laughing faces and hanging around the necks of teens and adults alike, makes my anxiety rise.

If only I could buy one of those stupid blood bags to calm my nerves.

"Are we ready?" Mom asks.

Sebas tightens his soft grip on my knee. Nadia gives a little smile from my other side. I can see Orion swallow from the front seat.

"I think so," I say.

Mom turns in her seat to speak to all of us. "Remember the plan. CJ, Sebas, and Nadia, stay together and look out for signs of the killer. Orion and I will be close. First sign of anything strange, you call. You get broken away from your squad, you call. You have the slightest bad feeling, you call. Keep your location shared with the group and your phone on you no matter what. Stay within plain sight of others. Even if you see the Wolf Man, you under no circumstances go off after him alone. You let me know, and I'll get the motherfucker. Got it?"

We all nod.

"We're targeting the book's death locations, right?" Mom asks.

I nod. "While the victims have changed, the locations of the murders have been consistent with the book."

We don't know who the Wolf Man will target now. The Slasherfest victims in the book weren't all related to Taylor; most were just random out-of-towners. Sticking to the crime scenes is the better choice.

"Got it." Mom's eyes are hard. "Then keep focused, eyes everywhere for any signs of danger. What do we do if we get separated or lose our phones?"

"Come back to the car and set off the alarm," Orion answers.

Mom pats his head. "That's right. And what if someone tries to lure you away from the crowd?"

"Say 'fuck off' and kick them in the crotch," Orion answers again.

"Or elbow to the solar plexus," I add.

"Or mace," Nadia continues.

"All good," Mom says happily. "The important thing is to get away, get back to visibility, and get to the car as soon as you can."

With another promise, we all get out of the car. Then it's time to split off into our groups. Normally, that would be a terrible idea, but we need to lure the Wolf Man somehow, and in these kinds of crowds, it's not as easy to keep all five of us together. As long as we aren't alone, keep to the Slasherfest venue, and stay focused, we should be okay.

At least, I hope so.

"First death location was in the theater, right?" Mom asks.

I nod. "Second was less clear, just said in some alley near a cavatelli stand."

"Orion and I will check out the theater together, you three look around the stands. Again, anything weird, you let me know right away. Do *not* engage the Wolf Man. Your weapons are for self-defense only. Got that?"

"Got it."

Mom turns to Sebas. "You too, Jiu-Jitsu. I don't want you running after him again. Better he gets away than you get stabbed to death."

Sebas nods. "Promise."

She eyes him for a moment, questioning whether to believe him.

"I'm not asking you to protect CJ by putting yourself in danger. I'm asking you *all* to try to avoid it."

He swallows. "Okay."

Orion adjusts his backpack before turning to me and awkwardly reaching an arm out.

"What?" I ask.

He narrows his eyes. "I'm trying to give you a hug, freak."

Right. I'm the weird one in this scenario. Whatever. I pull him into a hug.

"Don't die," he says, "or I'll kill you."

"Literally same."

After that, I pull away. Mom immediately locks on to me, hand on my cheek. I lean into her touch. I am scared, I am nervous, but she feels so strong. It's almost like a little bit of that strength could rub off on me.

She kisses my cheek, and she and Orion head off in the direction of the movie theater. Outside, they're selling kettle corn and snacks, but inside, there's a free horror movie marathon going. Taylor discovered the first body there.

I'm not religious, but I give a little prayer to the universe that Mom and Orion will be okay.

"Are you ready?" Nadia asks.

No.

In front of us, as people walk by in their Wolf Man masks and "I Survived Slasherfest" T-shirts, I want nothing more than to run back to my apartment and hide under the covers. Or better yet, get on the first bus out of Satterville and never look back.

Sebas reaches out and takes my right hand. Since my phone, mace, and knife are in a convenient (if perhaps a bit nerdy) fanny pack with little cats all over it, Nadia reaches out and takes the left.

Together, it feels like we are more than just extras.

It feels like we're motherfucking Final Girls.

"Yeah," I say. "Let's get this bitch."

27

Meatballs, Marinara, and Murder

After doing a quick walk-through of the main street, we narrow down the potential crime scene to two locations: Mamma Mia's Italian restaurant stand and another booth toward the west side of the street closure simply called Joanna's Cavatelli and Meatballs. We decide to put most of our attention on the latter, as it seems to match the *Return to Slasherville* text better and also has fewer people than Mamma Mia's, which is right in the middle of the street.

Sebas and Nadia both bought a bowl from Joanna's to make it less strange that we're hanging around the stand. As much as I love the doughy pasta, eating anything will just cause me to immediately vomit into one of the already overflowing trash cans on the street. My senses are in overdrive. There's so much going on, with the crowds of people, the wolf masks, the nearby screams from the carnival rides in the parking lot behind city hall.

A part of me feels like I'm in a dream, or some strange in-between state.

Focus.

I force myself to keep at attention. To look for the smallest details of everyone passing, anyone around us who might look a little too long or behave a little too strangely. It doesn't help that some of the attendees donning wolf masks have already had one too many of the boozy blood bags.

I'm not sure whether it provides relief or just makes it worse to see one dude, wolf mask dangling from the top of his hair, puking into a trash can.

I'm even more grateful now that I'm not eating, but neither Sebas nor Nadia seems to notice.

"This pasta is amazing," Sebas says. "It can now justify the price."

I roll my eyes. "Come back next week, everything here will be better quality and half the cost. All the restaurants jack up prices for the tourists and Slashervillains."

He bites the last of his meatball. "Well, it's still good."

"Are you even paying attention?" Nadia asks him, despite seeming to be focused on her own dish of pasta.

Sebas looks at her. "I've counted eight people around us currently in wolf masks. Five are old enough to actually be a problem. Two of those five have glanced over at us more than once, and the one at . . . your four o'clock keeps looking toward the cop car parked next to the roadblocks and is my current biggest suspect. So, yes. Are you?"

Nadia bites her lip before looking back at her fork. "Of course, I noticed all that, too. Obviously." She swallows another noodle.

I try to casually bring my gaze in the direction Sebas mentioned. I'm not as good with translating Nadia's four o'clock to mine, but after studying the general area, I find the person he highlighted. It seems to be an adult male, dressed in dark jeans and a black T-shirt, Wolf Man mask over his head. It sort of seems more like a cheap knockoff mask (which says something, since the original isn't exactly a work of art), but that doesn't mean he isn't our guy.

He's alone, leaning against a telephone pole as the crowd moves around him, occasionally eyeing the police car.

My heart races.

He does seem nervous. Did he just kill someone? Is he looking for his target?

My throat seizes with the loud *thump, thump, thump* of my heart that leaps into it. This has to be him. It has to be starting.

He moves his arm into his pocket.

What is he getting? His knife?

The man pulls out a small joint, wolf head checking around him for cops before he pulls up the rubber mask and lights up.

Oh. Maybe that isn't our guy.

My phone rings. It's Mom, so I immediately pick up.

"Are you good?"

"We're safe," Mom says. "But we found the body."

My heart rate spikes back up immediately. "Someone we know?"

Her voice is controlled over the phone. "No, a Slashervillain tourist, it seems. Cops are congregating here but keeping things hush-hush for now. No sign of the Wolf Man. Where are you?"

"We're right in front of Joanna's cavatelli stand."

"We're on our way. Don't move."

She hangs up. Both Nadia and Sebas watch me carefully, so I give them the details. While it isn't much, if it is like *Return to Slasherville,* it is likely that the body was found slumped over in the back row of the movie theater, blood spilling down the aisles and making the floor sticky.

"Hold on," a girl says next to us. "It's too loud here, I'm going to walk somewhere quieter."

I look up. She's probably in her twenties, dressed in normal clothes rather than the Slasherville gear so many have. Her phone is pressed to her ear as she walks in the direction of the nearby alley.

Shit.

I gesture to her. "Tell me that's not horror story victim behavior."

Nadia and Sebas watch her slip into the alley.

"Fuck," they say at the same time.

I swallow. "We have to help her."

"We *can't*," Nadia protests. "Your mom's already on the way, right? We're not supposed to put ourselves in danger."

"She could die, Nadia."

"We don't know her."

"I didn't know you!"

She swallows. I blink. I'm not sure if I went too far, but in the moment I don't care what I promised Mom. I have to at least go and warn this girl. I'm sick of people dying. Nadia might not know what it's like to lose someone to a monster like that. But I do.

I can't keep letting this happen.

Neither Nadia nor Sebas says anything, so I keep my voice hard.

"Nadia, you stay here. Tell Mom and Orion once they arrive. Get help, whatever. Sebas and I are going to get her away from that alley."

Nadia finally nods. "Okay, but run if you see him."

I don't make any more promises. Instead, I take Sebas's hand and we follow the girl.

It's a little wild how much everything changes once we take that first corner. Her voice carries from her position at the end of the alley, but the background noise is already muted, the flashing lights and laughter and thrilled screams faded from behind the thick walls on either side. The ground is littered with trash, but there's no sign of anyone else.

"Hey!" I call once we see her.

She looks over at us, the same time as a shadow appears behind her.

The Wolf Man. The real one.

I scream. Sebas yells at her to run.

She looks behind her, her own mouth forming an O at the same moment the knife is sunk into her throat, the blade handle protruding from her neck right behind her jaw. Blood spurts everywhere, coating the mask in sprays of red as the girl falls to the ground, phone smashing into the puddling blood on the ground.

The Wolf Man howls, looking right at us, then turns and runs away.

Sebas starts after him, but I stop him. "You can't go after him alone!"

His eyes are wild as he looks at me. "No, but we should go to her."

He's right. We hurry toward the girl, but there's so much blood. Too much blood. By the time we reach her, with the full gruesome scene laid out in front of my eyes, she's gone. We didn't have a chance.

Sebas calls for help. My phone buzzes. I expect it to be Mom, but it's a message from an unknown number. I open it.

There's a picture of Uncle Ian in his living room with Leo and Lyra. The three of them are laughing and watching TV. It's candid, none of them seeming to have any awareness of the camera on them.

But based on the angle, it wasn't taken from a window. There's no glass, it's too close.

It was taken from inside the house.

It's time, little sheep. Come to the below coordinates
ALONE or all three of them die.

The coordinates come through, along with one more message.

Checkmate, Cassie.

28

The Part in Which the Audience Would Yell at Our Final Girl

Anger rushes through me, overtaking the worry. How dare he threaten my family like this and *how dare* he fucking call me Cassie.

Of course, the rage burns out quickly and sheer horror bubbles up in the space it leaves behind. Someone is inside Uncle Ian's house. I don't give a shit about those coordinates, I have to get to Uncle Ian to make sure they're all okay.

A police officer runs up to Sebas and the girl on the ground. He's distracted.

I know I shouldn't.

But I run.

It takes a moment, but I think I hear Sebas call after me. I ignore him. I have to. It's not like I'm going after the killer, not exactly. Besides, my location is shared with all of them, so if they want to come after me, they can. What's important is protecting my family, like I promised Dad all those years ago.

I don't have time to wait for Mom and Orion.

As I turn the corner of a street, I notice a discarded bicycle on the ground.

"Goddamn it," I mutter. "I knew that was going to come back and haunt me."

I keep running, pushing myself until I feel like throwing up, although to be fair, I was already halfway there before I started my sprint. Fortunately, Uncle Ian's house isn't *that* far away. It's far enough that a bike would have been helpful, but now would not be the time to try and learn.

My mind is practically blank. It's like I black out somewhere along the run, and my awareness doesn't catch up with me until I'm looking at Uncle Ian's house. I run up to the front door, but it's locked. While I have a key, I didn't think to bring it with me.

I pound on the door.

"Uncle Ian! It's CJ, let me in!"

Nothing.

Shit.

I try to peer through the living room window, but the curtains are closed. I move around the house, looking for any sign of movement inside. Uncle Ian's car is still in the driveway, which means they should be home. Unless . . .

I swallow, my chest tight.

I have to get inside. In the back of the house, a window is opened a crack. It's the best chance I have. I'll just have to apologize to Uncle Ian later, but I'm sure he'll understand given the circumstances.

I pull out my knife and slice open the screen. Once I'm able to get my fingers in and pop the screen out, I push open the window. I hoist myself up onto the window ledge, the toes of my sneakers scraping against the side of the house until I'm able to duck my head inside.

The fall is far from graceful. I tumble inside with an awkward forward roll. At least the jiu-jitsu warm-ups helped prepare me to tuck my chin for that. I catch my breath, sitting up. I take in my surroundings and realize I'm in Uncle Ian's office. I've never actually seen it before, which is maybe weird but he usually keeps the door locked—even Chekov doesn't go in. I always figured it was because of his job's client confidentiality. It's a solid office space. Nice lighting, comfy reading nook, a big desk and dual-screen computer setup, and . . .

Multiple copies of Moon Satter books?

"Uncle Ian, what the fuck?"

I can understand Uncle Ian owning *Camp Slasherville* and *Welcome to Slasherville*. Most people in Satterville do. And after reading the first book myself, I kind of get it. It would make sense for him to want to revisit the stories looking for a piece of Dad, like I did. What I don't get is the sheer number of the books he has. It's not just a copy of each of the two. It's like every edition, hardcover and paperback, even all the translated versions.

A full Slashervillain collection.

But that doesn't make sense. It always felt like we were in agreement about the books. Like he hated Moon as much as the rest of us. Is this some kind of know-your-enemy obsession?

I shake my head. I can't focus on this now. Grief makes people do weird things and the fact is he might be in danger.

I step out of the office and into the hallway. The house is silent. It's the kind of silence that feels heavy, like something is wrong. That bad feeling is confirmed when I step into the living room. It's interrupted, suspended in time. Snacks are still out on the coffee table, two cups of juice where Leo and Lyra were sitting. Uncle Ian's phone is still out on the other side of the table. Blankets are strewn across the couch like someone hastily threw them off.

"Uncle Ian?" I call.

There's no answer.

"Leo? Lyra?"

Still nothing.

Then, a meow.

"Chekov? Is that you?"

Chekov's Gun slinks out from his hiding spot under the couch. His fur is completely on end, tail twice the size it normally is.

Something happened.

My eyes burn and I scoop up Chekov, holding him to me. "I'm so sorry, little guy. It's going to be okay, though, all right? I'm going to get them back."

Chekov starts to purr.

I need to get to the location from the text. But I can't do it alone, regardless of what it told me to do. Shifting Chekov's Gun to one arm, I take out my phone with the other and immediately call Mom.

"Cassiopeia Jane, why are you at Uncle Ian's?" Mom snaps immediately. "What is going on and why did you not wait for me?"

I swallow. "They have Uncle Ian and the twins. They're not here. The killer wants me to go to a location alone. If anyone else shows up, they'll hurt them."

Mom's good at hiding her panic. "Text me the place. We'll meet you there. You can go in first to make it seem like we're following their instructions and get a grasp of the situation, but you aren't doing this alone. I'm going to protect you and your siblings, okay?"

I almost want to agree, to ask her to just go instead because it seems like, no matter what, I'm always too late. One step behind.

But this is getting personal. When Taylor was the Final Girl, people still died before Mom was able to stop the Wolf Man. Maybe it's impossible to save everyone, to control everything and have it go according to plan.

That doesn't mean I can't keep trying to change the story.

"Okay," I say, "but you're not doing it alone either."

There's a pause as she considers my tone.

"Fine," she finally says. "Families that slay together stay together or whatever."

I forward her the coordinates.

"I'll see you soon, Mom."

"Be careful."

"You too." My throat feels choked up. "I love you."

"I love you too, CJ." I can almost hear her smile. "More than anything."

Immediately after we hang up, a notification ping sounds. But nothing comes up on my phone. I turn to the table, where Uncle Ian's phone is lit up. Chekov's Gun jumps out of my arms and I lean over to check the notification.

An email from Ron J. Cunningham.

Wait. I know that name.

Why is Uncle Ian emailing Moon Satter's agent? Was he trying to get info on them, too?

I press on the message to open it, but the phone is locked. I don't know his passcode. I try Uncle Ian's birthday. Doesn't work. Dad's birthday. Still locked.

I type in my birthday, and it opens.

"Asshole," I say. "Don't make it so obvious I'm the favorite."

I open up the email.

Hi Moon,

I really think you should reconsider this third book thing. I know you were on the fence about doing another Slasherville book, but I just don't think people are interested in a Moon Satter romance. I happened to bring up to your editor that you were considering writing about the new events with the Smith kid consulting, and he is all for it!

Want to set up a call soon to discuss?

Ron

What the fuck.

My hands shake as I look through the rest of the emails. All of them are addressed to Moon Satter. This is Moon Satter's email.

Why would Uncle Ian have access to Moon Satter's email?

He must have been looking into Moon, too. Hacked their email to see if they were behind the most recent murders. He was probably trying to protect us like he always does.

Still. I click on the next app. Google Drive.

I scroll past something entitled "Untitled Romantasy Project—Moon Satter" and past "Welcome to Slasherville Final," "Welcome to Slasherville Final FINAL," and "Welcome to Slasherville Final FINAL (1)" before I see it.

The publishing contract for *Welcome to Slasherville.* With a whole lot of zeros next to the payment amount and Moon Satter's legal name.

Ian Henley.

Uncle Ian.

No.

My eyes burn. My mind spins.

This isn't right. This can't be right.

But there's no other explanation.

The phone slips out of my hand, smacking to the floor and causing Chekov's Gun to jump and look over with wide eyes. I can't pretend anymore, the evidence is clear.

Uncle Ian isn't a Moon Satter superfan. He is Moon Satter.

29

What Kind of Book Club Is This?

The thing is, while I don't have my license, I did start learning how to drive. Mom wanted me to have an idea in case of an emergency. I'm pretty sure this is that exact emergency. Sure, I'm technically stealing Uncle Ian's car, but the keys were left out, and considering he hid the fact that he's Moon Satter for years, I honestly don't give a shit and also think he owes me *at least* this much. Especially since I'm leaving to go save his ass.

I kiss Chekov's Gun and snatch the keys, running outside.

I fumble my way through adjusting the mirrors, strap in, and start the car. It feels so weird to be in the driver's seat, and I'm definitely panicking. But I put it in reverse and slowly back out the driveway. While I get the lawn a bit, I don't hit anything as I pull out onto the street.

So far, so good.

While a part of me wants to crawl along at a slow pace because I'm terrified of the other cars coming, I press on the gas. I don't have time to waste. The coordinates are plugged into my phone, and it looks like I'm headed right back to the center of Slasherfest. There's not much parking left in the closest lot, but it's also not my car, so I pull over at a curb that has a resident-only parking sign.

Technically, Uncle Ian is a resident. Just not of this exact street.

Whatever, he can use his Moon Satter money to pay for the ticket.

In the short time I was gone, Slasherfest already turned into an entirely different scene. Aside from the sun setting and the daylight fully replaced with bright festival lights and the blues and reds of more cops arriving, the place is even more packed.

I don't know if word got out about the murders yet, considering all the people still around. I'm surprised they haven't shut down the festival, although based on the police blockades, it looks like they may not be letting people leave the main street.

Fortunately, I'm able to get back in.

I push past the energetic crowd to get closer to the coordinates on my phone. Once I'm in the right spot, I look up. It's Red Page. Only, the store is closed, the front door is covered, and there's a padlock on it. This doesn't make sense. Ms. Maeda said she wasn't going to close for Slasherfest.

What is going on?

I scan the crowd around me. I figured Mom, Sebas, Nadia, and Orion would have arrived before me. Maybe the police are holding them up. They did find bodies, after all.

My phone buzzes.

Another text from the unknown number.

6572.

Someone knows I'm here.

I enter the code into the padlock and it pops open. Without thinking, I step inside.

As the door slowly shuts behind me, I take in the setting. The store is set up like it usually is for a book event, with rows of chairs lined up in the middle of the store. But not all the chairs are empty.

Three people are scattered across the seating, all of them clad in dark clothing and wolf masks.

My eyes catch John Doe, still hanging in the corner with his "I Survived Slasherville" cap. His presence almost makes me feel better. Like he's watching over me just like he watched over Dad.

Like if he survived Slasherville, hell, maybe I can, too.

Under him, the Wolf Men all face the small stage Red Page has for events. There, Leo and Lyra are tied to the chairs with what looks like ribbon, but both of them have ice cream cones in their hands, which seems like the weirdest hostage situation ever.

Leo sees me and smiles wide. "Hi, CJ!"

None of the scary shit around me matters. They're okay. They're alive.

I rush past the still Wolf Men to my siblings, pulling them into an awkward hug that slides their chairs closer together and nearly spills their ice cream on my shirt.

"Are you both okay?" I ask, pulling out my pocketknife to cut the ribbons around their ankles.

"Yep," Lyra says, licking the cone. "We have ice cream."

"We're playing a game before the event," Leo adds. "It's called Secret Spies. We had to wait to try to escape until you got here!"

I swallow. At least they don't know what's actually going on. We can't afford a child psychologist at the moment.

There's a loud bang from the front of the store. I turn to where a fourth Wolf Man is hammering a board across the door. Shit. I grip my knife tighter. Two more Wolf Men flank either side of the stage.

"Welcome, Cassiopeia Jane," one says.

"Welcome," they all say as they pull out large knives.

I don't feel very welcome. The knives sort of kill the vibe. But none of the Wolf Men are making a move. If not for the unwanted greeting and the one still hammering at the door, they would almost seem like statues.

It's so strange, it almost distracts me from the fact that there are way more of them than expected and I am almost certainly going to die.

"What's going on?" I demand.

"You have been requested by the Creator," one answers.

This guy again. "What does that mean?" I snap. "Who is the Creator?"

No answer. My chest feels like it's filled with lead. They aren't going to tell me anything else, although I'm not sure they need to at this point. The creepy religious murder cult theory seems to have hit the nail on the head.

I focus back on my siblings.

"Where's Uncle Ian?" I ask the twins.

They both shrug, more focused on their ice cream.

"I think he's playing the game, too," Lyra says.

"You might have to rescue him," Leo adds.

Fuck. I don't know whether to be relieved he was also kidnapped or terrified he could already be dead. And where is Ms. Maeda? She said she would be working today, right? Did they do something to her, too?

None of the Wolf Men are talking, my backup is nowhere to be found, and both Uncle Ian and Ms. Maeda are missing. This is really bad. Everything in me is telling me to grab the kids and run, but there's no escape. All I can do is keep hold of my knife and keep myself between these freaks and my siblings.

I point my knife at the Wolf Man in the front row.

"Where's my uncle?" I ask.

He doesn't answer. Instead, he uses his own (much larger) knife to point toward the door behind me. It's the back room where all the shipments come in and that Ms. Maeda uses as a greenroom for author events.

Do these people know Uncle Ian is Moon Satter? Is that why they're doing this? Is this some kind of fucked up event for him?

Maybe they found out he was helping us, sending all that info on Brett Miller. This could be some kind of revenge for him potentially turning against their Creator or whatever.

Shit. I hope I'm not too late.

I rein Leo and Lyra in close to me, take a deep breath, and open the door.

In the back room, Uncle Ian is tied up to another chair. He has a gag around his mouth, but he starts making noise when he sees us enter.

I turn the twins away. I'm glad he's still alive, but they still don't need to see this. "Hey," I tell them. "I have to rescue Uncle Ian for the game, okay? You two stay in the corner and finish your ice cream."

They nod, skipping off in the direction I pointed, sitting on a bench. I rush to the back of the room where Uncle Ian is trapped.

"Uncle Ian . . ." I cut off the gag. "What's going on?"

His eyes are wide, frantic. "I don't know. A bunch of Wolf Men just showed up at my house and brought us here. Are you okay?"

I nod. Swallow. My heart is pounding in my throat, and my eyes burn just looking at him. "Uncle Ian, when were you going to tell me that you're Moon Satter?"

He blinks, expression a mix of shock and almost horror.

"CJ, I . . . I'm so sorry."

I can't help my tears from falling. Even though I already knew, it's still something totally different for him to confirm it. He lied to me, to all of us, this entire time. And for what?

"Why?" I ask, eyes stinging. "Why would you even write those books?"

Uncle Ian swallows. "The Wolf Man took so many lives. And no one cared that they were *people.* They were just victims, a name in passing. Both times, all the attention was on those fucking Miller brothers. I couldn't stand it. Especially not after losing Christian." His voice breaks. "I needed him to be remembered, CJ. But no one wanted to listen. I didn't have the voice, the reach, to make a difference. I hated that only *we* seemed to care. Writing has always been my outlet, and I just started writing the story, with Christian as I knew him, as I wanted him to be remembered . . . Before I knew it, I had a whole book. And I wanted to share it. For his legacy."

I don't know what to say. My eyes are flooded. I think of the feeling I got reading that first book. That Dad's character was so much more *alive* than everyone else. That he felt like a friend. A best friend.

Of course.

Uncle Ian shakes his head. "I should have been honest with you, with your mom, talked with her about it first, but . . . I thought it was what Christian would have wanted. Especially when I saw how much money they were offering. Your mom was working her ass off, but there was debt. I needed to make sure there was a cushion for you kids, that things would never get too desperate and you would be taken care of financially. I felt like . . . it was the one way I could help."

I sniffle. When he puts it like that, I get it.

"I don't think he cared about having a legacy," I say softly. "I don't think he'd give a shit about random people remembering him. He just cared about us."

Uncle Ian's eyes are soft. "I'm sorry, CJ. I never imagined it would end up like this."

He seems so sincere. And it makes sense. How could he have imagined any of this? There's no way Uncle Ian could have controlled the reaction of fans. He couldn't have known it would take on a life of its own. He was trying to help us solve it, even. Plus, it's like Sebas said, his books did help people.

Now it's my turn to help him.

My chest tightens. I have to get us out of here. All of us.

"Uncle Ian, where's Ms. Maeda?" I ask.

At that moment, a Wolf Man crashes into the room. They pull off the mask, revealing a crazed-looking Ms. Maeda underneath. She steps forward, locking eyes with Uncle Ian before slapping him right across the face.

Then she looks at me with a soft smile. "Hi, CJ. Lot to explain, huh?"

30

Who the Heck to Believe

I want to throw up.

Ms. Maeda? No way. She can't be involved in all this. She's been there for me over the years. This place has been like a second home. Her own daughter was caught up in one of the attacks.

But she's a horror fan. She has access. Hell, Chekov's Gun even loves her—that's probably why he didn't hiss at the Wolf Man in the library. It was someone he knew.

"CJ, I'm gonna need you to come over here," Ms. Maeda says, reaching her arm out toward me. I lean back.

"Ms. Maeda?" I squeak. "You're behind this?"

She gives me a look. "What? No. What would make you think I have anything to do with these freaks?"

"Um . . ." I gesture to her outfit. "You're dressed like a Wolf Man. And you just hit Uncle Ian, who is tied up in the back room of your bookstore?"

Ms. Maeda nods. "Fair. But, honey, I swear I have nothing to do with this. I was working the cash register when this piece of shit came in with his little troupe of animal assholes, knocked me out, and tied me up!" She glares at Uncle Ian. "Clearly you didn't go to Camp Satterville, because those knots were shit!"

I look between her and Uncle Ian.

"CJ, c'mon," he pleads. "She's lying. I have nothing to do with this."

Ms. Maeda slaps him again.

"Stop!" I yell. They both turn to me. Even Leo and Lyra look up from the back. I twist toward them. "Back to your ice cream! This is grown-up stuff."

They shrug, already bored. I turn back to Ms. Maeda and Uncle Ian.

One of them is lying to me. That much I know. And regardless of who it is, the betrayal is already causing a sickening hollowness to grow in my chest. But I need to figure out who is actually behind all this. I need to remain calm and levelheaded and go at this with a clear and logical mind.

I start crying more.

"CJ," Uncle Ian says softly. "I'm so sorry you have to go through this. Just let me free and we'll stop her together. I'll protect you."

Ms. Maeda rolls her eyes. "CJ, he is lying to you. He's been lying to *all of us*." She frowns at me. "How can you think I'm trying to kill you? Your recommendations are my bestsellers. And I don't even like Moon Satter books. Their writing sucks."

"They're actually critically acclaimed, so," Uncle Ian starts.

I take a shaking breath. I don't know what to believe—or what I want to believe. Both options suck. Except the things that are nagging at me are too big to keep pretending like I don't notice them.

"Ms. Maeda never knew Dad," I say.

Both of them look at me like I fully lost my mind.

"What does that have to do with anything?" Uncle Ian asks.

"It means she wouldn't know to call me Cassie."

I've only ever gone by CJ. "Cassie" was reserved for Dad, and he really only used it at home. Ms. Maeda doesn't even use my full name. She wouldn't even think of me as a Cassiopeia, let alone a Cassie.

But Uncle Ian would. He heard Dad call me that nickname plenty of times.

I stare at Uncle Ian through my tears, waiting for him to say something. Anything. To tell me I'm wrong. That I'm crazy. Ask me why I could ever think he'd do something like this when he's been nothing but good to me all these years.

After a moment, Uncle Ian lets out a long sigh. With barely a shake, his restraints fall right off. They were never tied. He stands, pulling a knife from his belt. "You are too smart for your own good, Cassie. I thought my performance was pretty great. You know I was an acting minor, right? But fine. Fine. We'll stop pretending." He points the knife in the direction of the twins. "Ms. Maeda, you watch the kids. Take them back to the stage. This is between me and CJ."

Ms. Maeda's eyes cut to me. I nod to the twins. Considering she has no weapon, it's better for her to follow his instructions.

With the twins taken care of, I turn back to Uncle Ian. He seems like a completely different person. He looks the same, from his shining eyes to the T-shirt he wears with a cat playing drums that says "Purr-cussion." But it's hard to connect the uncle I knew to the person in front of me now. It doesn't fit. To have him be Moon Satter is one thing, but to have him be doing all this . . .

My world is crumbling around me and I can't make sense of any of it.

I sniffle. "Why?" I finally ask.

"Well, everything I told you is true," he starts. "This was all for you kids. But to write the Slasherville novels, to become Moon Satter,

I had to really immerse myself in the story. Understand the killer's motivation. As I was looking into the Miller brothers, I came across a certain belief they held."

My heart pounds. "The Creator."

Uncle Ian nods. "The Creator, exactly."

"So you're some kind of born-again Christian?"

He makes a face, chuckling. "No, hell no. It's not like that. Didn't you read the manifesto? That's part of why I sent it to you—I was hoping you'd start to understand." Uncle Ian speaks with passion, like he desperately needs me to get it. "The Creator might be like a god, but they aren't one, really. The Creator is the one controlling all this. This world."

I take a step back. He actually believes in Brett Miller's simulation bullshit? "Um . . . I'm pretty sure you're describing God."

"No, because this . . ." Uncle Ian gestures around to everything. ". . . is all just a story. And the Creator chose Moon Satter to tell it."

Oh, hell no. Has he been listening in on my conversations with Nadia?

"That's ridiculous," I say.

"Maybe," he agrees. "But that doesn't mean it isn't true." Uncle Ian sighs. "I was like you at first, CJ. Skeptical. Angry. So fucking angry. I mean, those Miller shitheads. They took my best friend, my *brother.* And for what? No reason? I couldn't accept that."

My hands tremble, but Uncle Ian continues.

"I was in a bad place after Christian's death. I was drinking all the time, depressed, angry. I didn't let it show in front of you kids, but I wanted to die, CJ. It was my duty to you and your siblings that kept me alive. And then I found another reason to live. The Creator. Brett Miller didn't kill those people for no reason. Christian didn't die for no reason. It was a painful part of the Creator's plan. Losing him like that . . . it was hard. But I realized he had to die, because that's what the Creator wanted. I couldn't have saved him even if I wanted to. Because it was the story they wrote."

"There's no story, Uncle Ian," I say, my voice pleading. "Bad things just happen sometimes, and there's no reason. The Miller brothers were sick assholes and we're just unlucky."

"No," he snaps. His voice lightens again. "No. It's fate. It's the predetermined plot. And once I realized that, it all made sense."

"How does any of that make sense? Dad didn't *have* to die. He just *did*."

Uncle Ian's eyes water as he shakes his head. "No. Even if there were a world where Christian Smith died for no reason, I wouldn't want to exist in that world."

"Neither do I. But we have to. That's all we can do. Keep living in this world." Maybe I can get to him. Maybe I can help him come to reason. He's been dealing with this Creator shit on his own. Maybe I can help him snap out of it.

"This world is a *story*!" he barks at me. "One where everything is planned and predetermined and we have a role but we don't have a choice. I hoped it was over. That the rest of the story could play out without violence. But just like Brett said, the Creator came to me in my dreams. And I knew it wasn't over." He laughs. "I mean, it's a horror story, there's always a fucking reboot."

I blink. "So it *was* you who wrote *Return to Slasherville*."

He nods.

"And you got some Slashervillains to help you make it come true," I say, putting more of the pieces together, my eyes darting to the Wolf Men throughout the bookstore. "Using the forums."

"Doing the Creator's work," he confirms. "I only got close to a select few. You can't imagine how annoying the logistics can be in keeping this all untraceable, but everyone brought their skills."

That explains how they managed everything. There weren't just two Wolf Men, there was an entire pack working together to make the story real.

"Why the hell did you send the manuscript to me, then?" I ask.

"I wanted you to be prepared, so you could keep yourself safe. I didn't want you to accidentally get hurt."

Some good that did. "So when you realized I was getting involved, that I was interfering, why did you go off script?" I ask. "Why kill Taylor?"

Uncle Ian laughs. "Because I realized I got it wrong." His eyes are glassy and wide. "I learned the truth. After I sent the manuscript, I had a dream about the police reports. That there was something I missed. I immediately went back to them and realized the dream was a message from the Creator. Because there was something. Something everyone chose to ignore. That's when I realized it. You were always supposed to be the Final Girl, Cassie. *You* are who the Creator chose to be the lead of this story. It was easy enough to switch gears the next day and target Taylor instead. That girl was chronically online. It was helpful at first when I was writing from her perspective, but it also made it much easier to find and kill her that day."

Guess Nadia was right about that. But that doesn't explain what the hell he was talking about when he said he noticed something in the police reports.

"What do you mean? What did you find?"

He looks at me with pity. "I put together what really happened the night Christian died. What no one else knows except us and the Creator."

I shake my head back and forth. "Everyone knows what happened. Dad killed the Wolf Man, but his wounds were too severe to survive."

Uncle Ian takes a step toward me, his gaze intense. "No, CJ. No. Because the wounds on Evan were consistent with someone who was right-handed."

"So?" I ask.

Uncle Ian smiles. "Christian was left-handed."

My stomach twists. "That . . . that doesn't mean anything. They must have got it wrong." Bile rises in my throat as I instinctively step away. "Or maybe he could only reach his knife with his right hand. Maybe his left arm was injured. Maybe—"

"CJ. Think. What actually happened that night?"

My hands start trembling and I try to still them. I don't know what he's talking about, and I shouldn't care, but for some reason, it's like alarm bells are going off in my head.

"I'm not doing this."

Uncle Ian reaches out to grab my arm. "C'mon, CJ, remember."

I push him off me, tripping over my feet and stumbling to the ground.

"I don't know!"

"Yes, you do. You know."

Images flash through my mind. So much blood. Something in my hand. Bright lights.

"Shut up."

"What happened that night, CJ? What happened?"

"Shut up, shut up, shut up!" My throat is raw. My knife clatters to the floor, slipping from sweaty hands. I slap my hands to cover each ear but his voice still cuts through.

"What happened to Evan Miller?"

I scream and scream and sob. Dad, I'm so sorry, I'm so, so sorry. I broke my promise, but I didn't mean to. I swear, I didn't mean to.

Uncle Ian is patient, waiting for a break to interject.

"What's the most important trait in a Final Girl?" Uncle Ian asks.

I shake my head. No. No, no, no, no, no. Uncle Ian picks up the knife I dropped.

His voice is hard. "They're the one who stops the killer . . . by becoming a killer themself."

31

What Really Happened That Night

"Go," Dad said. He put a pocketknife in my hand, closing my fingers around it. It was exactly like the one his fingers gripped. His hand was warm, but his eyes were panicked. "You have to protect your brother, okay, Cassie?"

"Dad, what's happening?" I asked. My eyes burned from tears. He was leaving me. He wasn't supposed to leave me. I didn't want him to. I couldn't do it alone. My breaths came out faster, panic lacing each inhale.

"Hey, hey, hey," he said quickly, voice a controlled whisper. His hand cupped my face. "You're my strong girl. It'll all be okay. You know this. We planned for this, didn't we?"

Tears leaked. I shouldn't have believed him, but Dad was the kind of person who could make you believe anything. I nodded.

"What do we do when Daddy says to go?"

A crash from downstairs. Glass breaking. Orion started to cry.

"I take Orion and I hide."

"And when do you come out?"

I swallowed. "Only when you or Mom comes to get us."

"No matter what you hear?"

"No matter what."

He kissed me and Orion big and wet on our foreheads and pulled us in tight. I thought it was to make us brave. I think it was to say goodbye. I didn't want him to go. I wanted to stay with him or I wanted us to all leave together. Footsteps thundered, someone howled like a wolf.

"*Go,*" Dad said.

I didn't want to go.

But that time, I knew there was no question, no argument. I took Orion's hand and I ran into the closet. Through the slotted doors, bits of the room were in view. I pulled Orion back into the shadows, clothing draping over us. I covered his mouth with my free hand, not moving even when snot and spit dripped onto it.

I held out the pocketknife with my other hand. Between that and my brother against me, I told myself that everything would be okay. That Dad would protect us, no matter what. That Dad knew what to do. Because we had prepared for it. And I had to focus on the next step. The one task I had.

Don't move and don't leave. No matter what.

So we stayed quiet and still.

Even as the man in the wolf mask walked into the room.

Even as we heard them fight, shadows moving across the closet floor in front of our trembling feet. Even as a sourness filled the air and I felt Orion's pee warm against me. Even as, through the slots in the closet door, I saw the Wolf Man take the knife and stab it right through my dad's chest. Even as I saw him crumple to the floor. Even as I had to bite my own hand, pressed over my mouth, to keep myself from crying out. Even as the blood poured under the closet door, staining my pink pterodactyl socks a sickening red.

So much blood. Too much blood.

My heart was thundering in my chest as I tasted metal and salt. The Wolf Man turned toward the closet, like he knew we were there. He took a step closer.

I covered Orion's face with a shirt. I felt sick. I bit down on my hand harder until it bled.

The door opened. The Wolf Man, covered in my father's blood, found us.

I didn't think.

I just reacted.

I slammed the pocketknife into his chest. I felt it sink into his flesh, blood bubbling up from the surface and spewing out onto my face. The Wolf Man roared, but he was too slow. I was possessed, or something like it. I sunk the knife into him again. He stumbled, falling to the floor. I leapt out of the closet and onto him, crying and screaming and bringing the knife down on him again.

Again.

Again.

Again.

I kept stabbing until it seemed like the entire floor was red. Until it felt like I had more of his blood than he did. Until he was long past still and my adrenaline dropped and I was left only with the shocked horror of what I had done.

I promised Dad I wouldn't leave the closet.

I promised.

I choked, dropping the knife. It fell right next to Dad's lifeless hand.

His gift to me. I ruined it. I didn't listen to him and I ruined it.

That's when I saw Dad's knife. The exact copy, but with a clean blade, a foot away from his outstretched arm. I didn't think. I picked it up.

“CJ?” Orion sobbed from the closet. The shirt was still over his face.

I walked back into the closet, a zombie, and shut the doors. Then I hugged my brother tight.

“It’s okay,” I said. “He didn’t see us. He didn’t see us. We just have to wait for Mom or Dad to come get us, okay?”

I said it enough, I almost believed it, too.

32

The One, True Final Girl

Uncle Ian watches me carefully as I sob. He knows I'm remembering. He knows he's right. I didn't just avoid the Wolf Man the first time. I killed him. Everyone said it was Dad because that's what they wanted to believe. They didn't want to see the broken, terrifying rage of that eleven-year-old girl because it wasn't supposed to exist.

That wasn't an ending anyone wanted to hear.

Not even me.

"It's okay, CJ." Uncle Ian's voice is soft as he reaches out to me. "No one blames you. What you did was incredibly brave and, honestly, very understandable. You were protecting yourself. Your brother."

I sniffle, slapping his hand away. "Why are you doing this? Why are you killing people?"

He smiles at me pityingly, like I should understand this all by now. "You had to be the Final Girl. That was the most important thing. The Creator wanted it. So, someone needed to be your villain. There was no one else but me. It wasn't what I wanted, really. It's just the way the story was written."

"There is no fucking story!" I snap. "It's *your* story and you can change it. That's what you did when you had your Wolf Men target me instead."

"No," Uncle Ian says in his eerily calm voice. "I told you. There's always been a story. There's only ever been *this* story. It's just that the draft you had was the wrong one. That's my fault." He turns the knife in his hands. "You can't change what was destined to be. I tried, by keeping the family out of the first draft of *Return to Slasherville,* but that's not what the Creator wanted. That's not what anyone wanted because it wasn't the truth. And who would want Taylor as a lead anyway? She had the looks and the popularity, sure, but she sucked. Outing someone like that? She's not even a fun mean girl. I can't tell you how hard it was to write that. You're a much better option, trust me." He stops moving the knife, instead pointing it right at me. "Not even a better option. The only option. The truth is you are the one, true Final Girl, CJ, and I am here to help you complete that destiny."

He doesn't give me an opportunity to answer. To try to convince him that these are all delusions he got from getting in too deep into the minds of deeply troubled, fucked up people. I guess there is still a part of me hoping I can change his mind, make him realize how utterly outlandish this all is. To allow my uncle to still have some kind of happy ending.

Instead, he grabs my arm and leads me back to the stage. Ms. Maeda has Leo and Lyra in the corner. I look at her with desperate, sorry eyes, but there's nothing either of us can do. Uncle Ian seems distracted, looking toward his Wolf Men as if admiring his fans, and I manage to reach into my pocket and unlock my phone.

All the Wolf Men in the audience are standing now, still completely motionless, still holding their knives in place.

I press on Mom's name just as Uncle Ian looks back at me. I snap my hand away from my pocket. I turn to the crowd.

"So you're all seriously doing this, *killing* people, because you think we're living in a fucking horror story and it's what some god wants?"

They don't answer. Of course, Uncle Ian does.

Uncle Ian laughs. "I mean, it's not for the Creator. Not only, at least."

I turn toward him. "Then who the hell is it for? You don't have to be doing any of this! You can just let us all go and pretend this never happened!"

Uncle Ian shakes his head. "We can't. That's not what they want."

"They?"

"The audience!" Uncle Ian gestures big with his hands. *"That's* who this is all for. The people invested in our story, Cassiopeia. Your story. They want you to suffer, so they don't have to. They need you to survive, to show them they can, too. You have to defeat your demons so *they* can experience that, learn from that, and defeat their own Wolf Man in whatever form it may take. They don't want to see a happy ending. Not without blood." He smiles, pointing the handle of his knife toward me. "I'm the villain. They want to see me die. That's the destiny of the Final Girl. *Your* destiny."

It's then that I realize he's offering me his knife. My skin grows cold.

"You want me to kill you," I say.

"It's how the ending is supposed to go."

I stare at him in disbelief. "Look, Uncle Ian. I get it. You don't want to believe Dad died for no reason. You don't want to believe it could have been prevented, because it's so easy to blame yourself. I know, because I do." I can't see him well through my tears and smudged lenses, but he lets me continue. "It's not fair. It's not. But that doesn't mean the answer is that his death was inevitable. Dad shouldn't have died that night. It was the evil actions of one person that took him from us. But that doesn't mean he died for nothing. He died to protect us. He died because he loved us more than he loved himself. That was the reason. Not some fucking Creator."

Uncle Ian is quiet, gently shaking his head before speaking. "He did love you, CJ. But it's more than that. It's fate." He wipes his own eyes.

"Uncle Ian . . ." My heart sinks further at my inability to get through to him. It's like a stranger standing in front of me. Some doppelgänger or body snatcher or anyone but the person who's been there for me my entire life.

"I know you're scared," he says. "You're allowed to be scared. It's okay. I'm going to make it a little easier for you. I'll make you want to do it."

My heart jumps to my throat. "What do you mean by that?"

"Why does the Final Girl have to kill the big, bad Wolf Man?" Uncle Ian asks. "It's simple: because he keeps destroying what matters to her most."

With that, he lunges toward Ms. Maeda and the twins.

33

The Supporting Characters Strike Back

At that moment, multiple loud *bangs* thunder through the air as wood snaps and glass shatters. We all duck, instinctively turning to the source of the sound at the front of the store. Half of the boarded-up door has been blown in, and Mom stands in the rubble, shotgun in her arms. Behind her, Sebas, Nadia, and Orion all grip their weapons: a knife, something like bolt cutters, and a baseball bat. Mom takes in the scene, eyes locking on Uncle Ian.

"Ian, you delusional son of a bitch," she snarls.

He feigns innocence, body language immediately changing from heartless puppet master to cowering family member. "What are you talking about? I'm protecting our family."

"Not yours," I say. I pull out my phone, still connected to Mom's in a call. "She heard everything, asshole."

He rolls his eyes and lets out a groan. "Well, that doesn't change anything. This is why we taught you to not go places alone." He gestures to the Wolf Men.

Immediately, they spring into action, and all hell breaks loose.

The Wolf Men rush toward Mom and the others. She wastes no time in firing off rounds. Sebas, Nadia, and Orion stay close behind her, fending off Wolf Men on all sides. It's truly something to behold, but I don't focus on them for long, both because I need to stay out of the line of fire and because Uncle Ian is once again heading for Ms. Maeda and the twins. I sprint toward them, getting there first.

"Go for help!" I shout to Ms. Maeda, taking over my siblings.

It's my job to protect them anyway. I made that promise to Dad and I plan on keeping it, no matter what.

Ms. Maeda finds a clear path to the front door. Both Leo and Lyra have their hands over their ears, crying out at the loud noises and chaos around us. I pull them both into me, arms around them.

"It's okay," I say. "I'm gonna take care of this."

I don't know if they hear me. They open their eyes and I force them to look only at me and the wall. I reach out to the display of toys and collectables. The options aren't great, so I end up with a plushie of Chuckie and a xenomorph and hand them off to the twins.

"Hold on to these and stay in that back room, okay? Close your eyes and your ears and don't come out until me or Mom gets you. No matter what."

They both nod, faces streaked with tears and snot as they clutch their horror icons. I push them into the storage room.

"I don't want to hurt them, CJ. They really feel like my own kids. You all do."

I turn around. Uncle Ian stands there. Watching. He pushes aside the chair where I usually read, looking like a true villain with John Doe the stag hung overhead.

"I won't let you hurt them," I growl.

That only makes him smile.

This is what he's been planning for, after all. Believing I'm *actually* some kind of protagonist. That he is the enemy I have to stop, at any cost. I hate him. I really do.

But not completely.

At the end of the day, it's still Uncle Ian. Who has always been there for me. Who took me to the shelter with him to adopt Chekov's Gun because he wanted me to help choose his cat. Who would take us out to dinner and make sure we had up-to-date phones and laptops for school and new shoes before the current ones wore out.

Against my best wishes, my eyes start leaking again.

"Aren't you supposed to try to kill me first?" I ask, lifting my chin at the knife still in his hand. "Isn't that what the villain does?"

Uncle Ian laughs. "Maybe I'm just not that good of a villain."

"Guess not."

Behind him, I see a Wolf Man lunge for Nadia, but Sebas jumps onto their back, locking them in a rear naked choke. Nearby, Orion swings his bat at another Wolf Man, knocking the mask sideways as drops of blood fall down their pale neck.

"You know, your dad texted me. The night of the break-in."

My heart stops. I look back to Uncle Ian. "What?"

"He said, 'Promise you'll protect my kids.' I didn't know what he meant until after I learned what happened. But I've kept that promise. You can hate me, you can argue that I haven't done it in the right way, or even a good way, and that's fine. Hell, I might even agree with you. But I've kept that promise."

I see him there. The Uncle Ian who I love.

"I know," I say. "I just wish that changed anything."

"I know," he repeats. "I do, too."

I think he says it as a goodbye. I take it as one. A goodbye to the Uncle Ian I love. The one who is like my second dad. The one who I believed in more than anything. And all the moments we've had together.

Including this one.

"I was never going to hurt Leo or Lyra," he says. "But someone has to be the bad guy, and I didn't make any promises about your boyfriend."

That's when I see Sebas heading toward us, eyes filled with worry. Time seems to slow as Uncle Ian grips his knife and lunges. My heart pounds. I can't let him hurt Sebas. I can't let him hurt anyone.

I tackle Uncle Ian, slapping him to the floor in front of the cushioned chair. Some instinct in him fights back for a moment, but he stops after I wrestle his knife away and point it directly at him.

It would be so easy. I have the knife. The upper hand. He's not even trying to stop me. All of this could be over.

Uncle Ian and I both breathe heavily, chests rising and falling in unison. He closes his eyes as if preparing himself for what's to come next.

But I can't do it.

I can't fucking do it.

"CJ!"

I turn to the voice. Orion runs up onto the stage, baseball bat splattered in red but looking almost clean compared to the total bloodbath behind him, where another Wolf Man grabs Sebas's arm before Mom shoots the attacker in the chest.

Orion looks between me, Uncle Ian, and the knife. Finally he says, "Can I tell you something?"

It takes everything in me not to roll my eyes. "Orion, it's not exactly a good time."

"I know you killed Evan Miller."

This gets both Uncle Ian and me to turn to him.

"I saw it happen," he continues quietly. "That shirt you put over my eyes was see-through as shit."

"No," I say, shaking my head. "You didn't. You would have said something."

"I think I'd know," Orion says, slightly annoyed. His eyes fill with tears, though. "But I couldn't say anything. I thought I'd get you in trouble. And I . . . I had to protect you like you protected me."

"Orion . . ."

"I know you think you should be ashamed or that you did something wrong. But you shouldn't. You didn't. I'm glad you killed him. He would have killed us if you didn't. And that's what got me through all this."

"What?" I ask.

He sniffles, cheeks turning pink. "Knowing my big sibling would always be there to stop the Wolf Man."

Orion is right. I'd repressed the memory for so long because it'd felt like a mistake. I hadn't listened to Dad. He'd given his life for us and I couldn't even do the last thing he told me to do. But it wasn't a mistake. I saved him. Orion. I saved both of us. This entire time, I've been so convinced that I couldn't do it. That I was a failure, that I could never beat the Satterville Wolf Man.

But I already had.

"I don't want to kill Uncle Ian, Orion," I mutter, my knife drooping in my hand.

"It's messed up," Orion agrees. He gives me his usual shit-eating grin. "But it's always been messed up."

I know what he's saying. He wants me to stop this, like I did last time.

But that would be fulfilling the fate these freaks want to give me. And I won't do that.

It's like something snaps within me. I can almost hear it.

I step away from Uncle Ian. He doesn't move, but I still keep the knife in his direction. I reach out my hand to my brother.

"I wasn't alone that night," I say. "We both survived the Wolf Man, which means there isn't just one Final Girl here."

Orion's eyes are watery, but he looks determined. He grips his own bat.

"No." Uncle Ian leans on one arm, getting up. "No, it has to be *you*, CJ. Only you. The Creator has destined it! It's how it must be written!" He looks crazed, ready to jump at us. "I'll do it, CJ. I will hurt him." Looking at Uncle Ian now, I believe him. He'll do anything to have this go the way he wants.

I keep my knife at the ready and squeeze Orion's hand. "Sorry, Ian. But I'm writing my own story now."

Uncle Ian lunges.

SNAP!

Orion and I jump at the sound of John Doe's chains breaking free from the wall. In a flash, the stag head drops onto Uncle Ian. The antlers plunge through his back and neck, impaling him, pinning him to the floor. He chokes, blood gushing from his torso and spurting from his lips.

Orion and I can only watch as the life leaves his eyes.

John Doe's baseball cap, stained in red, glides in front of the gruesome scene.

"I Survived Slasherfest."

And just like that, Uncle Ian didn't

34

I Survived Slasherfest and All I Got Was This T-Shirt

The room goes silent, all fighting coming to a standstill. My mind refuses to work right away. There's a storm of emotion that swirls inside me. Horror, fear, sadness, and, above all, relief. John Doe killed the Wolf Man so we didn't have to. Two more Smith kids saved by a badly taxidermized stag.

"Was that . . . Dad?" Orion whispers. He glances up as if we'll see Dad staring down at us from the great beyond.

A voice does respond: "Not quite, but I like to think I'm as charming and handsome."

Orion and I look over to the left. Next to where the chains were once secured to the wall stands Nadia, holding the huge pair of bolt cutters.

"Damn, Nadia," I manage to say. "Looks like there really is more than one Final Girl in Satterville."

With that, I drop my knife and rush over, throwing my arms around her. Her bolt cutters clatter to the floor as she hugs me back.

"How's that for main character energy?" she asks. After a short laugh, her voice changes. "But holy shit, I didn't think it would fall like *that*. I didn't mean to kill him. Jesus Christ."

"It's okay." I squeeze her, burying my face in her shoulder. "Thank you."

We didn't let Uncle Ian's version of the story come true, but he might have been right about one thing: the Wolf Man has to die at the end.

It's Satterville tradition.

Cops finally arrive at the scene. It was unfortunate Mom didn't just bring them in the first place, but apparently, there's a procedure to things and she had no intention of waiting or following said procedure. The store is a complete mess. Aside from the horrific sight of Uncle Ian and John Doe, at least two other Wolf Men are down, possibly dead, and the others are injured. It's all sirens and blinding lights.

Once Nadia pulls away, Mom and Orion are piling onto me. The three of us are covered in blood, and the group hug only makes it worse.

"Cassiopeia Jane, I'm going to kill you for not waiting for me, but I'm so, so glad you're alive," Mom says, placing about a dozen little kisses on top of my head.

"I can't believe Uncle Ian would do this to us," Orion mutters. "He was like a dad."

I pat his head. "That's why I'm the only dad you'll ever need."

"Fuck off, CJ."

"I thought we just had a moment!"

"Yeah, until you had to be annoying again."

Mom shakes her head. "Is that how you talk to your sibling who saved your life?"

"Mom, were you here? We saved her ass first! I had to do the whole motivation speech, too, what a fucking drag."

"Language, Orion. Stop swearing like you're a damn teenager."

"I *am* a damn teenager."

"You're in middle school, that hardly counts. You're a baby to me."

Ah, family. Things would already feel back to normal if not for the bodily fluids coating our clothes and skin.

"We should get the twins," I say.

Nadia goes to check on Sebas, who throws me a relieved smile through the crowd of police and EMTs, while the three of us walk over to open the door to the storage room. Leo and Lyra both cling to their horror plushies. I'll have to pay Ms. Maeda for those later.

"Is it over?" Leo asks.

Lyra holds up her xenomorph. "I love him. I named him Gary."

I don't even bother unpacking that. The future therapy these two will have to go through thanks to Mom and me can handle it. Instead, I pull them into another hug. Mom and even Orion follow.

It's a touching family moment, until the cops come to question Mom about potential child endangerment and manslaughter. In her defense, Uncle Ian was the one responsible for bringing us all here, and it was in self-defense. The Wolf Men were trying to attack them with knives.

I'm not sure how all the legal stuff will pan out, but I have to have faith it will be fine. At the very least, it can't be worse than what we've already been through. No one will be trying to kill us, so that's something.

And it's easiest to just believe Uncle Ian and his Wolf Men were responsible for it all.

"CJ!" Sebas runs up to me.

I immediately pull Sebas into a hug and melt into him. Despite the sweat and blood, I nervously rise to my tiptoes so I can kiss him. His lips are warm and sweet.

"Gross," Orion says.

I should punch him.

"I'm so glad you're okay," Sebas tells me.

"I'm glad you're okay, too." I make a face. "Probably not exactly a fun date, huh?"

"I'd do anything with you," he says. "But, perhaps we don't include serial killers next time. Or ever again."

"Couldn't agree more."

Nadia pushes past him to step back up to me. "So, now that some time has passed—"

"It's been literally one minute."

"—I'm not saying I told you so. Or that I think the freaky cult is right, because I more than proved that I'm not on their side. But if this is a story? That means my chances of being reincarnated as the hot villainess in one of the webcomics I'm reading are definitely greater than zero."

I glare at her. "Don't go summoning truck-kun now."

"I'm just *saying*," she repeats. "Greater than zero."

"You may have saved the day, but you still need to cool it and stop agreeing with the murder cult."

Nadia thinks it over. "I believe I'm charming enough that I will retain my status as the fan favorite. The gays will understand my delusion stems from love, not hate."

I throw my arms around her again. "I'm so glad I saved you."

"You and me both, friend. Even if it means I have to hold off on truck-kun sending me to my sexy tsundere duchess with black hair and red eyes."

"I hate you."

"I know that means you love me."

"You're not wrong."

I hug her tighter. With both of us alive, there'll be many days ahead talking about all the different webcomics we read and which characters are our biggest crushes. The important thing is that everyone is okay.

My eyes fall back to Uncle Ian, now covered with a sheet.

Well, mostly everyone.

Nadia checks her phone. "Sebas, Samuel and my parents are here. We should go meet them."

"It's fine," I say. "I'll see you both later."

Sebas kisses me on the cheek. My skin buzzes.

"How about a real date sometime?" he asks. "One with less blood?"

"That would be great." I shrug. "I don't want my boyfriend to think this is all we do in Satterville."

I'm nervous, but Sebas smiles wide.

"Of course not, just . . . more than usual."

"Yeah, probably," I agree.

The two of them head off. I hope their family isn't too hard on them. If anything, they should blame me for getting them involved at all. Although I'm not sure exactly how much Sebas and Nadia will tell them.

With all my adrenaline gone, I feel myself starting to crash. I'm so tired, I have to take a seat on the floor. Once she's done with the cops, Mom joins me, Orion, and the twins.

"Are we going to be okay?" I ask her.

"Yes and no," she answers. "It's gonna be hard. Of course it is. But we'll keep going. As long as you survive, you can keep going." She gives a small smile. "In fact, you don't have much of a choice."

It's true. No matter who we lose or what hell we go through, time keeps on. While it feels kind of ridiculous that after all this, I'll have to go back to worrying about school and college apps and prom, time will pass, and those will be my big concerns.

At least it's summer now. The idea of driving to the lake with Sebas and staying out late as we steal kisses, catch the warm air, and fight off mosquitoes already has me buzzing with excitement. It feels nice to be excited about things. About the future. My emotions went on such a screwed-up roller coaster, it sometimes feels like they've kind of just abandoned ship altogether.

Maybe Mr. White was right and I do need to talk to someone.

"How's family therapy sound?" I ask Mom.

She laughs. "I think that's a great idea, CJ."

Done with her own questioning, Ms. Maeda steps up to us.

"I'm so sorry," I tell her. "I didn't mean to suspect you."

She waves it off. "I don't blame you. And you got it right in the end. You all really do have main character energy."

"We love a bisexual genderqueer and a lesbian Latina Final Girl," Mom agrees.

"Stop," I groan.

My eyes, desperate to look away from them, land on the store. It's a disaster. While there are still shelves of books that look mostly undamaged, there's the complete destruction of the front door, a ton of blood, and general havoc and debris.

"I'm so sorry about the store," I say.

"Are you kidding?" Ms. Maeda smiles. "Once news gets out, do you know how much business we're going to get now that we've been a legitimate Wolf Man crime scene?"

I laugh.

She's right.

You can stop the killer, but Satterville will always be Slasherville.

35

The Final Chapter

It's almost strange how quickly things seem to go back to normal. Although, I guess if any place was prepared to absorb another movie-monster-esque masked murder cult into the norm, Satterville is it. When the story drops, it's huge. Despite all Uncle Ian's talk about fate, it was clear that his Slashervillain goonies orchestrated everything, from the clogged toilet in the girls' room to getting Taylor in the right location. Everything. They made the story real.

The full story wasn't made public, though. We wanted to squash all references to the Creator. That shit dies with Uncle Ian. Police took credit for stopping the Wolf Men, aside from the "accidental" death of one Ian Henley.

As far as anyone knows, I'm just an extra.

I don't mind. In fact, I prefer it.

The news did bring a spike in sales of Moon Satter books. Their identity wasn't actually revealed, although even if it had been, I'm not sure that would have stopped anyone from getting the books back on bestseller lists. It wasn't all bad, since Uncle Ian did leave his estate to us. The least he could do.

My phone lights up with a text from Nadia.

Nadia: Beach party tonight. You lovebirds in?

Sebas responds before I do.

Sebas: That's not a real beach.

I'm in:)

Sebas: well, obviously i am too

Nadia: i thought it's not a real beach

Sebas: it's not, but I can still party

Nadia: you're so whipped

Can y'all pick me up?

Sebas: ofc love

Nadia: UGH I NEED A GIRLFRIEND

I like the idea of that. Double dates with Nadia and the girl she'll like. Discussing webcomics and watching horror movies and pretending we have nothing to do with them. Talking about the future and how it's okay that I don't have it all figured out.

Because what actually matters is that I have one. And I get to have Sebas and Nadia in it.

Chekov's Gun's hiss startles me from my spot on the couch. I look over to the door where he's growling. Must be a delivery person.

I open the door. No one's there, but a thick envelope was left in front of the apartment. It just has my name and address on it, no return label.

I rip into it. The first page is a letter.

Cassiopeia Jane,

I'm sorry for the way that everything happened. I know you must hate me, but I do hope that in the years to follow, you will come to realize that I loved you like my own daughter. That I always will.

I'm sure the recent events will sensationalize everything again and you'll have to deal with the limelight. Sell the film rights or something. I want you to have that money. Make sure they cast someone handsome and charming for me in the movie, and that they don't cut Chekov's Gun as a character. That would be bullshit.

I've included the real Return to Slasherville. The story as it always should have been. Despite my prayers to the Creator, I wasn't able to get a vision or a sense of what happens after I die, so you might have to edit some little details, but I think I got the big things right.

I hope you heal from my death. Don't blame yourself. It's how we were written.

I'd like to think, in another story, in some distant universe, things are different. Christian is alive, I'm alive, and I can actually support you in the way an uncle should. Instead of a horror, maybe it's a cozy mystery. Or a family comedy. I think I'd like to read that.

This is your story, CJ. I want you to profit off it.

I want you to control the ending.

Love always,
Uncle Ian

I hold the letter for a long time, almost like I'm in a daze. Finally, I look at the pages underneath. It's the revised manuscript of *Return to Slasherville,* just like Uncle Ian promised. This time, the events match what actually happened. Taylor's death, Mr. White's death, Hana's near-death, the horrible events of Slasherfest. It gets it mostly right, like he said, with the exception of some minor details and the ending he couldn't get right.

In it, I'm the lead. The Final Girl.

"I'll be right back," I tell Chekov. "You're in charge."

After grabbing a few things, I walk out of the apartment with the manuscript in hand and head to the back of the building. I open up the communal grill, remove the grate, and use the lighter I snagged from the kitchen drawer to get it started. Once the fire begins blazing, I toss the letter and the full manuscript inside.

I watch the paper curl up and blacken, falling to ashes inside the dancing flames. The fire crackles and rages, swallowing up the story with it. I don't need Uncle Ian's words. I have my own.

I keep staring until there's nothing left of the pages.

It's over, finished, up in flames.

Maybe not forever. That's the curse of having a life that's like a horror story. Even at the end, there's always a possibility the threat could come back. There can always be another Wolf Man. Another money-grab sequel.

But regardless of what my future holds and what happens next in Slasherville, I know I'll be okay.

Because I'm a fucking Final Girl.

Acknowledgments

This book has been a wild ride of a process, and it almost feels weird to have reached the "fade to black" moment of this horror, but I am so grateful to be doing it. There are so many thanks already bubbling up that it is hard to know where to begin, so I might as well start from the beginning, where I had the seed of an idea that involved "extras" being thrown into main character roles and the person who inspired it.

Thomy, I wouldn't have been able to write anything resembling romance without you. Thank you for helping me with my Spanish and my jiu-jitsu, for cheering on my ideas, for picking up the slack when I'm on deadlines, and for accepting me and loving me for me. There is no one I'd rather have to survive a slasher with than you.

This book ended up being far more emotional than I intended and a big part of that was losing my sweet kitty, Kana, while I was first drafting the book. Kanita, this book wouldn't exist without you. I love you and I miss you. Thank you so much for choosing me.

To my boys/writer's assistants/loves of my life/best cats ever: Jasper, Twinklepop, and Kimura. Thank you for always being there, and also for doing the heavy lifting of just about all marketing posts on my end.

I cannot give enough thanks to my incredible team at Bloomsbury. I want to cry thinking of how you have all championed me and my work across categories, even when it's really, really meta. It truly means the world to me. To my editor, Alex Borbolla, for being just such an icon and genius and getting my stories to where they need to go. I am the biggest fan of you and literally your entire list! To Kei Nakatsuka, for also being a genius and awesome and giving invaluable notes. Also to Diane Aronson, Lex Higbee, Lily Yengle, Erica Barmash, and Phoebe Dyer: I could go on and on about how amazing you all are and how much I appreciate you but I'm trying to maintain some self-control. Huge thanks to Jeanette Levy and Aleksey Rico for designing and illustrating the perfect cover for a teen slasher!

Thank you to my agent, Patricia Nelson, who supported this project and worked with me on a faster timeline to get it ready. You are the absolute best! (And not just because you always appreciate my army of fictional cats across my books.) Thank you for everything!

To my early readers (who I am going to refer to as the original extras): Edward Underhill, Emery Lee, Chloe Maron, Birdie Schae, CL Montblanc, Carlyn Greenwald, and Jen St. Jude. I would not have believed in this book without you all!

To my friends who have continued to give support throughout our publishing journeys, I don't know where I'd be without you. I love you (and your incredible books)! I can't name everyone and I already named some of you literally in the paragraph above this, but special shout-outs to Alex Brown, Joey Comes, Ronnie Riley, Caroline Huntoon, Kate Fussner, Hannah V. Sawyerr, Christen Randall, Shelly Page, and Leanne Yong.

To all the slashers I loved before. And all the queer people writing horror. We're (sort of literally) killing it, in my so humble opinion.

Lastly, to all the amazing booksellers, librarians, teachers, and readers who support my work. Whether you came here from my silly mysteries or my spooky middle grade, or if this is your first time reading a book I wrote, I am so grateful that you are here. Book lovers are my people (especially, but not limited to) queer and horror book lovers, and I am always excited and honored to get to meet you and hear from you! Everything I write is for you, and I sincerely hope you are able to enjoy the ride. Thank you, thank you, thank you! I hope to see you again with the next one. (In which there will probably be more cats.)